WINDSONG MANOR

WINDSONG MANOR

PROPER ROMANCE

JULIE WRIGHT

SHADOW
MOUNTAIN
PUBLISHING

To my Mr. Wright

Thanks for always answering "Polo!"
when I call out "Marco!" in the store.
It really is the little things that
make up a good husband.

Library of Congress Cataloging-in-Publication Data
Names: Wright, Julie, 1972– author.
Title: Windsong Manor / Julie Wright.
Other titles: Proper romance.
Description: Salt Lake City: Shadow Mountain, [2023] | Series: Proper romance |
    Summary: "When the baroness—and newly widowed—Eleanora Coventry moves
    her family to her country estate of Windsong Manor, she doesn't anticipate falling
    in love with Ridley Ellis, a lowly stable master who is hiding a secret about his
    past."—Provided by publisher.
Identifiers: LCCN 2023013435 | ISBN 9781639931569 (trade paperback)
Subjects: LCSH: Widows—Fiction. | Stablehands—Fiction. | Nineteenth century,
    setting. | England, setting. | BISAC: FICTION / Romance / Historical / Regency
    | FICTION / Romance / Clean & Wholesome | LCGFT: Historical fiction. |
    Romance fiction.
Classification: LCC PS3623. R55 W56 2023 | DDC 813/.6—dc23/eng/20230407
LC record available at https: //lccn.loc.gov/2023013435

Printed in the United States of America
Lake Book Manufacturing, Inc., Melrose Park, IL

10 9 8 7 6 5 4 3 2 1

Chapter One

Eleanora Coventry blinked at the housekeeper, Mrs. Herold, and tried to not frown at the request made of her. She stood, smoothed her hands over her skirts, and followed Mrs. Herold out of the drawing room and up the stairs to her husband's bedchamber.

Of course, he would summon her. She was his wife, and he was dying. Of course, he would want to hold her hand and say his farewells. He would want to give her a message for their nearly twelve-year-old son, who was away at Eton. So why did she feel like a child being summoned to her father's study?

Nora hadn't thought marriage would be this way. She had thought it would be endless flowers and declarations of love.

The reality was a disappointment that left her feeling inadequate and useless once she had produced the required heir, the only child she'd been able to carry to term. Her husband was old, had been old from the day her father arranged the match. She had been young. Far too young, she now understood. She'd been fifteen when the banns were read and barely sixteen when the ceremony that made her a wife took place.

She entered the bedchamber and offered the physician, Mr. Perkins, a trembling movement of her mouth that started as a smile but ended more like a grimace.

"He has been calling for you," Mr. Perkins said as he stepped back, allowing her to move to her husband's side with greater ease.

She did not want to move to his side.

She shrank back when her husband crooked his finger and beckoned her over, but with Mr. Perkins standing witness, she had no choice but to obey.

He is dying, she thought. In truth, he looked like a corpse already, and it frightened her in ways that made her feel more like a child than a wife. When her parents had both passed and Lord Coventry had become her only family, she felt how truly lonely death made a person. And now, Lord Coventry was leaving her as well. She wanted to hide from this unsettling event.

"Closer," he whispered.

It had to seem strange to her husband's physician that she was not weeping over his ailments and professing her love, but she could not make herself feel it.

She did as directed. The automatic obedience familiar.

She lowered her head to hear him better, holding her breath against the stink of his sweat-soaked nightshirt. *I am a baroness*—she drew the words around herself whenever she faced a challenge that seemed beyond her.

"In the wardrobe. In the box," his voice rasped.

"What is in the wardrobe? Would you like me to fetch something for you?"

"Eleanora." The word of frustration came out in a gust that smelled of the hard liquor he'd acquired from Ireland. He took it to ease his pain. "Do as you're told, girl."

She pressed her lips into a tight line and stepped away from the smell of her husband's sickness and his simmering impatience. She crossed the room and opened his wardrobe. The polished mahogany box was one she'd seen many times over the course of their marriage, often in his office. Its small silver handles made it easy to carry back to her husband. She noted the handles were polished to perfection, which meant the oval box had been cared for by his valet, which meant its contents couldn't have been so private if it was to be handled by anyone.

But not anyone.

This was the first time *she'd* handled it.

"My solicitor knows my affairs, but I do not want you embarrassing me with your ignorance when they are made known to you. There are settlements to be made upon my death. And my wishes *will* be respected."

Nora stifled a sigh at the words that had been declared to her many times over her years of marriage. The baron *will* be respected. He *will* be obeyed. He gave her tasks to complete in the same way he gave them to the housekeeper or the butler. She carried out those tasks as if she, too, was a member of his household staff. Though she believed she sighed a great deal more than any of those in her husband's employ. She had married so young that she felt she'd been sighing away the greater part of her life.

"Open it," he wheezed.

She didn't know what she'd expected to find. Perhaps opals or gold coins, perhaps crystal or silks from faraway lands. Those were the things of her ridiculous fancy. That's what her husband always called her wandering thoughts: ridiculous fancy.

And she supposed he was right. Those same fanciful thoughts had led her to believe matrimony would be filled with bliss, love, and harmony.

The box held nothing more than papers, drafted out in an elegant hand. She looked up for him to explain.

"You did not produce a child after Edward. While I am glad you provided the heir duty required, I would prefer the security of more than one child in line to inherit." His tone was pragmatic and direct, without emotion, even if it was weaker than ever before.

He coughed, new flecks of blood spotting his handkerchief. "I expect the girl to be raised in your household. I expect you to act as her mother; her actual mother passed on several weeks ago."

Nora felt ice shiver up her spine. "The girl?"

"Yes. The girl. My daughter. What other girl would there be? Pay attention, Eleanora. She is eight years old, and I have chosen to acknowledge her and offer her legitimacy in this world."

Nora knew of his wandering, of course. He'd hardly hidden his indiscretions, and she wasn't stupid no matter how often he made her question her own intelligence.

But she had not known there had been a child.

She glanced at Mr. Perkins to see if he'd heard the insult. He was looking out the window with far more determination than such a task required. His ears were bright red beneath his graying hair that curled over the tops of them. He had definitely heard.

Her son, Edward, would inherit everything upon the death of her husband, and she would be provided for only because she was the boy's mother. How strange to think that this illegitimate child, whoever she was, would suddenly be thrust into notice and rank. Nora would have pitied the poor creature for having to endure such a world except she was far too busy pitying herself for a circumstance entirely out of her control. She was to raise another woman's child as her own? How was such a thing to be done?

But acknowledging Lord Coventry's daughter gave the barony a chance at real survival through his lineage. It made a twisted sense even as it twisted her insides.

Mr. Perkins cleared his throat, probably hoping to remind Lord Coventry that he was not alone with his wife as they discussed such delicate matters. "You should rest, sir," he said.

"Won't there be time enough to rest when I am dead?" Lord Coventry asked, though how he could be so calm was a wonder. Nora certainly was not calm.

Mr. Perkins, wisely, did not respond.

For Nora's part, she could only think that, even with the new burden of raising a child not her own—a child who came from infidelity—*she* would finally get to rest once her husband was dead.

She felt certain that was one of her most wicked thoughts, which was saying something, as she'd had a great many wicked thoughts since her father and mother had arranged her union with the Baron of

Kendal. The match had been fortuitous in all the ways a mother and father could have wanted for their young daughter. The baron was an old man, but he was also titled and wealthy.

Nora had thought him distant and chilly when she'd first met him, but she'd been sure she would be able to tease a smile from his mouth and thaw his icy demeanor.

She had not been able to do so.

Her parents' relationship, while not doting, had still seemed like a companionship. And her childhood home felt like a summer sun warming her from the inside out compared to the heart of winter that had become her life with the baron. Not that he'd mistreated her exactly, but more that she was never given a moment where she felt like his companion.

"You will raise the girl as your own," Lord Coventry repeated his wishes with a deep, wracking cough.

Nora said nothing, and her heart felt hollow. *Of course I will. Don't I always do what I am told?*

Don't I always?

Chapter Two

Ridley Ellis breathed in the morning air and sighed happily. His muscles ached from the repairs he'd made in the stables over the course of the last year. He'd added a few windows to allow the horses better access to fresh air during good weather but made sure the windows could also be snugged tight during a storm.

The windows were open to let in the breeze of a fragrant spring. The stable master, Mr. Daw, had initially scoffed at the idea of more ventilation and natural light, but when Ridley hinted at how pleased Lord Coventry would be to see the tremendous care that his prize horses had been given, Mr. Daw seized on the idea as if it had been his own.

Daw had been deeply disappointed to hear of the baron's passing. Not because Daw cared for the baron, but because he had not had the chance to show off the improvements Ridley had initiated. A year later, credit or no credit, the upgrades were complete, and the effect was magnificent.

"Don't you have work to do?" Daw barked from the doors. His sparse gray hair stuck out at ridiculous angles, likely from a recent nap. The carriage's velvety interior had been a favorite of his of late.

Ridley bit back a retort that he was the only one of the two of them who did any work. He had known that making his living on his own would be difficult. He had known that men of rank and notability could be harsh and cruel masters. But he had not known that members of the staff could be so relentlessly tyrannical.

"Yes, sir. I do."

"Then get to it before I turn you out of this estate, and then where will you be?"

Ridley didn't bother looking back to the ruddy-faced man. "Yes, sir."

He entered the tack room and pulled a saddle from the cast-iron saddle racks located below the row of bridle hooks. It was time for General's daily exercise. As Lord Coventry's prize hunting horse, General had to be in perfect condition. The dark bay stallion was getting older though, which made Ridley secretly relieved that the baron would never be returning to the estate. If General's performance faltered, the baron would have had no issue with putting the horse down. The late baron was not one for sentimentality. However, Ridley had grown irrevocably attached to the animal and would be broken to lose him.

Daw's bootheels clicked on the cobblestones as he left the stable. Ridley sighed in relief. It was so much easier to tend to his responsibilities when Daw stayed out of the way. He hefted the saddle back into the main room of the stables.

"Do you know what my favorite memory is?" George, one of the undergrooms, asked, emerging from where he'd ducked into the shadows to avoid Daw.

"I don't. Tell me."

"The time old Daw thought to take a horsewhip to you, and you caught the whip and pulled him right down with a spin on his great bottom, and then you lectured the horrible man on how Lord Coventry wouldn't much like returning to the estate to find that his horses were suddenly in a state of decline just because you'd decided you were done taking orders from a barely sober thug and had sought employment elsewhere." George laughed, showing his crooked teeth. "*Barely sober thug*. Ah, those words still give me comfort when the nights are particularly cold."

"That moment certainly didn't earn me a friendship with the man." Ridley cinched up the saddle and patted the Belgian stallion's flank.

"But you didn't get the whip either. Not then. Not ever. None of the rest of us could've gotten away with that. We'd have been whipped double for showing such cheek. But not you. It makes me wonder how you're not the stable master here when you know more'n that man and when the horses do so well under your care. Everyone in the stable and carriage house knows the horses are jumping higher and running faster now that you're here. And they're more sure-footed than ever, even with a clumsy rider, and less cantankerous when they're pulling a heavy carriage. I bet you could sweet-talk the horses into making us dinner."

"Well, that *would* be something. But then we'd work in a circus, not a stable. No animals doing silly things here."

"Point is," George said, "you're much better at training the horses than old Daw." He nodded, his mop of brown hair flopping over his forehead as if he'd spoken a royal decree of truth.

"Rank is not always given to the deserving," Ridley said with a laugh. "But if you're going to sharpen your tongue on Daw's character, you should keep your voice low. If he hears you, even I won't be able to intercede. Keeping employment is sometimes the same as keeping your tongue."

That wiped the mirth off George's face. "Sorry, sir. I meant no disrespect." The young man got to work pulling at a bale of hay and filling the horses' feeding troughs.

"I know you didn't. And I mean not to lecture. I merely want to see you thrive in your work and have good references to go where you please."

"I'd be pleased to work where you're working. You've a way with the animals, even the nasty ones like Bonnie."

"Bonnie is as sweet as her name indicates if you treat her right."

George looked as though he'd been told a whopper of a lie, but he didn't argue. The boy was a valuable undergroom and a hard worker.

He'd be a strong stable master someday if he stayed his current course and learned to keep his tongue.

Ridley climbed onto General's saddle and was about to leave for a run through the woods when George said, "Did you hear?"

Honestly, that boy had his ear in every room of the great house despite never having stepped foot in most of those rooms. "Hear what?"

"The baroness is coming to live at Windsong. Permanently. They say she'll not be living in London at all, 'cept maybe to visit every now and again."

The news surprised Ridley. The baron's neglect of the property over the last few years had been part of its charm when Ridley had decided to accept employment. And in all that time, the baroness had visited the estate only once, to inter the late Lord Coventry. But her stay had been too short to even call a visit. He'd barely had time to care for the horses that had pulled her carriage before he'd had to hitch them up again. For her to claim Windsong as her permanent residence when she had no real attachment to the place made little sense.

He'd thought that with the baron passed, he'd never see a member of the family again until the Coventry boy had grown to fill his position and take over as baron.

"And she's bringing the children," George continued.

He frowned. "Of course she would. Why would they not be at their mother's side?"

"Right. But imagine that. Children. Not child. The girl, too. Seems strange, don't it?"

The household had whispered about the girl being brought into notice by her father on his deathbed. Ridley raised a brow at George to let him know he didn't approve of that sort of speculating.

"I just meant it's strange that the family will be living in the house all the time."

"It *is* their house, so it hardly warrants amazement. This does mean I'll have to scrub Daw's drool from the velvet cushions in the carriage before the family arrives. But not before the horses get their exercise. See that you wash down General's stall before I return. Maybe such work will keep you from gossiping with the maids." Ridley clucked his tongue, and General moved out into the yard.

It wasn't until Ridley had reached the edge of the wooded trail that he considered it might be time for him to find employment elsewhere.

He worked hard to keep his head down and stay out of the way of the members of high society. He was willing to allow Daw to take credit for his work and he was fine to collect wages for his work, but earning money from the elite so he could eat and have a roof over his head was not the same thing as being forced to be so near them that they knew his name or poked about in his affairs.

Leave the elite alone, and they usually returned the favor.

It was an ideal arrangement for Ridley. He hoped it would stay that way. If the family would be permanently relocating to Windsong, there might be complications for Ridley.

His heart thrummed harder at what the coming change might mean for him.

General tensed as a roll of thunder rumbled in the distance.

Ridley patted the horse behind the ear. "You sense it too then, old boy? There's a storm coming."

Chapter Three

"She cries all the time." Edward lounged in front of the fire, sitting in the chair that had once belonged to his father.

Edward's observation of his sister, Amelia, was not wrong, but neither was it the compassionate response Nora felt the poor girl deserved. It had been a year since Lord Coventry's death, and it seemed that each day brought her son closer to fitting the chair in the way his father had—a way that had been making Nora worry for months.

"She has had to undergo a great many changes," Nora said as she scanned the room to see what things she might want to direct the servants to pack away for her to take to their country estate. "She's lost her mother and—"

"What of that? I've lost my father, and you don't see me weeping until my eyes look as though they were bleeding."

Nora did not remind him that his sister had also lost her father. She hated the implications of it all and hated more that her young son should be exposed to such scandal. Wasn't he too young to know of such things? Nora felt *she* was too young to know of such things.

"We've had her for over a year. A good hunting dog takes less time to train. I'm barely older than she, and my behavior is infinitely superior to hers. Lia acts like an infant." He tapped his foot with an intensity that made him seem nervous and insolent—hardly superior qualities.

Nora hated how she eyed her own slouching son with such

suspicion. She hated how much a stranger he'd seemed to be when she'd pulled him out of Eton to attend his father's funeral. She'd noticed the changes in his personality right away, but it had taken her a few months to find the courage to remove her son from the school altogether.

Mr. Ashby, her husband's solicitor, had been determined to thwart her efforts to bring her son home. Nora feared Mr. Ashby and the power he wielded over her. In many ways, he reminded her of her late husband—exacting, dismissive, assuming she was incapable of the smallest tasks. Mr. Ashby had finally relented to Nora's wishes when Edward had fallen ill and was unable to continue in school.

She shuddered as she considered what could have happened at the school to have altered her son so completely. The changes in him filled her with dread. He'd always been a somber child, but now he was sharp, arrogant, and intolerant.

She'd convinced Mr. Ashby that it wasn't enough for Edward to no longer be in school, but that he needed the fresh country air to fully recover, though, in truth, she was sure he no longer suffered any lingering effects from the illness.

"Sit up straight, or no one will believe your boast of superior behavior," Nora instructed.

Her son glowered at her. "I'm the man of the house. I will sit as I wish, given the company I'm currently keeping."

Out of well-formed habit, Nora did not react to the words that stung so very deeply. Might she have been able to guide her son into a gentler shape if she'd spent more time with him personally, rather than acquiescing to her husband's command that he be trained by a governess before his schooling at Eton? "You will do as you are told, or you will not get dinner tonight. You may be man of the house, but you're still young enough to be scolded by your mother."

He straightened slightly. Nora decided to take the small motion as a win. The last year had nearly been the end of her, what with Edward so enraged after his father's death and with her new task of rearing Lia, who really *did* cry all the time. The girl missed her real mother, not the imposter she felt Nora was in her life. Lia hated being called "Miss Amelia." She hated all the servants. She hated that she wasn't allowed to speak to them as she had in her previous household. She hated Nora.

But the child hated her brother most of all.

And he deserved it.

He teased, taunted, and tortured his sister.

"I think we should stay in London," Edward said, sitting straighter still, as if that extra inch might give him some authority over the matter.

"Staying in London does nothing to prepare you for your future as the Baron of Kendal. Windsong Manor is where your land and tenants are. A good landowner oversees his land and assets." In truth, the move was a last desperate grasp for her son's love. She hoped he would find something in the country estate that would soften the edge of his persistent anger.

They had buried her husband in the Coventry family mausoleum at the church cemetery. The tenants had lined up along the roadside with candles to light the funeral procession on its way in the dusk. Every drip of wax from the candles had mimicked the tears on her face as she'd ridden past in her carriage. Those many candles—which must have cost her tenants dearly to light for her—had felt like a pathway toward something gentler, kinder. It had amazed her that these people had come out. Her husband had not been an attentive baron. He had certainly not been fair or just. From whispers she'd heard, he'd treated his tenants with the same sort of cold dismissal as he'd treated her.

But upon reflection, she felt certain the tenants had not lined up for her husband in much the same way she had not wept for her husband. Her tears and their melting candles had been a symbol of shared relief and a joint hope for something brighter. That was why she was moving the children back to Windsong. Something had stirred in her during that procession. Though she and the children hadn't stayed at Windsong for more than a day, she thought of the estate constantly, and now that she had put off her mourning clothes, it was time for a new beginning, time to see what the feeling that beckoned for her to return might actually mean.

London had been a cage for her. She hoped to find freedom at Windsong.

"I hate it there." Edward's sullen tone pulled her from her memories.

"You haven't been there in years aside from when we buried your father. How can you know if you hate a place when your memory of it comes from the time when you were still learning to walk?"

Instead of responding to Nora's question, Edward popped to his feet. "There's the crybaby now!"

Nora turned to find Lia standing behind her, her large eyes sad. The girl's light-golden hair as pale as her face.

Nora gave her son a disapproving frown for teasing the girl. "Edward." She put as much warning as she could into her tone.

"What?" Edward said. "You can't punish me more than you already are by forcing this move."

Nora pressed her lips together at how her son refused to be mollified when it came to the move. Why Edward wanted so desperately to stay in London baffled her. The move had been a source of contention between them since the moment she'd brought it up. The fact that he remained so stubbornly set against it was the reason she remained so stubbornly insistent that they go. He mentioned at least once a day how he wished to return to Eton, but how could he wish to return there when whatever had happened there had created this ogre he'd become?

She gave up on the puzzle that was Edward for the moment and turned back to Lia. "Do you need something, dear? Any help packing?"

Lia shook her head.

In truth, the move was as much for the girl as it was for her son. The pale, sad little creature might be brightened with fresh air and fields to roam.

"What can I get for you then?" Nora asked.

Lia glanced at Edward, obviously not wanting to speak in front of her brother. She finally focused on her feet. "I wondered if we might stop at Sheffield on our way to Windsong."

Sheffield was where Nora had gone to collect the girl. She had wanted to tend to the task herself in the hopes it might bring her some kind of peace with the situation. She'd been wrong. The grandparents had looked at Nora as if she had been the one to cause such wreckage under their roof. But they also knew Nora was a baroness, and, as part of the working class, they understood the opportunity for what it was. They allowed Nora to take Lia, and the girl had been a ceaseless puddle of tears ever since. The request to return to her homestead could not have been easy for Lia to make, and Nora wanted to find some sort of common ground. She wanted them all on the same side.

"I don't see that as a problem. We can even find an inn and stay the night if you'd like." She knew Lia's request was more about seeing her grandparents than anything else, but she didn't see the harm in a visit. They likely missed their granddaughter as much as their granddaughter missed them.

"Thank you! Thank you ever so much!" Lia exclaimed, offering up a rare smile.

Edward snorted in disgust from behind Nora.

Ignoring her son's rudeness, she smiled at Lia, who darted off to hasten her own packing.

When Nora turned around to deal with Edward, she realized he, too, had slipped from the room. For a moment, she was alone. She closed her eyes and listened to the sounds of London coming through the open window. Horse hooves clopped on the cobbled stones, and birds sang in the trees. The smell of cherry blossoms floated in on the breeze, and for a moment, all seemed right with the world.

She had believed her husband's death would equal an easier life for herself. And she'd been mostly right, but the children had proven difficult for her to navigate. She wished she had help, but she did not want to risk sounding incompetent regarding child rearing, and she dared not trust any governess or school setting after seeing what had happened to her son.

Not for the first time, she thought of her mother and how much easier the entire business of raising children would have been if her mother were still alive to offer help and advice. At no time did a woman need her mother more than when she became a mother herself.

She breathed deeply of the spring-blossomed air and reminded herself to count her blessings. Her life *was* much improved, if more complicated. She was well provided for financially. She had a roof overhead and food in the pantry. And she had two children she cared about—even while worrying about them and, occasionally, fearing them. Emotions were a quandary sometimes.

The quiet clearing of a throat brought her focus back to the room.

Gates, the butler, stood in the doorway. "I'm sorry, ma'am. I did not mean to intrude, but Mr. Ashby is waiting in the parlor for you."

The moment of peace was over. She nodded at Gates and steeled herself for the meeting with her husband's solicitor. *I am a baroness,* she thought.

She'd been furious with Mr. Ashby since the moment she realized that Lord Coventry had not put aside a settlement for her, nor had he provided her with a jointure. She had been left entirely to the whims of her inheriting son.

She wondered why her parents had not seen to any sort of settlement for her when the marriage contracts were drafted. *She* could not have paid attention to those details. She'd barely come out of her own childhood when she'd married. But it did not serve any purpose to be angry with her mother and father; they had been blinded by the baron's title. So had she. The prospect of marrying a baron had seemed exciting at the time. Who could think of settlements when such high-ranking titles awaited them?

"Lady Coventry." Mr. Ashby bowed in deference when she entered the parlor.

Her soul bristled at his voice. "Mr. Ashby."

"I wanted to see you before you traveled north in order to set your mind at ease that all is well with young Lord Coventry's inheritance. My responsibilities will keep me in London for a short while, but I will come along soon to check the boy's progress and help prepare him to take up the mantle of his father's affairs. I wanted to be sure you could do without me in the interim."

Do without him. She would love to show him how well she could do without him except she didn't understand enough to do well at all. She had not known how involved the solicitor would become in their lives with her husband gone. The move to the country had been hotly contested by Mr. Ashby, the man whose position should have entailed giving advice, not keeping her life in a stranglehold. Mr. Palmer, the estate steward, did not act with such high-handedness.

"I'm sure we'll be quite well, Mr. Ashby. I have things well in hand. The children are sincerely looking forward to their time at Windsong."

Edward's voice shouted an insult from upstairs, followed by Lia's cry.

"Yes, I see." Mr. Ashby smiled tightly. "Well in hand, Lady Coventry."

Nora's anxiety spiked. Would he insist on Edward's return to Eton? If so, she could do nothing to stop him. The will gave Mr. Ashby total control over the futures of her children. She needed to get him out of the house before the children did anything that would require his intervention.

"I don't wish to keep you from your duties, Mr. Ashby. I would hate to see you fall behind in your responsibilities simply because I trespassed too long on your time. Thank you for coming. I will look forward to seeing you at Windsong." She bobbed her head in what she hoped was a polite dismissal and rang the bell to summon Gates.

She left the room with the unhurried, untroubled discipline of a lady even though her mind was already racing up the stairs to quiet the children. She could not let him see where she was failing.

Mr. Ashby's voice rose behind her. "There are many wonderful governesses I could recommend to her ladyship if you would like."

She grit her teeth and said over her shoulder, "Thank you for your thoughtfulness, but I do not require such recommendations at this time. I have had my fill of other people's interference in raising my children." She hadn't meant to say that last part out loud, and her heart beat faster at having asserted herself so boldly. It was not in her nature to be disagreeable.

"He requires instruction beyond that of his mother."

She heard the threat in the word "requires." She nodded. "Of course. And I intend to hire the best tutors once we are settled at Windsong."

She breathed much better when the parlor door closed behind her—until another scream of fury came from upstairs. "Please let Mr. Ashby be deaf to that cacophony," she mumbled as she climbed the stairs. She knew such a hope to be entirely fruitless, but she held to it with fervor.

She arrived in the hallway where Edward dangled a porcelain doll by its foot over the banister. Nora glanced quickly from Lia's panicked face to the tiled floors below and held her hand out to her son. "Edward, give me that doll this instant."

"Or what?" the boy asked.

"Or we will leave right this instant for the country, and you will not be allowed to say farewell to any of your schoolmates." Her voice did not shake, nor did her outstretched hand. She felt fury to her fingernails. She was tired of this boy—*her* boy—mistreating this girl who was not hers but with whom she shared so many miseries.

Uncertainty crossed Edward's features. His blond eyebrows scrunched into a knot above his nose. "We aren't ready to leave. We're not even packed."

"No. We're not. But what is that to us? We have servants enough to finish such chores. They can bring our belongings later. And you will not be allowed to hold them accountable for anything they may fail to pack, because *you* will be the one responsible for our leaving in such a ridiculous hurry. And I will make certain each and every servant within our household is aware of your folly."

His lips thinned to a hard slash. He jutted out his thin jaw before he stepped closer to the banister. Lia gasped in horror, and Nora inwardly seethed, but he didn't drop the doll. He thrust it into Nora's hand.

"Take it, then. What do I care?" He turned on his heel and ambled to his rooms as if he hadn't a care in the world.

Nora began trembling as soon as he walked away. She waited until he was behind his closed door and then took several steadying breaths before she dared try to hand the doll to Lia. She feared her shaking hands would make her drop the toy. How Edward would gloat if she were the reason for the porcelain face shattering to pieces instead of him.

It was a pretty doll with rosy cheeks and a lovely cream-colored evening gown. A lorgnette hung from the doll's wrist by a ribbon that matched the gown. Nora tried to remember if she'd seen the toy before as she passed it to Lia's waiting hands.

Lia hugged the doll fiercely to her chest. From within a chalky face, forlorn eyes stared up at Nora. "Thank you." The small, timid voice felt like an echo from deep within her own soul. "My mama gave this to me."

Nora understood. A gift from a beloved mother who was lost to her made the doll so much more than a toy. It was a treasured memory of love. If Edward had broken it . . .

"I'm sorry—" Nora started to say but didn't know where to go from there. She was sorry for so many things. There was not enough time in a day to recount them all.

Lia nodded and scurried toward her own rooms.

"I am not old enough for these responsibilities," Nora murmured before heading back down to the drawing room.

Once there, she stared at the great chair in front of the fire. The chair that used to be occupied by her husband. The chair that her son seemed to fill up in the same unreachable way.

The door opened, and Mrs. Herold entered, carrying a small silver tray with a glass of creamy golden liquid. "My apologies for being late with this, m'lady," Mrs. Herold said.

"I did not request anything." Nora eyed the steaming liquid with no small degree of curiosity.

"Not in so many words, no. But old Nan used to swear by this restorative. And I thought you might want for a bit of freshening."

"You heard the disturbance upstairs," Nora said.

Mrs. Herold ventured a smile on her warm, round face. "I daresay the entire neighborhood heard."

Nora sighed and accepted the drink. She sniffed at the glass. "What is it?"

"A hot milk posset."

"What is in it?"

Mrs. Herold made a *tch* sound. "Best not to ask."

Nora nodded and drank with no further questions. The liquid burned unpleasantly down her throat. "The sooner we remove ourselves from London to Windsong, the better. We all need a fresh start," she said, handing the glass back to Mrs. Herold.

Nora glanced out the window. The cherry blossoms were a sign of new beginnings for the earth. She hoped the earth had saved some of those new beginnings for her little family. She had languished in the cold of her husband's shadow for far too long. But no longer. She would rise into the light. *I am a baroness.* She would find a way to take control of her own life.

Chapter Four

Ridley stood in line with the other household servants while they waited for the carriage to come to a stop in front of the house. He'd had years of training standing at attention and had no trouble holding still without fidgeting. Young George could not say the same.

"You want to stand like a soldier in ranks." Ridley kept his voice low to avoid being overheard schooling the undergroom.

"How long can a carriage take to make it up the drive?" George muttered under his breath, though he still slouched and shifted from foot to foot. "I could walk this bit faster. *Angel* could walk this bit faster."

Angel was a mare who'd rolled an ankle a few weeks prior. Though healing nicely, she was certainly not fast at the moment.

Ridley meant to further chastise the lad into straightening up and quieting down, but the carriage finally came to a stop. The line of staff felt absurdly large when seen all together at once.

The footman climbed down from the carriage, pulled out the step block, and opened the carriage door.

True to George's rumors, two children—a boy and a girl—climbed out of the carriage. Household gossip declared the girl to be the illegitimate offspring of the late baron, who'd decided to acknowledge her on his deathbed.

The staff had been instructed to treat the girl as Lady Coventry's natural daughter. They were also told to refrain from all gossip, though much good that bit of instruction had done, since tongues had been wagging. Nash, Windsong's butler, would not be pleased if he heard of the staff's indiscretion.

The children had been such a curiosity to Ridley that it almost startled him when he came face-to-face with their mother. He had expected Lady Coventry to be the same age as the late baron, but she appeared to be closer to Ridley's own age. Not a wrinkle on her brow or at the corners of her eyes. Not a gray hair on her fair head. She couldn't have been older than eight-and-twenty. As she inspected the household staff, her pale blue eyes briefly met his. Pain weighed heavy in their depths, a pain that was at once as familiar and heavy as the pain he'd known in his own past.

Her lips parted as if she meant to speak to him. Ridley almost opened his own mouth to speak, almost lifted his hand to take hers, almost told her he understood how she felt, but he managed to catch himself just in time. Her lips closed, and her eyes darted to young George, who was now standing as still as a tree on a windless day.

The family made their circuit past the staff and then entered the house. Everyone was excused to return to work, which Ridley was only too happy to do. Anything to take his mind off the strange feeling of compassion and commiseration that had come over him when faced with the mistress of the house. So what if she felt sadness and was near his age? What had that to do with him?

Nothing.

At the carriage house, he and George helped unhitch the horses and then walked them for a few minutes to let them relax and cool down before returning them to the stable.

"The family didn't look anything like I thought," George said, looking up from where he picked out the hooves to remove any pebbles or debris.

"How did you think they would look?"

"I thought Lady Coventry would be old. And I thought the new Lord Coventry would be a touch older—more my age instead of such a little 'un. They were certainly a somber group. I half expected the church to ring out a death knell, they all looked so broken."

Broken. That was one way to put it. Haunted would be another way. Tired too. That seemed to fit the description for all of them, not just the mother.

Ridley ran his hands down the horses' legs to feel for any swelling or cuts. "Lord Coventry did pass recently."

George shook his head. "Over a whole year ago. They looked as though he died yesterday or maybe even this morning. He was such a blustery, frigid man that you'd think they'd be glad he's gone."

"Be respectful."

George fell silent. Though he didn't stay that way for long.

"Do you ever wonder at that?" He brought over a bucket of water and the currying brushes.

"At what?"

"At rich people all long in the face and looking like they want to kick at rocks and shake their fists at the sky. Doesn't it seem odd that they could feel sad when they have so much food and comfort and people fetching and carrying for them all the day long?"

"Not odd at all. They are people, same as you and me. No matter what's on your dinner plate or how many rooms the roof over your head covers, human emotions are the same. Bad days and good days and sad days, too. People are people regardless."

"I s'pose you might be right," George said. "It just seems like it would be a mite easier to be happy when your plate is filled with hot buttered beans and tarts and pheasant than when your plate has biscuits and cold turnips or nothing at all as may be. And it'd be a mite easier to feel happy if the roof over your head didn't leak when it rained or let in the cold winds."

"I see your point. But the current roof over your head doesn't leak. And you have hot buttered beans on your plate often enough."

George nodded and soaked his brush in the water bucket before giving the horse another once over. "True enough, but that's only because rich people are doing the feeding and housing. You should've seen the house I grew up in." He dunked the brush again. "What sort of house did you grow up in?"

Ridley hadn't expected that question. He avoided talking about his own upbringing as much as possible. "Not so different from where I'm at now."

"Did you always live in stables then?"

"Not always. Take this one out and let her get the kinks out of her muscles before we put her in her stall."

"I know what I'm doing. You've told me before."

As Ridley had hoped, the boy had been sidetracked with the instruction and abandoned his line of questioning.

George took the horse Ridley had already examined out to the corral, leaving Ridley to finish currying the last mare. Once the animals had been to pasture long enough, he and George could get them back in their stalls with nice mounds of hay to sleep on. A horse making the trip from London pulling a full carriage deserved as many luxuries as it could be given.

While he waited for George to return, Ridley's thoughts drifted to his past. His parents had both passed away, and he missed them. Well, he missed his mother. His father was the sort of man no one would truly miss—the sort who drank too much and shouted too much and stomped about too much.

But his mother had been gentle and soft like butterfly wings. She had favored him; he was certain of that. She had formed a connection with him that she didn't seem to have for his two older brothers, who had grown up hard and cold like his father. Ridley's brothers had tormented him unmercifully for hanging on his mother's every word, for following after her and taking an interest in those things that interested her.

Though his father had been the one to introduce him to his very first horse, it had been his mother who'd taught him how to truly care for the animal, to pay attention to signs of wear and exhaustion, and to look for clues regarding the horse's well-being. "All living things tell stories about themselves if we know how to listen," she'd said.

He had taken that lesson to heart, and he'd found that by listening to and meeting the needs of the horses, they responded better and were easier to train. He kept them healthy and *happy*. That happiness bred capability. The horses under his care *were* improved compared to horses in other households. He raised champions both in body and spirit.

From the moment he'd begun making his own way in life by working in the stables, the horses under his care had begun to thrive as never before. He had been promoted from a stable boy to an undergroom after just a few months, which meant both the other grooms and the other stable boys equally loathed him. He'd had to move to a stable on a different estate to keep simmering tempers from flaring.

After a few months at the new estate, they had tried to elevate him to stable master. He declined that position. Since then, he'd always declined promotions, no matter that it meant more money and softer accommodations. He had no wish to be the front and center of attention. And he didn't mind working under a stable master who treated him fairly.

When he'd arrived in Windsong, he'd been disappointed to find that Mr. Daw had no real concern for the animals beyond what his job required of him. Nor did he have any real concern for the grooms and stable boys. He'd jeered at Ridley's methods and clearly was determined to make working in the stable difficult enough that Ridley would be forced to move on quickly. But once Lord Coventry had noticed how well the horses were doing, Daw had become invested in Ridley's methods. Rather, he'd become invested in taking the credit for Ridley's methods.

Ridley didn't mind because now Daw basically left him alone, aside from yelling at him every now and again. Ridley ran the stables as he wished. He was his own man for the most part, and he lived his life by his own merit and work.

"Is she ready to go out?" George asked, interrupting his thoughts. The boy gestured at the horse.

Ridley tossed the brush into the bucket of water now dark with horse sweat and dirt from the trail. "She's ready."

George guided the mare out to the corral, leaving Ridley alone again. "I am my own man," he whispered to the stable. Even as he said it, he considered the jolt he'd felt when meeting Lady Coventry. Her evident pain had affected him.

He turned back to his work, refusing to allow that seed of emotion any space to grow. Lady Coventry's problems could not be his problems. The woman had nothing to do with him. He would stay out of her way well enough to maintain the status quo.

Chapter Five

They'd been at Windsong for less than a day, and the children had already engaged in three separate arguments. Nora had barely broken up one before it turned to physical blows. She had told herself Edward would not hit a girl, but just because a boy was raised as a gentleman did not mean he acquired all gentlemanly attributes. Her indifferent husband had taught her that.

But she would do better by her son. She would not allow him to neglect and ignore other humans like his father had.

She took a deep breath before knocking on her son's door and entering his room without his permission. She should have waited for his permission. As the heir and, indeed, the actual owner of Windsong, he had the right to order her out of his rooms if he so chose. But she was his mother. And no matter what he'd been taught by his governesses and schools, she was the one who would make decisions for him until she had retrained him on how to make decisions for himself. She would choose tutors who would align best with her desires.

"I hate it here," he said sullenly. He had flopped back on the pillows of his bed and was staring at his ceiling.

"You've not even seen the rest of the house. Why don't you come with me while I tour the house and the yard? We can meet the staff in a more personal way and see where each person belongs. It will help us to remember who does what."

"Why do I care who does what?"

"Because this is your household. These people are under your care. Getting to know them allows you to earn loyalty and trust. Earning their loyalty means they will keep your private affairs private and defend your name if it is ever besmirched in the town. One learns more about a man by the words of his servants than by a reputation gained any other way."

He grunted in resignation. "Fine. Let's go then."

She felt surprised that he agreed without arguing. It was an excellent first step in this new household. Maybe this change in atmosphere was just the thing they needed, despite Mr. Ashby's obvious disapproval. Mr. Ashby would see the change and understand how much her son needed her.

Edward dragged himself off the bed, inch by inch, in the way he had when he was a stubborn toddler being called back to the table to eat his vegetables. She quickly hid her smile lest he discern how much it amused her.

The tour went well enough. Edward acted engaged and interested, and Nora felt pleased with herself for conceiving such a plan.

As they were exiting the back entrance of the house to go to the carriage house and stables, Nora heard Lia's voice calling. "Nora? Is anyone home?"

She felt a pang of regret that she hadn't thought to invite Lia on the tour with them. It was hard to not feel a rising sense of betrayal whenever she looked upon the girl. She also felt a rising sense of guilt because it was not the child's fault any more than it had been her own that they found themselves in their current situation. They were both victims of the same cruel circumstance.

"Wait a moment, Edward," she said to her son.

"Why?"

"For your sister, of course. She'll want to go with us."

"I thought this tour was to help me be a better master. What has she to do with that?"

Nora should have anticipated the question and done a better job at making the tour seem like his idea. There had been a few times she'd made ideas seem like Lord Coventry's own when she'd been forced to put herself forward on important matters he otherwise would have dismissed. Her son would be much easier to lead.

But no. She didn't want to manipulate him.

She wanted him to make good choices that stemmed from being a good man.

"Your sister is a baroness. She has an interest in the affairs of this land as well. Besides, you have it in you to be the kind of older brother a young girl like her could look up to and admire."

"Fine. I'll wait."

Nora felt another flood of immediate relief. He'd agreed to wait. That was something. Then she realized he'd only agreed to wait because she'd appealed to his vanity. How was that not manipulation? It was. Of course it was. She would have to be smarter in helping him make choices that had nothing to do with manipulation on her part.

She found Lia at the bottom of the stairs, hugging her porcelain doll.

Nora held out her hand and told Lia where they were going and what they were doing.

"Will Edward go too?" Lia asked.

"Yes. He's waiting just outside."

"Please wait another moment for me." Lia retreated up the stairs, returning a few minutes later without the doll. Nora understood. Edward had proven himself untrustworthy where the doll was concerned.

Lia hesitated before taking Nora's hand, as she did every time Nora offered it to the little girl.

It was time to have a rather difficult conversation. "Lia?"

"Yes?"

"When you called for me a moment ago, you called for Nora. You can see why the housekeeper and everyone else would think it strange for a little girl to call her mama by her name."

"But—" Lia was likely going to argue, again, that Nora was *not* her mama. The conversation had been repeated more times than Nora could count. "Yes, Mama," Lia said after a moment.

Nora felt the pain of what it cost the child to obey. But she didn't know what else to do. Lord Coventry's wishes had been specific. Nora was to care for Lia as her own daughter. It was one of the few things she agreed with when it came to her husband's commands. If Nora and Lia did not perfect the act of mother and daughter, it would leave the child open to censure from all sides of society, from those who would scorn her to the darker elements of society who would use her weakness for their own purposes.

Nora didn't want to see the girl growing up with that sort of branding on her forehead. Heaven knew it was hard enough to fit in where you actually belonged. To force a fit was that much more difficult.

She thought of the German fairy story about the slippers of gold and the girl made into a peasant by her own family. The stepsisters had branded the peasant girl as someone who did not fit within the society the sisters believed themselves to belong to. Though, in the end, they were the ones who did not fit, yet the young girl had endured so much grief at their hand, how would meeting any prince or living in a castle ever allow her to recover?

She did not want Lia to undergo that same sort of torment, especially not from Edward, but thus far nothing had seemed to have encouraged a change. The siblings did not care for one another. And Nora seemed to be fulfilling the role of cruel stepmother in the young girl's eyes no matter how kind she was. How were any of them to make sense of their lives all twined together?

When Nora and Lia joined Edward outside, he rolled his eyes at them and muttered, "Finally." He headed toward the stables in a noticeable effort to keep a few paces ahead of them.

Nora did not mind his poor manners in this instance. Better for him to stay ahead instead of trying to trip his sister or tossing taunts in her direction about the way she spoke or how she did not always keep her shoulders straight, even though he was guilty of slouching far more often than Lia was.

In spite of the length of time they'd spent waiting for Lia, the young girl became distracted on her way to the stables when she'd spotted the fluffy tail of a rabbit and begged to go after it. Edward groaned at his sister's childishness, but Nora found the request charmingly innocent. She gave her permission. It would be just her and Edward after all.

At the stables, Nora called out for the attention of the stable master. She remembered from her earlier introduction to the staff that he was older with a sour expression, but the man who answered her call looked to be closer to her own age.

When their eyes met, his lips lifted in a smile, and she felt her stomach tug up as well.

He was attractive with his dark, wavy hair curling over his ears and his face lightly shadowed with stubble. His eyes were dark and contemplative, and he held himself erect and sure, like any gentleman she had ever met. A small, pale scar—obviously from some adventure or another—almost disappeared into his firm jawline as he smiled.

It was the smile that made all the difference, she decided.

Truly, she had known many attractive men, but never before had she *felt* an attraction, which was thrilling and new and dangerous and ridiculous all at once. As a widowed baroness, the last thing she could afford to do was behave like a morally bankrupt rake and fling herself at the staff.

She gave herself a mental scolding to snap herself out of her silly, fanciful thoughts. *Think of the future. Your future. Your son's future.* She was glad Mr. Ashby was not inside her head to scowl at her.

"We were looking for the stable master, Mr.—"

"Mr. Daw is who you are looking for. I do apologize, Lady Coventry, but he is not here at the moment. However, I am happy to help with whatever you need. Would you like me to order a carriage or fit some horses with saddles for you and the children?"

"No. Thank you. I was hoping to introduce my son, Lord

Coventry, to all the staff while they were in their element so he may have a knowledge of those on his estate."

The man's eyes shifted from her to her son, and she felt disappointed to have his attention removed. The idea that she would miss his gaze on her face was ridiculous, and her cheeks warmed as an outward revelation of the thoughts she inwardly entertained. Forget being in her head. She was glad Mr. Ashby was nowhere in the vicinity to witness her folly.

"Hello, Lord Coventry. My name is Ridley Ellis. It is a pleasure to meet you. I am at your service for anything you need here in the stable. Is there anything specifically you would like me to show you at the present time?"

Nora was glad he'd shared his name since she hadn't recalled it from when she'd met the staff. Now that she'd heard it from his own lips, she doubted she would ever forget.

Edward looked up and down the stalls. "Show me the horses."

Nora inhaled sharply, ready to reprimand her son for not asking politely, but she held herself in check. Edward was the baron, after all. It would not do for her to rebuke him in front of those he employed. But she would be certain to scold him later when they were in private.

"Of course, sir." Mr. Ellis was most attentive to Edward, informing her son of each horse's name and breed and temperament. He asked after Edward's interests regarding horses and in his abilities in keeping a seat, to which Edward lied and declared himself a far more skilled rider than he was in actuality.

Even with the lie, she was pleased to see Edward engaged and leaving behind his typical sulkiness.

"This," Mr. Ellis said to Edward, "is General. He was your father's favorite horse. I daresay you will find him an energetic and amiable companion."

Edward looked into the dark brown eyes of the horse with awe and whispered, "General." He scratched the horse's nose, and the animal didn't shy away or stamp in agitation. It was as if he knew he'd been claimed by his new owner.

Nora wanted to thank the stable hand for giving her son a connection to another living creature.

Mr. Ellis walked them back to the path that led to the house
when his eyes connected with Nora's again. She felt a tingle of familiarity again, and she wondered if they had met before.

But that was ridiculous. How would she have met him? She
hardly ever came to Windsong, and on those few occasions in the beginning of her marriage when she had been at the estate, she'd kept to
her rooms. When she'd buried the late Lord Coventry, she'd stayed the
night and left early the next morning. Mr. Ellis had not been present
at that time. She was sure she would have remembered.

Yet, she could have sworn she'd looked into those same eyes before. She could almost hear the faint strands of a violin as she looked
at him.

"Yes, m'lady?" Mr. Ellis said, bringing her out of her thoughts.

"Oh." She'd been caught daydreaming. "Thank you for your tour.
Do you know when Mr. Daw will return? I do feel it would be helpful
for young Lord Coventry to become familiar with those who help
keep his household running."

"I will let Mr. Daw know you were asking after him as soon as he
returns."

"Thank you." It was only when she was on her way to the carriage
house that she realized Mr. Ellis hadn't exactly answered her question
regarding Mr. Daw's return.

But surely he hadn't been avoiding the question. She hated how
uncomfortable she suddenly felt in the too-bright sun. Certainly it
was the sun that caused the flush of her cheeks and made everything
feel strained and pinched and too warm. It was certainly not because
of Mr. Ellis. But even so, she would have to be careful to avoid the
stables in the future. She needed to gain control of her life and situation. She had to stop the fanciful wanderings of her mind.

Later, after her children had been put to bed and Nora's maid,
Rebecca, had gone, Nora stared in the mirror at her dressing table for
a long time. When Lord Coventry had visited the estate, Nora had

preferred to stay in London, relishing the space that allowed her to breathe, to not be told she was silly, to not feel she was always in her husband's way. When he was gone, she had been able to be her own person for a short period of time.

Now, after spending a day at the estate, she admitted she may have been mistaken in not visiting more often. The gloriously clean air felt refreshing to breathe in and out. The birds were cheery in their songs, and the smells of spring in early blossom were mesmerizing. How had she let opportunities of taking in such refreshment slip past her?

She knew how, of course. She merely wished it differently.

"Ridiculous fancy," she said to the mirror. The echo of her words returned to her in her husband's voice.

She thought of the man in the stable. She thought of his kind eyes and attentive manner.

"Ridiculous fancy, indeed." She blew out the candle on her dressing table and made her way in the dark to her bed where she removed her robe and slipped under the covers.

She was almost asleep when Lia started crying from her room and Edward yelled from his room for her to be quiet. If they were loud enough for her to hear, they were loud enough to wake the entire household. So much for getting some sleep.

Chapter Six

Ridley oversaw the visit from the farrier who had arrived to repair some shoes on a few of the horses. The estate used to have a permanent position for a farrier, but after Lord Coventry passed, there was not so great a need, and Daw had dismissed their farrier.

Ridley suspected the steward, Mr. Palmer, had not been made aware of the dismissal at the time it had happened, as the farrier's pay seemed to be flowing directly into Daw's pocket.

He was certain Daw would no longer be profiting from such a ruse, not with the lady living at the estate and Mr. Palmer suddenly spending so much time at Windsong.

He laughed to himself at the thought. Old Daw.

He stopped laughing when he heard a sniffle from Bonnie's stall. It was not the sort of noise a horse would make, but more like the kind that came from a child. He peeked over the stall gate to see a small head of hair so fair as to be nearly white. The curls, which might have been tidy at some point, were in complete disarray and tangled about with pieces of hay.

He glanced over to Bonnie, who didn't much care for people, specifically strangers, but the horse blinked her big brown eyes and flicked her tail agreeably.

The little girl ran a hand under her nose as she sniffled again.

He pulled his handkerchief from his pocket, opened the gate, and approached the tiny figure. When she realized she wasn't alone, she shrank back into the hay as if she could hide herself.

"Don't be angry," she said. "I didn't know where else to go."

"It's all right, Miss Amelia. I'm certain I could never be angry with you. I only wish to give you a handkerchief. Is that all right?" He held out the small square of white cloth to her.

She frowned before tentatively taking the handkerchief and wiping at her eyes.

"There now." Ridley leaned against the stall. "What has you in here looking so sad?"

"I miss home."

"I can imagine. London is quite different."

"Not London. My *home*. We saw Castle Rising on the way here." Her small voice held the smallest hint at happiness at that information.

"Well, that's lovely. I've been through there on many occasions. When I was a boy and traveling with my father, we once stopped there for a picnic lunch. My father let me play in the old ruins with my brothers, and it was great fun."

The tiny girl nodded. "My mama let me play there with my cousins sometimes. Not very often because she was afraid I'd become hurt."

"Your mama is a very kind woman."

The child narrowed her eyes and tilted her head; she looked very much like a white feathered starling puzzling out a noise in the distance. "Did you know my mama?"

"I work here in the stable, so I do not know her well, but she has been fair and kind to all of us who work here at Windsong."

The girl shook her head. "Not her. Nora is my brother's mama, only I'm not supposed to say it." She hung her head and frowned. "I am supposed to call her my mama, too, but it is hard even though I am good at pretending. Have you ever had to pretend too hard?"

Ridley felt an unexpected swell of compassion and empathy for the small figure. "I have," he said quietly. "But I've found that if you want something to be true, even just a little, it helps make the pretending easier."

"But what if you don't want it to be true?"

The question perplexed him. He had not expected to have so honest a conversation with a member of the household. "What is it that you don't want to be true?"

"I don't want her to be dead."

Ridley clucked his tongue. "That is an unhappy truth." He glanced over the stall gate to see if anyone else might overhear. He felt a need to protect the little girl from further gossip.

"Pretending that Nora is my mother is just hard to do sometimes," she said.

He thought about that for several moments before realizing he didn't know how to respond, and no amount of time would give him a right answer. So he did what he knew best. He went to work. "Would you like to help me exercise the horses?"

She nodded and scrambled to her feet, straightening a dress much too nice to be worn in a stable. He waited for Miss Amelia to leave the stall so he could lock it up again when she asked, "Are we not going to give her exercise?"

"Bonnie? No. I think not this time."

"Why not?"

"Bonnie is an extremely sensitive horse, and that makes her difficult to control sometimes. Beyond that, she doesn't take well to strangers. You might get hurt if we took her out, and that would be a very bad thing indeed."

"But I'm not a stranger. I fed her an apple so I could stay in here with her."

Ridley wanted to laugh out loud at the ingenuity of the child to think of bribing the horse for a place of refuge. "So you're friends now, the two of you?"

Miss Amelia stepped up and rubbed Bonnie's nose. "I think we are."

He watched the two of them. Bonnie not only did not mind the little girl but seemed entirely happy to have the child in her space. Bonnie *did* need to walk in the exercise yard, and they *did* seem to be getting on quite well.

"All right, Miss Amelia, let us walk your horse then."

He readied Bonnie, and then let Miss Amelia take the horse's lead. He kept his hand higher up on the lead in case Bonnie and Miss Amelia were not so good as friends as the young lady believed. He did not wish to see the child hurt by an overly rambunctious horse. And though *he* had never encountered troubles with Bonnie, he'd seen enough people struggle with the mare that he was careful about who he allowed to ride her.

Walking with Miss Amelia and Bonnie out into the sunshine, Ridley noticed both child and horse seemed content to be where they were and to keep the company they were keeping. Miss Amelia spoke to the horse in sweet tones, and Bonnie responded with happy tail swishes and gentle nudges of her nose into the girl's side.

"So what gave you a need to hide in the stalls this morning?" he asked.

"My brother doesn't like me."

"I doubt that is true. How could anyone not like you?"

"I don't think he likes anyone if you want to know the truth." Miss Amelia widened her eyes and nodded her small head emphatically. "He's mean, even to Mama."

Ridley smiled to hear the little girl call Lady Coventry "Mama" even after she had declared the woman to not be any such relation. The girl and the lady could have passed for mother and daughter given their matching fair hair and pale blue eyes fringed by dark lashes.

"Perhaps he has his own troubles weighing heavy on his shoulders."

"What troubles could he possibly have? He's a baron."

The conversation reminded him of George's amazement that wealthy people could have struggles. "You're a baron's daughter Yet you still found reason enough to hide out in Bonnie's stall."

"But I had to hide *because* of my brother. I don't trouble him the way he troubles me."

"What trouble was he giving you this morning?"

She shook her head and rested it against the mare's neck as they walked. "It doesn't matter."

She said it as if that were the end of the conversation, so Ridley held his tongue and asked no further questions, instead letting the girl lead the horse in silence. They'd made two full circuits of the pasture and were halfway through a third when Ridley heard shouting from the stables.

When they neared the source of the commotion, Ridley saw Daw standing next to Lady Coventry, who was frowning the way ladies did with only a slight crease in her brow. Daw frowned with his entire person, from his eyebrows to his crossed arms to his boot tapping that grew more agitated the closer Miss Amelia, Bonnie, and he came to them.

"How dare you!" Daw shouted, causing Bonnie to fidget.

Ridley murmured to Miss Amelia to relinquish her hold on the mare's lead even as he tightened his own grip. He edged the child to the side to keep her out of harm's way. He gave Daw a pointed look that demanded the man explain his anger.

"You took Miss Amelia out without notice from her mother!" Though Daw hadn't shouted, Bonnie sidestepped at the man's obvious undercurrent of fury.

"Stay calm, Mr. Daw," he said softly, keeping calm so as not to further agitate the horse. Miss Amelia turned worried eyes to Ridley and then back to Lady Coventry.

"It's not Mr. Ellis's fault—" she started to say as Daw whipped open the pasture gate.

His motion startled Bonnie, and she reared up.

Miss Amelia froze in place as the horse loomed over her.

Everything felt like it happened all at once with Miss Amelia rooted to the spot and the horse bearing down on her and Lady Coventry gasping aloud with widened eyes and Daw standing stupidly at the gate as he shouted something Ridley couldn't hear.

Ridley jumped into motion, snatching the little girl away from where the hooves were coming down and depositing her by her mother's side before whirling around to regain control of Bonnie.

It took him a few tries, but he managed to pull the mare back to some semblance of calm as he shushed and soothed her. He turned his glare to Daw who glared right back.

"What do you mean taking the young lady out with our meanest horse? You could have gotten the child *killed*." Daw nearly spat the last word.

"Killed?" Lady Coventry repeated with obvious alarm.

It occurred to Ridley that Daw meant to see him terminated. With no need to impress the late baron, Daw no longer had use for Ridley.

Lady Coventry had her arms around Miss Amelia as if to comfort the child, but she also turned her own glare at Ridley.

Ridley knew better than to try to explain that taking out Bonnie had been the young lady's choice, not his. He also knew better than to try to explain that Bonnie had been perfectly docile and that Miss Amelia would have been safe if Daw hadn't bumbled into the situation.

"Well?" Daw growled in a low voice. "What do you have to say for yourself?"

"The young lady has taken a liking to this horse. If Bonnie is to be her horse, it seemed fitting to have them become acquainted with one another in a controlled environment."

"You call this controlled?" Lady Coventry asked with no small amount of shock and disbelief in her own tone.

Ridley knew not to contradict the baroness of Windsong. He maintained her gaze. "I'm sorry m'lady. It will not happen again."

"True right it won't!" Daw snapped. "You're sacked. Collect your wages and your belongings and then be on your way."

The young girl's eyes widened in horror. "Mama! Please don't let that happen! Mr. Ellis was only doing as I asked. Bonnie is my horse, and I wanted to walk her. You cannot let him be turned away because of me. Please, Mama! Please!"

While Lady Coventry looked pleased to be called "Mama," Daw

looked anything but pleased to see that Ridley had found an advocate among the family.

Ridley looked from Daw to Lady Coventry, curious to see what would happen.

Lady Coventry swept her hands down Miss Amelia's arms. "Well, it seems no harm has come to you." She straightened and met Ridley's gaze. "I trust you will be more careful in the future. And you will not allow my children out on the horses without my express permission."

"Of course, m'lady."

She nodded her dismissal, so Ridley bowed and moved with a tight grip on Bonnie's lead back toward her stall.

The little girl, who apparently had the power to control worlds with her words, said, "Thank you for letting me walk Bonnie."

He stopped, and Lady Coventry tightened her arms protectively around the girl, despite the danger having passed and despite the way the girl squirmed to be free.

"It was a pleasure to meet you, Miss Amelia. I'm sorry you were frightened."

"I wasn't frightened. Bonnie was frightened because he startled her." She pointed at Daw.

Ridley wondered if the child's testimony would result in a rebuke for Daw from Lady Coventry, but the woman made no move to admonish the stable master. Ridley wasn't surprised. For the most part, society people were not observant. He clucked his tongue and guided the horse away.

Lady Coventry had not allowed him to be fired, but she *had* allowed him to be scolded like a child. Such an action would embolden Daw and make life a trifle more difficult.

As if to prove his point, he'd barely finished latching the gate to Bonnie's stall when Daw stomped into the stable.

"I've had enough of you, Ellis!" the man growled. The words were kept low, likely in case the young lady and her mother were still about.

Ridley turned to Daw but said nothing.

"I'd have you gone in two shakes if I had my way—if that brat of a girl hadn't interfered."

"You should be grateful, Daw. The young lady did you an incredible service. If you had your way and were finally rid of me, you might have to actually do some work. And once the family realizes you're incapable of such action, then it will be *you* seeking employment elsewhere. I daresay employment would be difficult to find for a man with idle hands and a drunken temper."

Daw raised his fists, but Ridley held his ground and merely lifted his eyebrows.

Daw glared at Ridley, a flash of fear on his face. "I've had enough of your cheek. You watch yourself. Because you know I'll be watching."

He turned and strode from the stable.

"Watching me work, you mean, since heaven knows you aren't doing any of it," Ridley muttered when the man had gone.

Some time later, George and Robert, another of the undergrooms, entered the stable. "Daw's in a temper!" George exclaimed.

Robert nodded. "Best stay away from the carriage house. No reason for him to be cross with all of us."

"He's cross because of me. I'm sorry if he took it out on the two of you," Ridley said.

"*Tcha!* Like he wouldn't be gnashing 'is teeth at us either way," Robert declared. "But he's got it in fer you, Ridley. Make no mistake, he's planning something. I can see it in 'is eyes that he's thinking up something."

Ridley smiled at the two young undergrooms. "It is generous that you believe he thinks at all."

The boys laughed, but their brevity was cut short when Daw entered the stables.

"Ellis." Daw said Ridley's last name as if it were a curse. "Come with me."

George and Robert hung their heads as Ridley passed them, almost as if they felt he was being led to his execution. Seeing the glint in Daw's eye, Ridley wondered if that just might be where he was headed.

Chapter Seven

"N—Mama?"

Nora looked up from her letters to give Lia her full attention. The girl had worked with diligence to call her Mama instead of using her first name. "Yes, dear?"

"I would like to learn to ride my horse."

"Your horse?" Nora asked.

"Yes. Bonnie. Mr. Ellis called her my horse because we became friends."

It had been three days since the incident at the pasture. Nora shivered, remembering her fear. "That horse might not be safe."

"Bonnie's safe. I promise."

"I don't know if I can arrange for lessons today. Mr. Daw is a busy man."

Lia scrunched up her face as if she'd been handed something bitter to eat. "Not Mr. Daw. George said that—"

"George? Who is George?" Nora had not yet accepted any of the several invitations to tea she had received to get to know the neighbors. She'd wanted to feel settled and in control of herself before venturing out into the society that had always belonged to the late baron.

"He's a stable boy."

Nora blinked in surprise. "What were you doing in the stables? Have you been bothering those who are working?"

"Oh, no. I didn't talk to George. I was hiding under the stairs and heard him talking to one of the maids. He said Daw has been working him to death, which was a strange thing to say since he was alive when he was talking. Anyway, he said Daw frightened all of the animals. And I've seen that to be true. I want Mr. Ellis to teach me."

Mr. Ellis. Nora had tried to put him out of her mind since the moment she'd left the stables the other day. He was far too handsome for his own good. And for her own good. "I do not know. It might be best to wait for Mr. Daw to recommend a riding teacher."

Lia's eyes grew large and luminous with tears. "But Mr. Ellis would be a good teacher."

"A good instructor would have sound judgment. Mr. Ellis took you out without permission, and he did so with a horse that clearly hasn't been properly trained."

"Bonnie *is* properly trained." Lia's innocent indignance regarding the horse's honor brought a smile to Nora's lips.

Even with the smile, Nora held firm. "If you don't care for Mr. Daw, we shall find someone else to teach you to ride. And what do you mean you were hiding under the stairs? Hiding from what?"

Lia's gaze dropped to the floor like a stone to the bottom of a shallow pond. She didn't need to answer. In truth, Nora shouldn't have felt it necessary to ask.

"I'm sorry," Nora said. "I'll speak with him."

Lia's gaze shot up. "No! Please don't. It's always worse after you've spoken with him. But, if you could, there is something you can do for me."

Lia's eyes so rarely filled with hope instead of tears that Nora felt herself soften. "Yes, dear? What is it?"

"Please think about Mr. Ellis as my riding instructor. You don't have to decide right this minute. If you promise to think about it, that will be enough for me."

Nora immediately shook her head. "I know this is hard to understand, Lia, but I must do what I think is best. You matter a great deal to me, and if something happened to you . . ."

Lia gripped her skirts tightly—a habit Nora had been trying to cure. "Nothing will happen to me. I promise. Besides, everyone speaks well of Mr. Ellis. George said there's no one in the whole of England who calms a horse the way Mr. Ellis does."

"Lia." Nora had to make the little girl let go of her fantasy that Mr. Ellis would be her riding instructor. Perhaps Nora ought to sell the horse Lia had claimed as her own. The horse was unpredictable, and Nora wasn't convinced the stable hand was much better.

Nora stopped her thoughts. Why should she make Lia give up on her fantasy the way Lord Coventry had always demanded of her? Shouldn't one of them have some slim grasp of her dreams?

"Please, Mama. Please think about it."

Those magic words settled everything. When Lia said "Mama" like that—not after being prodded or reminded, not as an after-thought, but sincere and hopeful—it was Nora's undoing.

"I will see what can be done," she said.

And she *would* see what could be done. Both about Mr. Daw and Mr. Ellis.

She returned her attention to the invitations for tea piling up on her writing desk. She would make some careful inquiries and hope the gossips would have something to say on the subject of both her stable master and the stable hand.

Nora smiled politely as Mrs. Spencer poured the tea. The woman was decidedly middle-aged with hair already graying. Her round cheeks and easy smile made her also decidedly pretty. Though Mrs. Spencer offered her condolences for the late baron's passing, she didn't seem to wish to dwell on that dark topic, much to Nora's relief, since she wasn't sure she appeared adequately mournful. She'd never had any useful talent for pretense.

Mrs. Spencer settled into her chair and took a sip from her tea-cup. "The neighborhood will be grateful for the improvement of a couple of new children. I daresay it is good for the young to spend time with the young. Spending time with generations wholly separate from oneself would become intensely tiresome, do you not agree?"

"I do agree."

Mrs. Spencer laughed. "My youngest daughter, Mary, would be very pleased to meet your Amelia."

Nora felt her smile slip and hid it by taking another sip of her tea. To hear Lia referred to as Nora's surprised her, despite the fact that she had done everything in her power to make everyone believe it to be the truth. With Lia still finding it difficult to call Nora "Mama," she worried about letting the girl spend too much time with others.

Except maybe Lia would thrive with another young girl as a friend.

Nora set her cup back on its saucer and placed it on the table. "I am sure Lia would enjoy a friendly face now that we're settling into Windsong. Tell me—does Mary enjoy horseback riding?"

"She adores horses, though she isn't a very good rider yet. We have a new instructor coming from Salisbury next month, so we're hoping to see improvements. It's just a shame, do you not agree?"

"A shame?"

Mrs. Spencer laughed. "It is a shame that the rest of us must make do with lesser instructors when it is well-known that your groom is one of the very best. Any number of us would snatch him up for our own stables if we could. My, my! Your horses are the fastest in all of England, I would wager, and it is all due to him. Mr. Spencer practically covets your groom."

"Which of the grooms did you mean?" Nora asked, wishing she had not put down her cup so she could hide her discomfort at pretending not to know. It was as if Lia had coached the woman on what to say to Nora regarding Mr. Ellis. "Mr. Daw?" She gave an apologetic wave. "We're still learning the staff."

"Oh my, my! No! Not your man Daw. No. He's simply awful, I've been tol—" Mrs. Spencer caught herself and widened her eyes. "I *am* sorry. I don't mean to gossip regarding your domestics. Please ignore me. I'm prone to prattle on and on with very little sense in my words."

"Thus far, you seem quite sensible, Mrs. Spencer. Please, if you have unpleasant information regarding my staff, it's fine for you to share it as I have yet to form an opinion of my own. I promise I will give my staff fair consideration before passing judgment on them, but I find it is easier to come to correct choices when one is working with the full spectrum of information."

With that permission given, Mrs. Spencer talked for a quarter of an hour, detailing all the ways she had heard how Nora's stable master was a brute to the horses and to the rest of the staff, a cheat at cards who had several outstanding debts to servants in several other households, and a layabout as well. Mrs. Spencer was certain Mr. Ellis did the bulk of the work within the stables. She praised the way he had with horses—and people too. He had come to Mrs. Spencer's husband's aid on a few occasions when their horses had some malady or when they required a gentler, but firmer, hand in their training.

By the time Nora left the Spencer estate, she was certain of one thing. She liked Mrs. Spencer with her quick smile and easy manner. She hoped she could introduce Lia to Mrs. Spencer's daughter sooner rather than later. She was not certain, however, that Mrs. Spencer's many compliments about Mr. Ellis were founded in reality.

Once Nora returned to Windsong, she went directly to the stables.

She did not see Mr. Daw or Mr. Ellis, but only two young men of the household staff whom she recalled meeting briefly.

The taller of the two was a gangly, gap-toothed youth who couldn't have been older than fifteen or sixteen. He looked up when she cleared her throat, and his eyes widened. He immediately went from open-mouthed staring to tightly pressing his lips together. He remembered to remove his hat after a moment, twisting it in his hands tighter and tighter until Nora feared he would permanently damage the item.

"Lady Coventry." He made a stiff bow before tossing a meaningful look to his companion.

The other boy hurried to bow as well, making a more awkward mess of the endeavor than the first had.

"Hello," she said. "Yes. Who might I have the pleasure of addressing?"

"I'm George, ma'am. This here is Robert. Is there something we can do for you?"

Ah. So this was George, the boy who gossiped with her maids. "I was looking for Mr. Ellis, but since I have you two fine fellows here, perhaps you could answer a few questions."

"Certainly, ma'am." George nodded and, if possible, twisted his poor cap even tighter.

She first asked about the horses—their diet, their exercise schedule, their overall well-being—and then about the stables. Having been trained as a rider when she was a child, she felt she understood the subject enough to know if Windsong's stables were being properly managed. George answered each question with confidence and competence, while Robert maintained relative silence.

"Hm. Well then." She could find no fault regarding the information she'd heard. She opened her mouth to ask questions regarding Mr. Daw—and Mr. Ellis specifically—when Mr. Ellis himself interrupted her interrogation.

"Lady Coventry." His bow was perfect as far as such etiquette was concerned. "What has brought you to the stables today? Would you like to order a carriage or perhaps the curricle?" He did not offer to saddle a horse for her, likely having noted she was not dressed for riding.

"I merely came for information," she said, feeling slightly foolish for having interrogated the undergrooms rather than waiting for someone with higher authority. The truth was that she felt more at ease with the undergrooms. She didn't have to worry about them noticing if she made a misstep. Mr. Ellis was in perfect control of himself—not pretending at control the way she did. She was sure he would notice her insecurities bubbling beneath her façade.

"I see," Mr. Ellis said. "I am most happy to oblige." He sent a meaningful look to the two young men and then back to her as if to ask her if they could be excused.

She clasped her hands in front of her as she inclined her head. "Thank you, George and Robert. That will be all."

George nodded, gave a hurried bow, and turned to leave. Robert's bow looked more like he was doubling over about to be sick before he, too, scurried off.

"Is Mr. Daw about the stables somewhere?" she asked when she realized that Mr. Ellis was waiting for her to say something.

"No. Not today." Mr. Ellis flashed an apologetic grin, the small scar on his jaw disappearing as he did so.

"He was not here the other day when I visited with the young baron either."

"No, ma'am. He was not."

"Interesting," she murmured, tucking that information away for later consideration. She felt certain Mr. Ellis was not the sort of man to abuse his superiors, even if they might be deserving. She wasn't sure if she found that personality trait infuriating or admirable. "Well then." She removed her gloves and tucked them into her pocket. The day had warmed too much for gloves. "We shall have to proceed, just the two of us."

The man made no show of curiosity. He simply stood at attention and waited for her to speak.

"I have heard from several sources of varying reliability that you are an adept riding instructor. What is your opinion of this?"

"I would say that your sources are not varying at all in their reliability. They are entirely reliable, and the information they've provided is entirely accurate."

She stared at him, surprised at his show of vanity.

"My response has displeased you," he said. "I am sorry for that, but you did ask my opinion, and I do not believe it is prideful to be honest regarding one's capabilities."

She decided to not address his lack of humility because really, what could she say? "How many people have you taught to ride?"

"Fourteen, ma'am. I've also helped at least a dozen more improve their skills, though I would not go so far as to say that I was their instructor but more that I was someone merely giving advice."

She glanced around the well-kept and well-lit stable. The horses all seemed healthy and happy, and the stables smelled fresh and clean. A black Friesian to her right puffed and stamped at her as if telling her to get on with her reasons for being in the stable.

"My daughter seems to believe you can teach her to ride the horse that nearly trampled her the other day. What is your opinion regarding such an endeavor?"

"I can teach Miss Amelia to ride a horse. And I can teach her to ride Bonnie at some point, but not now. While Bonnie is a sweet creature, she is not ready to trust. That will take time. I will not put your daughter in harm's way, Lady Coventry. But I believe you know that to be true already."

"Do I know that?" she asked. "You took my daughter out with that same horse just the other day. What is that if not putting her in harm's way?"

Nora's pulse quickened at her assertion. But she had to be strong. *I am a baroness,* she thought. In truth, the only times she seemed able to pull off pretending at control were when her children needed her strength. She could do it for them.

"I do see your point, ma'am. But Miss Amelia requested to go walking with Bonnie specifically. While I said that Bonnie does not trust easily, she does trust me, and she trusts Miss Amelia. Even so, I kept my grip on the lead at all times. I could not have foreseen that anyone would join us, as that is atypical when I am exercising the horses. And by *atypical,* I mean to say that no one has ever come out to me while I have been out with Bonnie. But I think you know all that as well."

Nora liked his answer. Well, most of it. She did not like his assumption that he knew anything about her thoughts. How could he when she barely knew them herself? "What would you say regarding Mr. Daw as an instructor?"

Mr. Ellis leaned against the stall where the Friesian had been making noise. He rubbed the horse's nose absently as if trying to compose an appropriate answer. "I have no ready opinion in that regard."

"Why not?"

"I've never seen him give riding instruction so I have had no way to form a fair opinion."

She studied him. And he seemed to study her in return. "Have we met before, Mr. Ellis?" she asked.

Surprise flashed across his face. "How could we have, Lady Coventry?"

"Yes, of course. You're right." She finally nodded sharply. "I will require lessons for both of my children. From you. Not Mr. Daw. They will start tomorrow if it is convenient."

"Yes, ma'am."

She nodded again, not knowing why she wished to stay, especially because she had clearly run out of reasons for doing so. His calm demeanor seemed to also calm her. Was that what Mrs. Spencer had meant when she'd said Mr. Ellis knew how to steady anxious animals? Did he know how to steady anxious humans as well?

When she entered the house, Nash informed her that Mr. Palmer was waiting for her in her late husband's study. It suddenly occurred to her that she likely should have sent Mr. Palmer to arrange for the children's riding instruction rather than go herself. She hadn't considered Mr. Ellis's other work or how her request might interfere with the rhythm of the stables' workflow. Would Mr. Palmer tell Mr. Ashby what she had done? Perhaps not. She was grateful Mr. Ashby had not yet shown up.

Regardless, there was no way to recall her actions. She sighed. She'd gone herself because she was curious. Because she wanted to see for herself what kind of man Mr. Ellis might be.

Mr. Palmer stood as soon as she entered the study. He was a tall man. He might have been able to pass for a younger man except for the gray in his beard and hair. "Lady Coventry. You're looking well. It would seem the country has agreed with you."

"Thank you, Mr. Palmer. I do believe it does."

Once they were both seated, Mr. Palmer handed her a letter. It was addressed to him, and the seal was already broken. She began to read, but barely a sentence into the letter, she felt the frown settle so deeply on her face, she worried it might become permanent.

When she finished, she handed the letter back to Mr. Palmer. "Is this even legal?" she asked.

"I don't know the law in such specific terms, but I believe it is. It is important that you prove to Mr. Ashby that Edward is being properly trained to take over the barony in earnest while you have him here in the country. Otherwise, I believe Mr. Ashby would be within his rights, as given to him by the late Lord Coventry, to take the boy under his own care."

"Who decides the definition or standard to be used in determining what is 'properly trained'?" Her head pounded behind her eyes. It took all of her effort not to press her fingers to her temples to ease the ache.

"Happily, I am part of that deciding factor, so you need not worry too much, Lady Coventry."

Mr. Palmer's assurances did little to console her. "Why would my husband do this to me?" she asked quietly.

Mr. Palmer blew out a long breath. "I do not believe he meant it as a personal affront to you, Lady Coventry. For him, his sole concern was to ensure the continuance of the barony. It is his immortality in many ways. It is why he decided to acknowledge Miss Amelia. Should something happen to Edward, it was important for a second heir to be established. As I said, I do not believe his actions were personal."

"No," she whispered. "Of course not." Nothing with her husband had been personal. Everything was a business transaction. Why should the rearing of his child be any different? She kept her thoughts to herself, worrying that Mr. Palmer was not quite the loyal confidant he seemed.

When Mr. Palmer responded, he spoke with determination. "You *are* the boy's mother. This means we shall do our best to help your son hit the necessary milestones so that when Mr. Ashby comes to survey our progress, Edward will be more than ready. Rest easy, Lady Coventry. All will be well."

She smiled and did her best to appear as though she had no worries.

But she worried a great deal. Even reminding herself that she was a baroness was not enough to ease her fear.

And later that night, when Edward scoffed at her suggestion of studying with her and then left for his rooms without so much as a backward glance, she felt that worry settle into her heart.

From beyond the grave, her husband had proved he had the power to snatch her child from her arms, and she wasn't sure she would be able to stop him.

Chapter Eight

Ridley finished the morning chores well before breakfast. Like Ridley, Daw never missed breakfast. Unlike Ridley, Daw never bothered to set foot in the stables until after he'd eaten.

When Ridley entered the kitchen, he was glad to see Mr. Palmer, who had taken to joining the staff for mealtimes when he was on the estate. Ridley found Mr. Palmer to be a well-informed conversationalist, which was why it seemed so strange that Mr. Palmer remained quiet through the meal in spite of the lively chatter flowing around him. He frowned at his plate so long and so hard that Cook finally jabbed a spoon in his direction.

"What's got you looking like the good food I've placed before you might bite you back?"

Mr. Palmer, pulled from whatever dark and brooding thoughts he might have been entertaining, looked up. "What?"

"Are you ill, Mr. Palmer?" Ridley asked, genuinely concerned for the estate's steward.

"Ill? No. I'm fine, thank you."

Daw snorted in derision. "Are you ill, Mr. Palmer?" Daw repeated Ridley's question in a high, mocking voice. "Does it bother anyone else that Ridley here talks like he's expecting an invitation from the prince regent hisself? Like he thinks he's better than the rest of us?"

"Did you not sleep off your night's indiscretions, yet?" Mr. Nash asked Daw with a sniff of annoyance at Daw's surly attitude.

"I ask a sincere question and all I get is aggravation from you lot," Daw said with a scowl.

Nathaniel, the young lord's valet spoke up. "If Ridley's refined speech makes you feel inferior, then maybe, if you behave like a good boy, you can ask him to teach you to speak better." Nathaniel seldom had patience for Daw, especially now that Daw owed him a fair amount of money. The entire staff knew Daw would never pay his gambling debts, so Nathaniel took it out of Daw one insult at a time. Ridley did not love that Nathaniel brought him into the center of their squabbles.

Daw's face darkened, but he fixed his attention on his plate, thereby missing the glances the staff passed around the table. Daw was not incredibly well-liked, and it seemed the others were waiting to jump in the fray at the slightest provocation. Ridley would have felt sorry for him, but the man was unwilling to offer a kind word to anyone at the table. He might have even found an ally with Ridley, but Daw seemed determined to be unpleasant.

Rebecca, Lady Coventry's personal maid, touched Mr. Palmer's arm. "Truly, you look as poorly as Lady Coventry."

"Is the baroness unwell?" Mr. Palmer asked.

"Not unwell exactly. Something troubles her. She's unhappier than she's been in a long time. She was all at sixes and sevens last night before she went to bed. Do you know what's bothering her, or what I might do to help?"

"There really isn't much anyone can do to help Lady Coventry except . . ." Mr. Palmer's frown deepened. "Except if any of you see an opportunity to assist the young lord in finding his footing as the baron, it would be a great help to Lady Coventry. Indeed, it would likely help all of us in time."

"What's she to do with us?" Daw asked.

"You mean besides paying you, feeding you, and keeping a roof over your head?" Rebecca retorted.

Daw mumbled something that sounded suspiciously like "Shove off." But he went back to his breakfast without another word.

Rebecca returned her attention to Mr. Palmer, the two speaking to each other in voices too low to be overheard. Ridley smirked as George leaned closer. He had every confidence in George's ability to ferret out the bulk of the conversation between Lady Coventry's maid and the steward. And once he did, George would surely relay his findings to everyone in the stables.

Ridley finished his meal, thanked Cook for her many talents in the kitchen, and headed back to work. He had much to do if he was to begin the task of riding instruction for the young baron and baroness.

He was in the stalls picking out Opal's hooves when Daw appeared. "Bet you're proud of yourself."

While Ridley took a great deal of pride in his work, Daw was certainly not complimenting him. It took a concerted effort to control his temper anytime Daw spoke. After the incident with Bonnie and Miss Amelia, Daw had given the undergrooms the afternoon off to go swimming in the nearby lake and had Ridley do all the work required in the stables. Though George had offered to help, Daw had growled and blustered until the frightened boy left. Ridley had still been working long after dark.

He hoped Daw was not creating a similar situation today since he already had so much to do. He waited for Daw to explain himself, which didn't take long. "Getting the baroness to let you teach her brats to ride horses is brilliant. I know what you're doing."

Ridley bristled at hearing Daw insult the children. "I also know what I am doing. I'm doing my job."

"No. You're trying to do *my* job." Daw snarled the words.

Ridley smiled patiently. "Yes. Well, somebody has to."

"Are you implying I don't do my own work?"

"I'm certainly not *implying* anything. I rather thought I'd stated the facts quite clearly."

"You're trying to make me look bad." Daw's complaint almost sounded like a whine.

"I believe you give me too much credit, sir, on accomplishing a task that you need no help to achieve."

Daw leapt forward with his hands balled into fists. Ridley didn't so much as flinch. Nash was likely accurate in predicting that Daw still nursed the aftereffects that came from a night of hard drinking, which meant he would be less efficient in a fight.

But Ridley did not get the chance to discover if Daw could land a blow or not because just then a feminine voice called into the stables.

"Mr. Ell-is?" The singsong, childish way Miss Amelia called his name was charming. The way her brother scolded her and said, "Don't you know anything? Ladies aren't supposed to raise their voices like that" was less than charming.

Ridley lowered the Friesian's foot to the ground and took up her lead. He edged himself and the horse past the stable master, who had not yet properly processed what was happening. "I love these little talks of ours, Daw, but, as you've kindly pointed out, I have work to do, so you must excuse me."

Daw frothed and foamed but said nothing as Ridley welcomed the children then ushered them and Opal out into the exercise yard. He'd chosen Opal for the lessons because there was no horse in the entire county with an easier temperament.

"Today, we will start with the basics of a proper seat."

The young lord balked at that news. "I already know how to keep a seat."

"And so you may, but it is still the lesson for the day."

"Then you're wasting my time. I'll come back tomorrow to see if you've anything new to teach me."

Ridley put his arm out in front of the boy to stop him from leaving. "Before you go, m'lord, would you be so kind as to show me what you know. It may be useful to help with your sister's understanding."

The boy seemed conflicted but finally agreed. He pulled himself up into the saddle.

It was as Ridley had feared. The boy had not the first clue

regarding a proper seat. "Excellent, now that you're up there, please show us how to be in a balanced seated position."

"I *am* balanced."

Ridley strained to not contradict the boy in such a way that would be insulting. "If you were bent over at the waist like that while you were standing on the ground, you would eventually topple over. You want to sit on the horse in such a manner that your shoulders, hips, and heels are in a straight line."

Though the lesson started poorly, the young lord clearly didn't want to be shown up by his little sister, so he finally did as directed and managed to achieve a proper balanced seat.

Miss Amelia, after having watched her brother and offered her encouragements from the side, achieved a proper seat almost from the moment she was on the saddle.

While Miss Amelia had cheered his efforts, the young Lord Coventry did not return the favor. He scowled and murmured and scoffed. Miss Amelia did not seem to be too hurt by the heckling; it was almost as if she expected it.

Once she was down from Opal's saddle, she asked, "When will I be able to ride Bonnie?"

"It won't be too long," Ridley assured her. "While you are learning to ride, Bonnie will be learning as well. She doesn't trust easily, so she must be taught that she is able to depend on us in the same way we will depend on her."

"Boring," the young lord said with an irritated huff before he left the stable and his sister.

Miss Amelia watched him head toward the house and looked up at Ridley. "Would you walk me back?"

"Of course, but surely you know the way."

She nodded. "I do, but Edward might be waiting in the hedge-row to jump out at me. Or he might be behind the stone wall. That's where he was last time. I think he's angry because I did better than he did, so I would feel safer if I did not have to return on my own."

Ridley thought back to his own troubled childhood and to the many times his oldest brother had waited to spring such traps on him. "Yes. I would be happy to escort you to your home, Miss Amelia."

He put out his arm for her, but before she took it, she ran to Bonnie's stall. She pulled a small carrot from her pocket and fed it to the horse. She rubbed Bonnie's nose and then hurried back to Ridley. "Don't tell anyone that I was running."

"And why would it matter that you were running?" Ridley asked.

"Ladies are not supposed to run." Miss Amelia's smile dipped into a momentary frown, as if not running might be the greatest loss conceivable.

"What is a lady to do if she is in a hurry?"

"I asked that question too," she said with a sigh that indicated she had not been given a satisfactory answer. She took his arm.

As they neared the house, Lady Coventry emerged from the door. She smiled at Miss Amelia. "There you are, dearest. I wondered what you were about since Edward returned without you. How was your first lesson?"

Ridley felt like he ought to extract himself from the conversation but could not think of how to do so without interrupting either the mother or the child.

"It was lovely, Mama. Mr. Ellis is the best teacher. I knew he would be."

"Is that so?" Lady Coventry met his gaze. "The best, is it?" She looked amused, which made him bristle.

Why he cared to impress the lady was something he did not want to examine too closely. He was glad to have done well by little Miss Amelia, but her mother was fascinating and infuriating all at once. Her status in society and the way she seemed controlled by that status made her more infuriating than fascinating. He needed to remember that.

"It does help to have such an eager and adept student," Ridley said, tearing his gaze from those pale blue eyes so he could look down at Miss Amelia.

"Since you are here," Lady Coventry said, "I wondered if I might request a horse to be readied. It has been a while since I've been riding. I would like to let that ability stretch so I might go riding with the children when they are ready."

"Of course, ma'am. Do you have a preference on which horse?"

"I'm afraid I don't really know the horses stabled here. I would prefer one who is good-natured and leads easily. I do not want"—she looked down at her daughter—"Bonnie, is it?"

Uncertain if the lady was making a joke or not, Ridley kept his smile in check. "I will be certain to not saddle Bonnie for you, ma'am."

"She could ride Opal," Miss Amelia offered.

"Who is Opal?" Lady Coventry asked.

The little girl sighed happily as she described the Friesian's glossy, jet-black coat and big eyes.

"Would she not be too tired after her exertions with the children?" Lady Coventry asked.

"No, ma'am," Ridley said. "She did not have the chance to get much exercise with today's lessons. She would be glad to have a rider take her out. Will it just be you, ma'am? Will there be any guests?"

"Actually, yes. My neighbor, Lady Spencer, will be joining me, but she will be bringing her own mount. She should be here inside of an hour."

"Of course, ma'am."

The lady nodded, took a hold of Miss Amelia's hand, and turned to enter the house. She had not made it two steps before Miss Amelia turned back, quite nearly dragging Lady Coventry with her. "Thank you, Mr. Ellis! I had a lovely time!"

He smiled and bowed. She giggled and let her mother turn them both back to the door, but not before he saw a small frown crease Lady Coventry's brow and lips.

Had she meant that frown for him?

Had he, again, done something to earn her displeasure?

Or was the frown because of the girl?

Was he not to bow to the child?

Perhaps she did not truly accept the girl as her own and disapproved of any gesture made to the child. But that made no sense. He was no one of consequence in Lady Coventry's eyes, so what matter would it be for him to bow to the girl?

"You're chasing ghosts, Ridlington," he muttered to himself, using his given name rather than the nickname he'd assumed when he'd left home. She likely wasn't frowning at all. And if she were, what would it matter to him? Not one whit.

He was entertaining such arguments in his own head when he arrived back at the stables and found Daw waiting for him, eager to continue their previous discourse.

"Since you've been ignoring your work while teaching the brats to ride, I expect you to catch up on your chores," he said.

Ridley gave the man a flat-lidded stare. How Daw could not consider what he'd been doing to be work truly defied all comprehension. "I woke much earlier than usual this morning to accomplish all my work in order to accommodate the lessons. What is it precisely that you feel I've neglected?"

"There's the mucking that needs done as well as replacing the hay."

Ridley gritted his teeth. "Those jobs belong to the stable boys."

"Not today they don't." Daw shoved a pitchfork into Ridley's hand. "Best get to it. The stable boys and undergrooms have the day off, so don't even think asking 'em for help after I leave." Daw smirked and clapped his hands together as he walked away.

Ridley could not let him leave without an attempt to prick the man's conscience. "And what will you do today, Daw? What labor is yours? What labor is *ever* yours?"

"I make sure that the likes of you remembers your place."

Then the man was gone. Ridley glanced to the many stalls. Eleven horses. He wondered how he had not noticed the stalls had not been mucked as soon as he'd entered. He'd also not noticed that George, Robert, and the two new stable boys that Mr. Palmer had recently hired were nowhere to be found. He had been thinking of Lady Coventry—that was how the situation had caught him so unawares.

Devil take him. How he had let a pretty face distract him was incomprehensible, especially since he was sure she had been frowning when she turned away.

Regardless of what chores Daw had left for him, Ridley's first responsibility was to prepare Opal for the baroness. He did so quickly, changing out the saddle to accommodate an adult instead of a child.

Lady Coventry arrived not too long after. He had not started mucking out the stalls because he knew he would need to help her into her saddle, and he did not want to be covered in filth when he did so. No woman of society would have ever approved of a dirty stable hand helping her up, which was silly because while out riding, she was quite likely to get very dirty indeed.

Not thinking, Ridley let out a breath of mirth.

"Is something amusing, Mr. Ellis?" the baroness asked him as he led her to the Friesian horse waiting for her.

Devil take him. He'd expressed his inner thoughts out loud with that one breath. "No, ma'am."

The baroness glanced around the stable. "Where are all the others?"

"Mr. Daw gave them the day off, my lady."

"Is such a thing merited when there is work to be done?"

"The boys work hard. They deserve a day off every now and again. Have faith, my lady, the work will be done." Ridley would not give the baroness any reason to find fault with the boys.

Mrs. Spencer arrived and smiled broadly at him. "My, my, Mr. Ellis. It has been an age since I last saw you. I thank you again for the help you have been to my stable master."

"I am happy to be of service, ma'am." Ridley gave a short bow to Mrs. Spencer.

"We are lucky to have such skills in the neighborhood, do you not agree, Lady Coventry?"

The baroness seemed startled by the question. "Yes," she said when she'd collected herself. "Lucky." She met his eye. "Indeed."

Mrs. Spencer laughed, making her Dartmoor pony twitch and sidestep. The pony was a good choice since Mrs. Spencer was a shorter woman, and the pony, at barely twelve hands, would have been easier to mount and dismount. "Indeed. My, my! Mr. Spencer says your horses are the fastest in all of England. Not that I worry myself over such things. I do not ride for speed but for pleasure."

After some general chitchat, Lady Coventry urged Mrs. Spencer that they should really get on with their plans to visit the lake. Ridley felt considerable relief once they'd gone. He had work to tend to.

He was glad Mrs. Spencer was accompanying the baroness on her ride. It was common for a lady to require company when she went out to ride, and often that company was given by the stable master. Ridley did not want Daw anywhere near the baroness.

It wasn't that he believed Daw would do anything to harm the lady. But Daw was a slippery sort of fellow, capable of working his way into situations where he did not belong. The fact that he had been named stable master was enough to prove he had an ability that defied reason. And though Ridley could not account for his wanting to protect Lady Coventry, he *did* want to protect her. Even while she vexed him.

He removed his waistcoat and switched his gaiters for an older set more suited for mucking and started on the first stall. Halfway through the second, the sound of footsteps on the flagstones rang through the stable. He peered out and saw Miss Amelia holding something in her skirts as she rushed to Bonnie's stall.

In spite of the child's obvious distress, Bonnie showed none of her own as the girl tightened one fist around the pouch she'd made of her skirts and the other around the latch of Bonnie's stall.

Ridley set aside the pitchfork and followed the little girl. "Miss Amelia?"

She looked up, her face streaked with tears. Without even asking, he knew her brother had done something.

"What has he done?"

"He killed her. She's destroyed entirely."

The news instantly alarmed Ridley. Had the little girl a cat or some such that her brother could have harmed? He was trying to determine the best way to ask when Miss Amelia laid out what she'd held in her skirts.

A porcelain doll, or what *had* been a porcelain doll, lay in pieces on Miss Amelia's lap. A triangle of pink cheek and an oval-shaped eye were readily recognized among the fragments that were once the face of a now-headless doll. The hands and body were still intact, and what appeared to be a still-unharmed lorgnette hung from the doll's wrist.

He still had nine stalls to finish as well as horses that needed to be fed and watered and exercised and saddles that needed to be washed and oiled.

Instead, he sat down next to the girl in the hay, grateful he had cleaned Bonnie's stall first. It was going to be a long day.

Chapter Nine

"My, my! What an afternoon, Lady Coventry!" Mrs. Spencer declared as they approached the stable.

"Would you like to join me for tea at the house, Mrs. Spencer? It would be lovely for you to meet my Lia. Then perhaps next time, you may bring Mary with you."

"That would be lovely, Lady Coventry. Thank you for the kind offer." They rode to the back entrance of the house where Lawrence, one of the footmen, helped them dismount.

Nora directed a second footman to take the horses to the stables and Lawrence to escort Mrs. Spencer to the drawing room. "I'll be with you in a moment. I'll fetch Lia to join us." She might have sent Lawrence to find the child, but she wanted to prepare Lia to meet the mother of a girl who might become a friend.

Lia was not in the nursery nor in her rooms. Nora found Edward in the library and asked where his sister might be. He didn't look up from where he sat in the armchair reading a book. "How would I know where that crybaby went? She's not my responsibility."

He had that hard look on his features—the look that told her his heart was at its blackest and that perhaps his sister had met with cruelty at his hands.

Nora narrowed her eyes at her son and put her hand on his book to force him to lower it. "What have you done?"

He shrugged and slouched lower in the chair. "I didn't do anything. It isn't my fault she can't take care of her own belongings."

"Edward." She inserted the tone of warning. "What happened?"

"Her doll broke, and she blamed me. I wasn't even in the room where she found it, so why she thought it was me I couldn't say."

Nora closed her eyes and counted to five. Tears built up behind her lids. Poor Lia. How many ways could a heart break and continue to beat? The child had been through so much already and losing such a precious gift probably felt like losing her mother all over again.

"I'll deal with you later, Edward, but trust me when I say that there will be a reckoning." For the moment, she had to find Lia. She wanted to hold her, to mourn with her, to try to fix what Edward felt determined to break.

She suddenly knew exactly where to look.

In the stable, Nora could not readily see anyone available. She fleetingly wondered why Mr. Daw never seemed to be in the stables, but when she heard the low murmur of voices, she forgot all about Daw and crept toward the sound. She felt silly for sneaking up on Lia, but she wanted to gauge the child's feelings before she rushed in. She wanted to use any information available to help her comfort the little girl.

"See there?" The voice was Mr. Ellis's. "When the Flanders glue dries, it won't be white like you see now. It'll be clear. That's not to say you will not see the cracks, Miss Amelia. What are we, any of us, but a collage of broken pieces glued back together with little more than our determined hope in a better future?"

"She won't be as beautiful with the cracks." The ache in Lia's voice tore at Nora's heart.

"I don't believe that is true. I think she will be more beautiful."

"But she won't be perfect."

"Miss Amelia, do you remember the first day I met you when we were out in the pasture with Bonnie, and you pointed out a twisted tree and declared it the loveliest thing you'd ever seen?"

"Yes," Lia's small voice answered.

"Was that tree perfect? Did its trunk stand tall and straight? Was its bark smooth? Were all the leaves found on the tree the exact same shade of green and of a perfect, uniform size?"

"No. That would be silly. No tree is like that."

"But if no tree is perfect, are you saying that no tree is beautiful? Not even one?"

Her little girl blew out a long breath as if she was thinking very hard. Nora could almost see the way Lia would bite her lip.

"Consider a sunset as well," Mr. Ellis continued. His voice sounded a little distracted, as if he was also focusing on something else.

Nora wished she could glimpse into the room without being caught eavesdropping.

"A sunset is never the same. So many different shades, all changing and shifting with each moment. The beams of light are not equal. The shades are not always complementary with the reds and pinks and oranges all slurring into each other as the wind pushes the clouds along. Sunsets are never perfect, so then perhaps sunsets are not beautiful either?"

"Mr. Ellis, you're being silly."

"No, dear. I'm not being silly at all. A tree is beautiful *because* of its bends and twists. It proves that it has persevered through heat and rain and lack of light. Those hardships shape every branch. Without the wind driving clouds across the sky, the sun setting would be rather unremarkable. It is the colors and clouds that make it an orchestra in the sky. These things are not beautiful because they are perfect. They are beautiful because they endure."

There was silence for some time before Lia said, "I think I understand."

Nora heard a small shuffling noise and carefully stepped back in case Mr. Ellis and Lia exited the back room of the stable.

Neither emerged, but she heard Mr. Ellis take a deep, satisfied breath. "There now. When the glue dries, your doll will be better than new because now her face tells the story that she has been through hard things and has endured."

Nora pressed her lips together to hold in the sob his words elic-ited. She quietly left the stable, composed herself, and then returned, making sure her footsteps rang out loudly enough to announce her presence. She called out, "Lia? Are you in here, Lia?"

"Mama?" Lia emerged from the room. "I'm sorry," she said im-mediately.

"Sorry? For what, dearest? You're not in trouble."

"I know I'm not supposed to be bothering Mr. Ellis when he's working."

Nora forced herself to smile and appear untroubled. "As I said, darling, you're not in trouble. Far from it. I have a friend visiting who has a daughter close to your age. I thought you might want to meet Mrs. Spencer so she might introduce you to her daughter. Would you like that?"

Lia's pale face brightened. "I would like a friend."

"Well, then, it's settled. Run along and wash your face and hands before meeting us in the drawing room for tea."

Lia went immediately to do as directed.

Nora turned to the stable hand. "Thank you, Mr. Ellis."

Mr. Ellis frowned. "Before you thank me, I think you should know—"

"I *do* know." She felt bad for interrupting, but she needed to say what she wanted quickly before she lost her nerve. "I know what Edward did to Lia's doll, and I know that you handled the situation as well as anyone could have handled it. I did not know what I would find when I came here for her, but what I did find warmed my heart and restored my faith in human goodness." She motioned toward the back room where Lia and Mr. Ellis had been talking. "May I?"

He moved aside to let her enter.

The room was neat with its rows of saddles, leads, and bridles. It smelled of beeswax and leather, a smell she was beginning to associate with Mr. Ellis. It was a fragrance she found she quite liked.

Lia's porcelain doll lay on a low shelf in a corner where it was unlikely to be bumped or found to be in the way. The doll's face had undergone quite a change with the many fine white lines running over its surface. If she had seen it without having heard the conversation between Mr. Ellis and Lia, she might have despaired over the marred face, but now, she saw all the ways that it was beautiful.

"You have worked a miracle," she whispered.

Their eyes met, and his gentle expression seemed to somehow engulf her worry and drown it out until there was nothing left but peace. She nearly caught her breath. If she did not leave immediately, she might never be able to. A woman could exist in such peace for a very long time.

"Thank you again," she managed to say. She stepped from the room and returned to the house.

No doubt Mrs. Spencer had begun wondering where she'd gone off to.

She hoped Lia would not mention the day's mishap. It was imperative that Nora continue to make a good impression, and that her children did so as well. Any hint of rumor that things might not be as they ought could result in word reaching the ears of the solicitor. Mr. Ashby might see the situation with the doll as some fault in how Nora was raising her son, and then he might take her son away from her.

Nora had no intention of allowing that to happen. She would behave perfectly and remain above reproach. She would find a way for Edward and Lia to do the same. She would.

So when she settled in the drawing room across from Mrs. Spencer and Mrs. Spencer gave a sly smile and said, "Mr. Ellis is certainly handsome, isn't he?" Nora nearly choked on her sip of tea.

"Mr. Ellis? The stable hand?"

Mrs. Spencer made a *psh* noise. "Oh, my, my! Lady Coventry! Please tell me you have eyes. It only gives me one more reason to lament that we could not get him for our own stables. I do believe you and I will have to become very good friends so that I might enjoy art in human form."

"Mrs. Spencer!"

Mrs. Spencer laughed and took a sip of her own tea before settling the cup back on its saucer. "Please do call me wicked. Mr. Spencer finds it so amusing when gossip of that nature reaches his ears."

"I don't really know quite what to say." Nora certainly felt no inclination to agree with Mrs. Spencer out loud even if she did inside her own head. She'd had enough acquaintances in London who baited women to say things that were then spread to the rest of society as gossip and rumor. She'd never been caught in such a trap, but she'd witnessed enough to know it was best to err on the side of caution.

Especially when her son's reputation, rather than merely her own, was on the line. She diverted the conversation to a safer topic. "Do you keep a governess?"

"Me? Oh no. I did when my children were quite small and into everything. I simply do not have the nervous constitution to allow me to manage the antics of a child who creates chaos with every breath and step. My, my, no! But I found I did not require such help once they were older. Indeed, I truly enjoy my children. They are great fun to tease, and, to be sure, they can do their fair share of teasing in return."

"Do you ever worry?" Nora asked, intrigued by the idea of a mother enjoying her children. Her mother had certainly not acted as though she'd enjoyed Nora's company, and none of the ladies in London had ever confessed to such a thing. For her own part, she had been so busy managing her husband's household in London and making certain her family maintained society's favor that she'd hardly had time to enjoy Edward, and then he'd gone away to Eton. By the time he'd returned so altered, she'd scarcely recognized him as her own.

"Worry, Lady Coventry?"

"Over doing everything right."

Mrs. Spencer smiled indulgently. "I don't believe there is one mother in the entire history of our world who has done everything right. My mother certainly did not. And I certainly have not. If I may be so bold, you should not expect to either."

Nora smiled, but it didn't feel genuine. She sipped from her teacup and wondered how to start a different conversation. She'd been good at small talk and frivolities in London, but for some reason, she felt inadequate at every turn of late. Mr. Ashby constantly peering over her shoulder to enforce her late husband's demands had exacerbated that feeling.

Fortunately, Lia appeared in the doorway and spared Nora from having to think up new topics. The girl herself presented many topics which were delightful. The rest of Mrs. Spencer's visit could be called a triumph. Lia's vibrant innocence was endearing. Mrs. Spencer seemed quite taken with her and promised to bring Mary the very next day for a visit.

When Mrs. Spencer had gone, Lia let out a contented sigh. "I thought today might be one of the worst days of my life. No—one of the worst days in the whole world. But instead, I found I have one good friend and that I will be soon introduced to another. Isn't it"—Lia looked up at the ceiling as if searching for the right word—"superb that a day can change so completely?"

"Yes, dearest. It is superb."

Nora looked to the ceiling as well, knowing that, for her, the day was to shift again. She had to discuss the situation with Edward. She felt deep in her soul that the triumph she'd felt with Mrs. Spencer and Lia would not be duplicated with her son.

She didn't wait to accomplish the task. She didn't want Edward to come down for dinner pretending that nothing was wrong, which would make her bringing it up later almost impossible.

She left Lia with her favorite tin box of crayons and a stack of paper. She took a deep breath. *I am a baroness.* She then went to the library to seek out her son.

He wasn't there. He wasn't in his rooms either. She finally found him in the conservatory in the middle of the gardens. She peered through the glass windows to see him on his stomach near the pool in the center of the conservatory. His eyes were trained on a frog who sat lazily on its lily pad. The frog hopped away when Nora opened the door and entered.

Edward grunted in irritation at her interruption. "Hello, Mother."

"Hello, Edward."

"Is this the moment of reckoning? Where you frighten away a frog?"

She sat upon one of the several chairs near the pond and tried to find the same peace she'd felt in the stable with Mr. Ellis. "Why don't you begin by telling me the truth?"

"Does it really matter?"

"Yes, it matters to me. It certainly matters to your sister. It should matter to you."

"To me?" he scoffed.

"Yes. If your word means nothing to you, that is what it will be worth to others."

"Are you saying I have no value?"

Nora gritted her teeth. She was doing this wrong, but she didn't know how to correct it. "I'm telling you that lies have no value."

Edward sat up. "All right. So, if I admit that I broke the doll, then you'll find value in me because I told the truth?"

"No, dearest. *You* will find value in you."

"And then I suppose I'll find comfort in valuing myself?" He leaned back on his hands.

"No." She thought of the many truths she had been forced to confront and how much of it showed her things within herself to value, such as her fierce determination to fight for her children's custody. It was a strength she hadn't known she possessed. "Truth of that nature is often uncomfortable, and it often leads to a great deal of work."

"Well." He swiped his hands together and stood. "You've convinced me then to accept all my truths."

"Did you break the doll?" she asked before he could take a step. She didn't want him to make it to the door and escape the conversation.

He plucked one of the white flowers from the vine climbing a nearby trellis and pulled at its petals, dropping each one into the water. "No."

The heat of the conservatory only added to her aggravation.

"Edward, it is not easy to recover truth from a lie. A lie complicates a life that could have been simpler. Not easier, but simpler."

"All right. And what if I did break the doll?"

"I would expect you to own your deed. To apologize. To make amends."

He crushed the remaining petals in his hand and flicked the ball of bruised velvet to the stones at his feet. "I did break the doll. But by the merit of this conversation, I will not apologize."

"You *will* apologize."

"I won't."

"Edward!"

"My word should mean something. Isn't that what you're trying to teach me? Well, an apology would just be a different lie because I'm not sorry. She's too old to be carrying around such a silly toy. Did you even ask her why I might have felt provoked to break her stupid doll?"

Nora faltered. In truth, she hadn't even mentioned to Lia that she knew the doll was broken.

"Start there, Mother. We can continue this discussion after that." He left, stepping on the ball of white petals and crushing them into a small paste on the stones.

Nora stared at the spot on the stones for a long time. She felt like her son had hopped away in much the same manner as the frog had. If only she knew how to reach Edward before Mr. Ashby captured him and took him away for good.

Chapter Ten

Ridley looked at the doll one last time before he took up the pitchfork and got back to work. His encounters with Miss Amelia and then with Lady Coventry had created delays he hadn't anticipated and certainly had no time for, but what else could he have done? He couldn't leave a child weeping in Bonnie's stall. He couldn't have dismissed the baroness when she'd asked to see the repairs on the doll.

The day had gotten entirely away from him. But Daw would not take excuses, even if those excuses came from the estate's family members. He would likely punish Ridley by assigning him even more work the next day.

As expected, when Daw showed up and Ridley was only on the fourth stall, Daw laughed. "What have you been doing all afternoon? Have a laze about, did you?"

"Hardly. Miss Amelia returned to the stables with her mother. They required assistance. And since you are never available when they need their stable master, their tasks fell to me."

It wasn't exactly true that they had wanted the stable master since Daw would never have helped Miss Amelia glue a doll back together, but Ridley liked to poke at the man where he could.

Daw's face darkened, his chin whiskers bristling as his mouth thinned into a hard line. "Is that what you been doing? You been telling the lady of the house that I'm never around? You been telling her that I'm not doing my job?"

Ridley nearly laughed at the idea that anyone would have to tell Lady Coventry something that would be evident to the most casual of observers, but something in Daw's tone and demeanor kept Ridley in check. Daw looked *desperate*. Ridley knew from experience that desperate men often committed reckless actions.

"Well?" Daw demanded, edging closer to Ridley.

Ridley remained silent.

"You've been filling the lady's head with lies," Daw snapped. "Turning her and Palmer and everyone here against me."

"I promise you I have done no such thing." Ridley shifted his stance, bending his knees slightly, preparing for the blow that was likely coming his way.

If Ridley felt secure in any of his own abilities, it was in reading a situation accurately. He felt the tension rising as easily as watching the water level rise in a bucket being filled. He knew how far that tension could rise before it broke apart into something else entirely. He held his hands into loose fists, lowered his chin, and kept his eyes locked on Daw.

The swing came from Daw's left arm, not a surprise since he'd hurt his right arm years before. That he immediately followed the swing with another from his right *was* a bit of a surprise. Ridley pivoted to avoid both attempts to hit him. Daw's fists kept swinging, however, forcing Ridley to back up.

"Daw!" Ridley said as he ducked a punch. "Daw, listen to me. I have never disparaged you to any member of the household." He tried to speak calmly even as Daw kept coming for him.

Ridley scrambled back. "See reason, man. I will defend myself, and you know you're outmatched." He maneuvered and ducked until Daw had backed him into a corner. The horses snorted in distress, clearly uncomfortable with the tension, but Daw smiled, not caring that the horses were unsettled.

"Where you goin' now, Ellis? You're out of places to run."

Ridley widened his stance. When Daw struck out, Ridley dodged left, then threw his own punch, connecting to Daw's face with a solid crack.

Daw's hands flew to his nose, and blood seeped through his fingers as he let out a string of expletives. "You broke my nose!"

While he was distracted, Ridley moved from the corner to a more defensible position. "I told you I would defend myself."

Daw pulled away his hand long enough to note the blood, and when he looked at Ridley again, there was murder in his eyes. "You're through here, Ellis. You pack your things and go. I'm through with you turning everyone against me and making up lies about what I do around here. And now you've gone and struck me. You could go to jail for that—might be locked up for a whole year. But I'll be fair. You just go, and I won't be pressing charges."

"You want me to go?" Ridley said and spread his hands wide to the stable. "You think you could handle that, do you? You think yourself capable of caring for the animals properly so they don't become ill or damaged by your neglect? You think you wouldn't be dismissed immediately when the place falls apart due to your indolence? If I leave, you would be ruined."

"I said leave!" Daw bellowed the last word, making the horses snort. Bonnie squealed outright at Daw's threatening tone.

Ridley weighed his options. He could petition Mr. Palmer for understanding regarding the situation. Mr. Palmer would likely side with him—except for the fact that Ridley had actually struck his superior, which *was* unlawful and would be hard to overlook. Compounding that was the fact that his contract-for-hire had only been for a year and had technically expired three years past. Ridley had no actual standing regarding his employment at Windsong. It did not help matters at all that, were he to have charges pressed against him, the unwanted attention he would receive would be his undoing—possibly even his death.

In truth, Ridley had few options. It was his word against Daw's when it came down to the events of the evening. And Daw, as the stable master, held the position of power as well as the proof of a broken nose.

"Fine," Ridley said. "I'll go. Though I do advise you to think."

"Think!" Daw spat. "Of what?"

Ridley reached a hand over Bonnie's stall to offer her reassurance. "Think of how your actions today will affect your tomorrows. Life is nothing if not a string of consequences we bring upon ourselves."

"Get. Out."

"So be it." Ridley left without another word. Daw wouldn't listen anyway so there really was no point.

But accepting the situation did not mean Ridley did not fume over the situation. He'd been fired. *Fired.* By a man who was incompetent by anyone's definition. Who did Daw think would do the work with him gone? Poor George and Robert. They'd be buried under Daw's demands. The two new stable boys would be equally overtasked.

Ridley didn't have many belongings, so gathering everything took little enough time. He hoped George and Robert would return before he left. He wanted to give the boys a proper farewell and to warn them of the change, but they hadn't returned by the time Ridley was done packing. Ridley wondered if Daw had sent them away so there would be no one to witness Ridley's departure. Perhaps Daw had intended that from the first moment. But no, that hardly seemed likely. That would be giving Daw far too much credit. The man couldn't outmaneuver an infant.

"I should be angry," he muttered to himself, and he *was* angry, but not in the way he'd expected. True, he would be required to seek employment elsewhere. He would have to start afresh. While that was never convenient, he was leaving behind more than just his position. He had come to feel responsible for the little girl, Miss Amelia. He had promised to teach her to ride her horse. With Daw in charge, it was unlikely the girl would benefit from competent training. Beyond that, Bonnie would likely be sold because Daw would never be able to train Bonnie well enough to trust that Miss Amelia would be safe on her back.

He again considered petitioning Mr. Palmer, perhaps asking him to vouch for his character to Lady Coventry.

But that foolish notion made him scoff out loud. Him piecing together a doll hardly merited a writ of pardon for striking a superior. What did she know of his character? Nothing. Nothing at all.

Such thoughts darkened his mood and deepened his anger.

With Lady Coventry.

Which was ridiculous, as she had nothing to do with the confrontation with Daw. But devil take him, had it not happened in her stables?

He expected Daw's incompetence. And though he had nothing on which to base his opinion, he had expected greater understanding and attention from the lady of the house than she'd shown. How could she allow one such as Daw to work for her estate? How could she not see that the man did less work than the fleas on the dog?

He left the rooms above the stables and made his way downstairs, quietly searching to see if Daw was anywhere about. Daw wasn't, of course. The man never was. Ridley took a moment to say farewell to each of the horses, rubbing their noses as they rested their cheeks against his arm. He checked on Angel, who was still healing after rolling her ankle. Would Daw have any idea how to care for her?

He shook his head. His horses were beyond his care now. He had to leave.

He hurried to scoop a bit of oats for each horse since he wasn't certain when George or Robert would return. He didn't want the horses going hungry.

"I will miss you, my friends," he murmured.

Ridley left the stable and turned toward Kendal. Perhaps he could find accommodations at the inn there. He took a shortcut through the fields of Windsong, but every footstep fueled greater fury. He'd been forced to defend himself, and for that he was the one to be punished?

How was Lady Coventry so obtuse as to keep a man of Daw's

character in charge of animals who required constant and precise care? He should have been fired as soon as the family arrived at Windsong.

Would Miss Amelia even be able to retrieve her doll?

By the time he'd made it into town, he'd determined that Lady Coventry was the last woman on earth he could ever esteem in any degree because she had allowed such a louse as Daw to remain on the estate though she had to know he did nothing to earn his keep.

Never mind that Ridley still felt a stirring of pity for the baroness. No. He would not feel pity.

He felt complete contempt for Daw. Moderate contempt for Lady Coventry. And even mild contempt for Palmer. He knew he was being unfair to all but Daw, but it was hard to be fair when one had been treated so unfairly.

"A room please." He handed the innkeeper of the Goose and Crown enough money to pay for several nights' lodging. He would need that time, and very likely more, to consider where he would go next. He wouldn't be able to expect references from Windsong, not while Daw remained as stable master.

He plunked down more coin to buy a bowl of stew and some bread, and the innkeeper pointed him to the common room where a few guests were already seated and enjoying their evenings.

Ridley chose a seat away from them so he could brood in peace rather than be obliged to talk with strangers. When his meal was placed before him, he muttered into his food about wretched people, the upper class who allowed wretched people to get away with wretched deeds and who themselves were often wretched, and the lower class who were treated wretchedly. Devil take them all.

He stayed in the dining room for a while longer before the exhaustion of his day, both physically and mentally, claimed him. He went to his own room and fell into bed.

Sleep did not come.

He'd been thinking of leaving Windsong, so why did he feel so unhappy about leaving now?

The answer was because he'd settled in Windsong in a way he never had before.

Not that such things mattered. Windsong was lost to him.

Would Lady Coventry miss him? It was a fool's question. She'd likely not even notice he was gone. Why would she? People of status never noticed anything beneath their status. It was the way of things. It was why he kept himself away from people of society as much as possible.

As his mind started to skip over the surface of sleep, he wondered if he should be grateful to Daw. Leaving Windsong had reminded him that people of society were the exactly the sort of people he wished to avoid.

Chapter Eleven

Lia was already dressed for her riding lesson though it wasn't to begin for another half hour. She and Nora were enjoying a stroll through the gardens. Nora glanced to the conservatory, wondering if Edward was inside. He wasn't.

"Lia?"

"Hm?" Lia paused, distracted by the butterfly fluttering over the white rosebush.

"I heard that Edward broke your doll yesterday while I was out with Mrs. Spencer."

Lia went still. "Yes. He did."

"Can you tell me what happened?"

Lia sighed and looked up from the flower and the butterfly. She began walking again along the path. "We fought."

"Over what?"

Lia shrugged. "What don't we fight over?"

That was true enough.

When Nora didn't respond, Lia continued. "He was angry because he'd lied about being able to keep a balanced seat in the saddle, and Mr. Ellis caught him in the lie and convinced him to learn to do it right."

That was something at least. Learning to sit properly was the first step.

"He told me he was better at horseback riding than I was, and I told him he was a liar. I told him Mr. Ellis knew he was a liar."

"I see."

"And then I told him that our father would be disgusted by such lies and that he would be a terrible baron because no one would trust a lie-mouth like his. And that's when he took my doll and hit her face on the banister."

Nora finally understood. Little Lia had poked the wound that lingered in all of them. They all wanted assurances that the late baron was pleased with their efforts, had loved them in some small way. Nora wondered if perhaps Edward felt he had been cast off by his father when he'd been sent to school at so young an age.

"How do you feel about that fight now that it is over?"

Lia peeked at Nora through her eyelashes. "Not very good. I was mad at him yesterday. But I've been thinking about what I said. He was not wrong to be mad at me."

"True," Nora said. "But he *was* wrong to break your doll. I am sorry for that."

"It's all right. Mr. Ellis fixed it."

"Did he now?"

Her sad demeanor was immediately replaced with one of happiness. "I think he could fix anything."

"You know, we could learn a thing from that." When she was certain she had Lia's full attention, she continued. "There are many things that can be fixed. Dolls with glue, clothing with a needle and thread, and words with apologies."

Lia's breath puffed out her cheeks. "I know what you're saying."

"That's because you're a very clever girl."

"I'll say sorry when I see him at riding lessons. It's probably time I go to the stable."

Nora checked her pocket watch. "So it is. Off with you then."

Lia hurried away, then turned back to Nora with a look of

remorse as if remembering running wasn't for ladies. She resigned herself to walking quickly, though it was so swift, her pace was nearly a trot.

Nora looked toward the house but didn't shift her course. Instead, she followed Lia to the stables; she wanted to check on Edward, who would also be preparing for his instruction. She wanted to tell him she understood his actions even if she could not condone them. She worked to convince herself she was going only to talk to Edward, but her eyes sought out Mr. Ellis.

Except she did not see him. She saw the stable boys and undergrooms, and she saw Mr. Daw, who was speaking to Lia and waving his hands at the horse he'd saddled for her. As Nora approached, she saw Lia burst into tears.

"You're a horrible, mean man," the girl said, before running off toward the house.

"What's going on here?" Nora asked loudly. She directed her words to her son because she felt no inclination to address the man who'd made her daughter cry.

"It would appear—" Edward began when Mr. Daw interjected, "She's just not getting her way, is all."

Nora threw a sharp look at Mr. Daw and was startled to see his nose purpled and swollen. She recovered from her shock long enough to inquire, "Are you interrupting the Baron of Windsong?" She would not let this man trample over her children.

"No, ma'am. Sorry, ma'am." Daw ducked his chin into his chest as though trying to resemble some form of humility, but he only came off appearing cross.

Edward started again. "It would appear that Mr. Ellis struck Mr. Daw last night. And he was dismissed."

"Dismissed? Without consulting me?" She narrowed her eyes at the man whose eyes were red, likely from too much drink and not enough sense. Every time she felt she was making progress, something happened to set her back again.

"I did consult with Mr. Palmer, ma'am. Mr. Ellis broke the law.

There's not much to be done regarding such a thing 'cept what's been done. But I'm here and ready to continue riding instructions."

"Continue riding instructions? You can barely stay on your own feet. How are you to instruct the baron and baroness to stay on a horse?" She referred to her children by their titles to remind the man who he was dealing with.

The stable hands were busy with their work, but she could almost feel their ears widening to catch every word uttered.

"I'm sorry, ma'am. I received quite a blow last night. My head is aching something fierce. I might have a con—" He frowned as he tried to think of the word.

"You feel you might be concussed?"

"Yes, ma'am. That." He dipped his head.

"For heaven's sakes. Edward, there will be no riding instruction today. Please return to the house with me."

Edward fell into step with her. "He's drunk, you know. Or at least he was."

"I do know. And such behavior will be addressed. But at the moment, I wish to discuss yesterday's incident, only I want to hear your point of view."

He rolled his eyes and made a sound of disgust in his throat.

She hoped he didn't see how his contempt distressed her. "Hear me out. I've asked Lia what led up to the doll being broken, and she confessed her unkindness to you."

"You're making this so much more ridiculous than it already was. It's not like I care what that crybaby said. Leave it alone." Her son hurried in front of her and was inside the house before she made it to the stairs.

"Will nothing go right this day?" she asked the sky. The sky, wisely, did not answer. As soon as she was in the house, she removed her bonnet and asked Nash to summon Mr. Palmer to the house.

She went to the study to wait—and pace. Mr. Daw had made her daughter cry and had interrupted her son. Her anger was reaching a boiling point.

When Mr. Palmer finally entered, he held up a hand in order to speak first. "I know what you're going to say, but the law is clear. The fact is that Mr. Ellis struck his superior. There are no witnesses to defend Mr. Ellis's actions, and Mr. Ellis himself has packed up and abandoned his post, making him unable to defend himself. We have only Mr. Daw's word."

"I don't like him." She'd paced for nearly an hour waiting to utter those exact words.

"No one does."

"I want him fired."

Mr. Palmer rubbed the bridge of his nose. "May we sit, Lady Coventry?"

Feeling suddenly unsure, she motioned to the chairs. Was she wrong to want Mr. Daw fired? She didn't think so. What would Mr. Ashby say if she allowed a man who had disrespected the baron to retain his employment? Surely that would be a more grievous course of action.

When they were both seated, Mr. Palmer steepled his hands on his lap. "If we dismiss him now, we may be without a stable master for some time. It would not reflect well on you or Lord Coventry to have no stable master in your employ."

"What does not reflect well on me is that a half-drunk man was stumbling about my stables in front of my children. Had Mr. Ashby witnessed such a display, Edward would be packed and on his way back to London already. I cannot afford such a misstep."

"What would you like me to do?"

Nora smoothed her skirts. It was not often that anyone, especially a man, asked her opinion on how to handle a situation. She had opinions, of course. But few people asked what those opinions might be. She'd half expected Mr. Palmer to have arrived with pretty words of how he would see to everything and how she should return to her menu planning, dismissing her in much the same way her husband had always dismissed her.

In much the same way Mr. Ellis had been dismissed.

"Can we not bring back Mr. Ellis?"

"If we did, Mr. Daw would be sure to press charges. We would have no way to prevent such scandalous news from reaching Mr. Ashby."

Mr. Ashby. She flinched inwardly every time she heard, or thought, his name. "Could we not promote one of the undergrooms? George is young but capable. He's been well-trained."

Mr. Palmer tapped his thumbs together while he mulled over her suggestion. "While that seems like it might work, he's still far too young and coarse of manner and language to be stable master."

Nora made a decidedly unladylike sound. "Do you believe Mr. Daw to have refined manners and language?"

"No, certainly not. But he has age to lend him credibility."

"Well, then, our hands are tied. Perhaps we could quietly inquire regarding any who are immediately available for such a post. It would be best to resolve this quickly."

Mr. Palmer agreed and left, though Nora remained in the study a long time thinking of her options.

As she replayed her one real interaction with Mr. Daw, she finally realized an important truth. Mr. Daw had been harboring some sort of deep anger toward Mr. Ellis long before now.

Looking back at the afternoon with Lia and her horse from the luxurious standpoint of information and distance, she could see the facts far more clearly. Mr. Ellis *had* taken the horse's lead when he'd seen Bonnie's agitation, as he had said. He had moved Lia to the other side to protect her as the horse grew even more unsettled. Then he had scooped the girl up and out of harm's way before regaining control of the horse. And all while remaining calm himself.

She remembered how Mr. Ellis had told her that no one ever came out while he was exercising the horses. She also realized that it had been Mr. Daw who had spoken loudly to cause the horse to become agitated in the first place. What was it Lia had said? "I wasn't frightened. Bonnie was frightened. He startled her." And she had pointed at Mr. Daw.

Had Daw known what he was doing? Had the man manipulated the situation to create the danger and find a reason to cast suspicion on Mr. Ellis's abilities?

She could not know for sure, but it seemed possible. Which made her decision easy. She couldn't let him stay, not when he'd purposely put Lia in harm's way. The longer she thought about it, the more furious she grew. He needed to be terminated immediately.

She required only a little more information in order to know what steps to take next. She prepared a list of questions and then sent for Mr. Daw. She considered having Mr. Palmer take care of this business, but she wanted to confront the stable master herself. The man believed she wasn't paying attention and thought she could be manipulated. But she'd had her share of such treatment from her husband. She would not let the staff treat her in that manner, not when her children were at stake.

I am their mother. It was the first time she'd thought such a thing to rally her strength, but somehow those words lent her more strength than she expected. She was their mother. She would protect them.

When Mr. Daw entered, he smiled in a way that felt oily and vaguely irritating. "You wanted to see me, m'lady?"

"Yes. I had some questions I thought you might be able to answer."

He bowed.

She began with the same questions she had once asked George regarding the horses and the stable and its management. She found Mr. Daw's answers less satisfying than George's had been, proving George to be far more competent when it came to the tasks such a job required. Mr. Daw scratched his head as he took his time giving answers he should have known as well as his own name.

"I was under the impression that the horses' feeding schedules and exercise routines were different than what you have described to me," she commented after Daw had given her another unsatisfactory answer.

"Oh, well, you see, there've been some changes of late, so I can't rightly be certain," he mumbled.

She lifted her eyebrows and waited in silence, watching him. She'd seen her husband do that very thing with enough people over the course of her marriage to know the intense effect it could have on a less-secure confidence.

"Mr. Daw, you'll recall a few weeks ago when I was searching for my daughter at the stables. You said you would help me find her, and when we couldn't easily find her, you suggested I look out in the gardens."

"That's right, ma'am. Lovely gardens would be a logical place to think a young girl might be off to."

"Of course. But it wasn't until you noticed that Bonnie's stall was empty that you suggested we search the pasture."

Perspiration popped out on his forehead, but she had to give the man credit, it was the only sign he might have felt uneasy with this new line of questioning. "Well, ma'am, I don't rightly know when I thought to mention the pasture. But it was good that I did, seeing that the little girl might've come to harm if we hadn't come along."

"No."

He frowned. "No, ma'am?"

"No. I rather think she almost came to harm *because* we came along. Going out to the pasture and agitating a horse put my daughter in harm's way, Mr. Daw. A horse that clearly finds you in particular to be threatening."

He shuffled back a few feet and then forward again. "Why would you think that horse finds me threatening? That horse is a bad one. She finds everyone threatening. I've been saying we should get rid of her for a while now."

"But you didn't get rid of her. You got rid of the one man who made her feel calm, didn't you?"

"I don't know where this is all coming from, ma'am. Is Ridley come back and said something? Trying to get me into trouble?"

"No. I've been speaking to the neighbors, to the estate's steward, and to the rest of the staff. I also took my own counsel regarding the matter. I find it interesting that you are never anywhere to be found when I am in the stables. You were not the one to saddle my horse on the occasions I have needed such service, and you were not there when I was searching for information regarding riding lessons. I've also spoken with my daughter who claims the horse was quite docile until you came along."

Mr. Daw guffawed. "As if she knows anything. You can't trust the silly fantasies of a little girl."

Had the man really said "silly fantasies"? In that same demeaning tone her husband had used with her during their entire marriage? Nora may not have had a lot of control in her life, but she would not allow anyone to disparage her daughter.

"Your general negligence of duty is quite enough reason for me to terminate your employment here, but as you were the sole cause my daughter found herself in a situation that could have proved fatal is the reason for your dismissal. You may collect your wages, sir, and then be on your way."

He stared at her with unblinking eyes. "You can't be serious."

"Do I have the slightest appearance of jesting, Mr. Daw?"

"It's Ridley who's done this. He put you up to this."

"I assure you, Mr. Daw, I am a baroness and capable of running my own household. More, I am a mother, which means I am capable of protecting the members of my household from you and your attempts to bring harm to them." She rang the bell for Nash. When the butler arrived, she directed him to remove Mr. Daw from her home.

Mr. Daw was most displeased if his loud vocalization about his new circumstances were to be believed, but she could not waste her thoughts on the man who was leaving or on her sudden doubts regarding her actions.

She had to turn her thoughts to Mr. Ellis. With Mr. Daw being terminated with just cause, he could not seek any sort of grievance against Mr. Ellis should she be lucky enough to find him and convince him to return to the estate.

Chapter Twelve

Ridley knew he needn't hurry along the task of seeking new employment. It was unlikely that he'd find a situation even half so amiable as what he'd had at Windsong—even considering Daw—but he'd saved up enough money to allow him many months of decent living. He'd traveled far from his childhood home with the intent to find anonymity and had enjoyed many years of blessed peace as a result. That he had been able to engage in labor he excelled at while also being in a comfortable living arrangement added to his happiness.

Even so, he was determined to begin searching immediately. Ridley had secured a map from one of the coach drivers on his first full day at the Goose and Crown. He spent the rest of the afternoon in his room, surveying the map for townships where he could avoid the prying eyes of London yet still stay on English soil. He hoped to discover that his new area would have a registry office that would help him find employment quickly. And this time, he would choose a household too obscure to entertain members of prominent society. He had assumed wrongly that Windsong was beneath any remarkable notice from its owners. He never would've imagined the family would choose to permanently reside in the house.

No matter. He was moving on. He would likely have to begin again as a basic groom, but he didn't mind. The work gave him a sense of purpose that he'd lacked in his youth. When he found a village that looked promising, he returned the map to the driver and fetched himself some dinner.

Once he returned to his room, he settled against his pillows and closed his eyes with satisfaction. He'd stay in town long enough to bid young George farewell and to buy a horse. After such an extravagant purchase, he wouldn't be able to afford the luxury of sleeping in inns, but he had a good bedroll, and the warmth of summer would be an excellent traveling companion.

The next morning, Ridley awoke in good spirits. Adventure was ahead of him, and only a fool failed to look forward to such an experience.

He left his room, eager to get a bite of breakfast and begin his search for a horse, but when he stepped into the open dining room, he stopped short.

Mr. Palmer, the steward of Windsong estate, stood up from his seat in the corner. He held out his hand to Ridley. "Mr. Ellis, it's good to see you. I'd begun to worry you were never coming down from the rooms."

Ridley shook Mr. Palmer's hand and smiled. "Then you don't know me very well, sir. I'm not the sort of man who is in the habit of missing meals. The food here is quite good. Would you care to join me?"

"I believe I will. I struck out quite early this morning for fear of perhaps missing you, and so had no time for my own breakfast."

Ridley motioned to the innkeeper's daughter to let her know they would both be dining. She nodded and scurried off to the kitchen.

Ridley sat at Mr. Palmer's table and leaned back in his chair. He eyed the man whose belly proved he wasn't used to missing meals either. "So what brings you out so early to see me? I do hope you're here to tell me how badly you feel that I was dismissed without being allowed to collect wages and that you have my last payment in your pocket."

Mr. Palmer smiled, the gray stubble on his cheeks and chin bristling with the motion. "I apologize that you were unable to collect your wages, but I believe I can offer you something better. Lady Coventry has requested you be brought back to work for the estate."

"Why would she do that? Does she not know I broke the law?"

Mr. Palmer's lips quirked up in a smile. "The lady knows a good deal more than I gave her credit for. Last night, she fired Daw and had him thrown from her house. She only notified me after the deed was done and asked me to find you and bring you back. We all know Daw deserved whatever happened and more—no one faults you for it—and now Daw is gone. He cannot trouble you or threaten you with a revenge that's no longer within his power to exact."

Ridley couldn't have been more intrigued that Lady Coventry had seen the truth of what happened on her property. He offered her a silent apology for recently thinking so ill of her. He owed Mr. Palmer an apology as well. "She didn't leave the task of Daw's dismissal to you?"

Mr. Palmer held his hands out as if to say he was as surprised as Ridley might be at such news.

Ridley felt the change in his luck. He could return to Windsong and perhaps work under a stable master worth working under. It was clear the mistress of the estate was worth working under.

"Lady Coventry would like you to return as her new stable master. She has become quite taken with Windsong and plans to entertain. She wants her friends from the neighborhood and from London to ride through her woods and see the beauty for themselves. What say you? Shall I congratulate you on a well-deserved promotion?"

Ridley thought of the storm he'd felt coming when he'd first heard Lady Coventry was making Windsong her primary residence. Thunder boomed within his bones. All of Lady Coventry's friends from London? Nothing more needed to be said.

"This is a surprise. And look, here is breakfast, so you can have my answer and then sit back and enjoy your meal."

The young girl laid out the plates and bowls in front of them.

Mr. Palmer waited until she'd finished and then asked, "And your answer would be?"

Ridley buttered his biscuit. "Please send my gratitude to the baroness for her offer. But I won't be returning to my employment at Windsong." He offered a smile to ease the sting of his words. "Now eat, while it's hot."

"I've just lost my appetite. How can you give such a poor answer? I don't think you properly understand. Lady Coventry means for you to return as the stable master, not as a groom. It would be more responsibility, to be sure—"

"More responsibility? Surely, you jest. You and I both know Daw did very little of the actual work in the stables."

"Yes. That is likely true."

"Not likely, sir. It is absolute truth." Ridley bit into his biscuit and frowned inwardly. The butter at Windsong was mildly sweeter than what was served at the inn. He hated how much of a snob he was when it came to butter, especially since he would not be resuming his post at Windsong. He couldn't mourn the loss of that butter for the rest of his life.

"But you see?" Mr. Palmer said. "As stable master, you'll receive higher pay and actually receive the credit for the fine work you do. Everyone knows how wonderful you are with the horses and with keeping the stables in such excellent condition."

Ridley stared down at his food, trying to figure out his best course of action. "Is my return dependent on my becoming the stable master?"

"Well . . . yes." Mr. Palmer's graying brow furrowed over his nose.

"Then I do apologize, but I cannot return."

"But to be a stable master!"

"I have no wish to be a stable master, Mr. Palmer. I have no wish to be forced to handle the members of society who visit the household. I was quite content in my position. And though I'm honored and humbled by your request, I cannot return. Please accept my best wishes for you all. And do eat your eggs. They were done to perfection this morning."

Ridley ate his meal with far more enthusiasm than he felt, but he'd paid for the food and letting things go to waste was a luxury he couldn't afford.

After breakfast, Mr. Palmer tried one more time to change Ridley's mind. "She really needs you to return," he said as he gathered his hat.

"A baroness could need nothing from one such as I," Ridley responded.

"You're wrong there, but I've said all I can say to change your mind. Thank you for the meal. And good luck to you, sir."

"To you as well, Mr. Palmer." Ridley felt a pricking of conscience as he watched Palmer leave. The man had looked almost woeful to bear the burden of Ridley's refusal.

He spent the rest of the day trying to quell his curiosity and shake off the feeling that he was missing something. The baroness's business had nothing to do with him, and by leaving the county, he would ensure it would stay that way.

After making some inquiries regarding horses for sale, he was directed to a man in Windermere who had several promising options. One of the grooms offered Ridley a ride since he would be traveling there on business, and Ridley gladly accepted.

He woke early the next day and went down for breakfast.

He had been surprised to see Mr. Palmer waiting for him yesterday, but he was completely confounded to see Lady Coventry waiting for him today.

"Mr. Ellis!" the lady called out.

Unable to mask his astonishment, he moved toward her direction. "Lady Coventry."

She motioned for him to take the chair across from her. He gave a low bow, then slid into his seat.

"I've come to offer you a position as Windsong's stable master." She looked nervous as well as pleased to be giving such news, though he could hardly understand what the woman thought she was doing conducting this business on her own instead of sending the steward again—even though he'd already declined Mr. Palmer. It complicated everything to have her in person.

"I'm terribly sorry that you've come all this way to pay me such a great honor, Lady Coventry, but I am afraid I must repeat the answer I gave Mr. Palmer and decline."

"Mr. Palmer told me you would say that, but I want to reassure you that Mr. Daw will no longer trouble you. He's a man without position or references. You are protected, Mr. Ellis. You have my word that I will not allow that odious absurdity of a man to bring any charges against you."

Ridley could not help but stare. She'd not only fired Daw, but she now offered him protection? She, a baroness, and he, nothing more than a stable hand? He had to admit that he was impressed. Never in his entire life had he seen a member of society offer a servant such a kindness.

"Ma'am, I do appreciate your generosity. Truly, but I do not—"

She offered a smile, likely to take the sting out of interrupting him. "You do not wish to be stable master. Mr. Palmer explained this to me already. Might I inquire as to why?"

"To explain my reasons would be like explaining directions through a labyrinth."

"Then we should order breakfast so we might discuss your labyrinth without further delay." She motioned to the innkeeper, who hurried over. Lady Coventry requested Ridley's meal be brought to him. "And bring a little extra. I find I could use some refreshment this morning."

Ridley's mouth dropped open in shock. He closed it immediately. She was requesting food? To be eaten at the same time he was eating? At the same table?

"Please, Mr. Ellis. It's imperative that you return. Windsong must be in perfect order, or . . ." She pressed her lips together.

He knew he shouldn't stare at her, but he couldn't help it. Far more than just basic beauty, which he'd noticed already, her eyes were mesmerizing. A blue as clear and bright as a lake on a cloudless day. In his determination to stay clear of her, he'd not allowed himself to pay attention to those details, but now with her before him in such a personal way, he could not help but notice.

He blinked and looked away. He gathered his wits before meeting her gaze again. "I must warn you," he said.

"Warn me?" She lifted delicate eyebrows over those lovely eyes.

"The butter here is not so fine as it is at Windsong."

Her lips curved in a sudden smile. It was the first sincere smile he'd seen on her, not one given to be polite or to appear happy, but one born from genuine amusement. The movement seemed to surprise her as much as it surprised him.

Her brightened demeanor forced him to offer a return smile. He realized he was not in a position to deny her what she wished.

"I think we can come to an arrangement, Lady Coventry. I will be your stable master, but I do not wish to interact with your guests directly."

"Then how are you to help them with their horses?"

"I will do all the duties of the stable master, including choosing horses for the guests and preparing them, but I do not wish to speak to the guests directly. George can manage that part well enough."

She tilted her head and examined him. "Not speaking to the guests is one of your terms? Might I ask why? Surely it is not because you fear appearing ignorant to them. You are very well-spoken."

And just like that, his irritation flared, and he was much less willing to come to any agreement. Why should he not be well-spoken? Working with one's hands did not make one ignorant.

"My reasons are my own, ma'am, a thing I hope you will respect."

And just like that, her smile vanished. He felt sorry to be the cause that it should go. Sorry and even more irritated with himself for having been pleased to be the reason it had shown itself in the first place. He was in no position to like the woman. His own affairs were complicated enough. His current happiness depended on his solitude and privacy.

"I can agree to that stipulation," she said. "However, there is one man to whom I do require that you reveal your position."

"Why would my position matter to this one man?" Had the woman tensed, or was the sudden strain between them his imagination?

"I fear your desire for privacy must be mirrored by my own."

"Who is this man?" Ridley asked.

"His name is Leonard Ashby. He is the solicitor over my late husband's affairs. Should he ever show himself on our property, I will require you to claim the title of your position." She lifted her chin. "Can you do this? Or will I need to seek a stable master elsewhere?"

He lifted his chin to match hers. "I can do this. I do ask one more thing, however. I ask to be trusted, to have my way of doing things respected. I do not ask such things with the intention of becoming lax in my work, but so that it may be known that I am not ignorant and that my work will be trusted to be held to my highest personal standard. Can you do that, Lady Coventry? Can you trust me?"

Her eyes were wide and unblinking as she stared at him. Several moments passed before she answered, and her voice had thickened for reasons he could not understand. "I trust you, Mr. Ellis."

The innkeeper approached with a food-ladened tray. Lady Coventry stood abruptly, forcing Ridley to scramble to his feet. "I'm afraid I must attend to matters at home. Please send the bill for your stay here to Windsong. Mr. Palmer will see to those expenses. I do hope to see you at the estate by morning, Mr. Ellis. If you'll excuse me."

For the smallest moment, he thought she had dipped slightly before leaving, as if to curtsy to him, which would have been entirely irregular and completely inappropriate. But no. He must have imagined that. A baroness would never curtsy to a stable hand, even if he had been newly appointed as a stable master.

The innkeeper had brought an abundance of food, likely hoping to impress the baroness. But Ridley, surprisingly, had lost his appetite. He should have been hungry now that his affairs were settled.

He asked for the excess food to be bundled to be taken back with him to Windsong. He would share the bounty with the stable hands, who would now look to him for guidance. Not that much would change. They'd always looked to him in the past, but now it was official. And he had the luxury of a private cottage in the bargain.

His affairs truly were settled. Why was it that his emotions did not feel the same?

Chapter Thirteen

Nora wondered at her own choices as the thick wooden door of the Goose and Crown closed behind her. Perhaps bringing a man such as Mr. Ellis back to the estate was a bad idea. He'd done something to stir up her insides, to make her feel . . . yes. To make her *feel*. Every time her eyes met his, she felt that tingle of familiarity she'd felt when introducing Edward to the staff of the estate, back when her son had become enamored with General, the horse.

And when Mr. Ellis had asked her to trust him, she found herself unraveling beneath his gaze. She did trust him, even without knowing him. But how could such a feeling occur so quickly? She'd never really trusted any man; she'd been given plenty of reasons to lose faith in the male half of the human race. But this one?

She'd had to leave immediately. If she'd stayed another moment in his presence, she feared she would have become lost entirely. Mr. Palmer had warned her against going to the Goose and Crown herself to convince Mr. Ellis to return to Windsong, but she'd not listened. Mr. Palmer had come with her, of course, but she'd asked him to stay in the carriage while she settled the matter. She'd wanted to prove herself capable of managing her affairs. She knew she was going about it all wrong, but when hadn't she gone about everything all wrong?

She arrived back at the carriage and was handed up. As she settled back in her seat, Mr. Palmer immediately leaned forward. "You are distressed. Did Mr. Ellis offend you when he declined your offer?"

"He did not decline," she said.

Mr. Palmer's eyes widened in near-comical surprise. "He did not decline? But how? Why, then, do you look so—"

Mr. Palmer was a smart man, smart enough to let his words stay on his tongue rather than rolling out insults to her.

She could very well guess how she looked to him.

He would have been horrified to know that she had asked the innkeeper for food for herself and that, for the smallest moment, she had intended to eat with Mr. Ellis as though they were equals. What had she been thinking?

A charming smile—one that made the scar on his jawline disappear even as it made a dimple appear on his cheek—and kind eyes were not enough for her to forget her station. Were they?

The man could be her undoing. She'd believed so before. Today's encounter proved it.

Her carriage gently jerked forward and pulled her from her private thoughts. She swallowed hard and raised her chin. "I do believe Mr. Ellis will be back to Windsong tomorrow morning, so please alert those at the stables and carriage house. Prepare the stable master's cottage for him. We must have him fitted for his uniforms immediately upon his return."

"Yes, ma'am."

"Also, please set up a schedule for Mr. Ellis to continue riding instructions to both Miss Amelia and Lord Coventry."

"Of course, ma'am."

Of course. She had a son to raise to become a baron. Any thoughts of overstepping herself would result in the loss of her own child.

She would have to keep her wits about her when Mr. Ellis was near. She might need to go as far as to avoid the stables despite how much she loved riding because she was now certain of all the ways he was a danger to her. She should have left well enough alone and not sought him out at the Goose and Crown. But she needed her estate in perfect condition for when Mr. Ashby visited.

"All you all right, ma'am?" Mr. Palmer asked.

"Yes. Of course."

Of course.

Once they were back at the manor, Nora walked through the front door, relieved that she had one problem solved. Nash greeted her with a grim look, and her relief immediately plummeted into dread.

"What is it?" she asked.

"Mr. Ashby is visiting from London. He arrived first thing this morning and was . . . unhappy to find you were unavailable."

Nora couldn't seem to draw in a breath. "Where is he now?"

"I have him waiting in the library. He wanted to wait in the study but as your papers were still on the desk, I thought it best to have him where he would have more appropriate and less invasive reading at his disposal. I told him the study was being cleaned."

"Where did you tell him I was?"

"I merely said you'd gone into town."

Nora flexed her fingers, trying to bring some feeling back into them. Her extremities had gone numb with panic. "Thank you. Good." There was no time to find Mr. Palmer and beg him to corroborate the lies she was about to tell. She could only hope he would keep her whereabouts during the morning to himself. She steadied herself, smoothing her hands down her skirts, then made her way to the library.

"I am a baroness," she whispered to herself. "I can be strong for my children. I am a mother. I will protect my family. I can be strong. *Please let me be strong.*" The last was a prayer, a plea to her maker that He would help her.

She straightened her spine and swung open the door to greet the man who terrified her more than anything else. "Mr. Ashby. I trust you enjoyed a pleasant journey to Windsong."

"It was tolerable, Lady Coventry. I arrived in town last night. Imagine my surprise to find you already out. Where were you so early in the morning?"

The cheek on that man to ask such a question. What business was it of his what she did with her time? She smiled. "A neighbor has invited me to a musicale, and I wanted a new hat for the occasion. I heard the milliners in town had some new fabrics and wanted to peruse the selection before anyone else." The lie tasted like acid. "I hope you were comfortable at . . . I'm sorry, where are you staying?"

"The Goose and Crown. The service is reprehensible. I mean to voice my displeasure with the owner."

The Goose and Crown? Mercy. They'd likely just missed each other.

Nora took a moment to seat herself on the blue velvet reading chair closest to her. She needed to compose herself and wipe the alarm from her features before she faced him again. What if he had witnessed her sitting at an inn with a stable hand, eating together as equals? She wasn't being careful enough.

She hoped Mr. Ellis would arrive swiftly. The household needed to be running smoothly. At least Lia and Edward would be happier with Mr. Ellis than they had been with Mr. Daw. That had to count for something with Mr. Ashby, didn't it?

She worried that it wouldn't count for anything at all with such a man.

Two weeks later, Nora sat at the pianoforte, practicing and venting her frustrations with Mr. Ashby's presence on the keys. She found that her life at Windsong now offered her time to do the simple things that pleased her. She had not been able to play very often after she'd married Lord Coventry. At least not when he was in town. He said the racket gave him a headache. It irked her that he'd expected her to perform when he'd had guests over but also deprived her of the practice that would have allowed her to perform well.

Now, she could play as much as she wanted. Often, the children would sit in the drawing room after dinner and listen to her while they read books, or, in Lia's case, drew pictures. It was something they all enjoyed doing together, even Edward, which had been a surprise to Nora. She had feared she would never find anything the boy liked to do that involved her. But the music seemed to calm him. It calmed her as well. She let her fingers stretch over the keys and felt the music swell within her. She needed to feel the calm of this music.

Mr. Ashby never learned about her visit to the Goose and Crown. He did make quite a fuss regarding Mr. Daw's firing, but Mr. Palmer explained that not only was Mr. Daw a slovenly stable master but he had also endangered the children. Mr. Palmer praised Mr. Ellis's skills and took the credit for having promoted him.

Mr. Ashby now came to the manor almost every day. He followed the staff around while they worked, pelting them with questions regarding Nora's handling of the children and their education. She kept waiting for one member of the staff to share some grievance or other that would lead to her downfall.

Just that morning, Mr. Ashby had voiced complaints that Edward didn't have enough tutors, which was absurd. Did the man want the child in lessons all day? Nora had enough trouble getting her son to mind the studies she'd arranged for him, not including the new mathematics tutor or the addition of a handwriting instructor. Mr. Ashby had declared Edward's handwriting to be "vulgar in its every line."

For once, Edward and Nora were on the same side of fury and indignation.

Nora played her music with greater energy, draining her frustrations from the keys to the strings.

"Mama!" Lia flew into the room with more excitement than Nora had ever seen in the child before.

Since Lia had started her riding lessons and become friends with Mary Spencer, she'd called Nora "Mama" almost exclusively without being reminded.

The endearment and the girl's noticeably brightened spirits had shifted things for Nora. She had begun to feel as if she really was Lia's mother. The two had grown closer. Nora only wished she knew how to develop that same relationship with her son.

Nora stood from the pianoforte as Lia hurled herself forward, wrapping her arms around Nora's waist. Nora's parents had not been physically affectionate people, and her rather chilly marriage had certainly lacked such things, so Nora wasn't so certain how to handle the sudden and unexpected embrace. She slowly wrapped her arms around the little girl. An immediate sense of relief and comfort flooded her. She could certainly get used to such affection.

"What is it? Is everything all right?" she asked.

"Everything is positively perfect!" Lia exclaimed.

"Perfect? Well, that is something to celebrate. What has everything so perfect, darling?"

Lia pulled away and twirled in small circles around Nora. "Mr. Ellis says I am *so good* at riding. He said he's never seen someone take to the saddle as I have."

"Well, of course, you're brilliant. No daughter of mine could ever be anything less."

Lia practically sparkled under such praise. But then her mouth turned down in a pout. "But he won't let me ride Bonnie."

That was a relief to Nora. She was not too keen on the idea of that horse, no matter how much Lia insisted Bonnie was sweet and gentle, and she wondered if the horse ought to simply be sold.

"We must trust that Mr. Ellis knows what he is about. If he does not think Bonnie is ready to ride, then she's not ready to ride." She had told Mr. Ellis that she trusted him, and she *did* trust him. Even if that trust had to be offered from a distance.

She had kept her word to herself and stayed away from the stables these past weeks. Her time with Mrs. Spencer and other ladies from the neighborhood had all been indoors while taking tea. She ached to be out riding again, but she dared not venture out, not when she wasn't sure she could trust herself around Mr. Ellis. Not when any inappropriate behavior could be reported to Mr. Ashby.

Mr. Palmer delivered reports of the estate affairs, and though she most keenly listened to the reports that dealt with the progress of her son's growing aptitude as a baron, she also paid closer attention than she knew she ought to regarding the children's riding lessons—and the one giving those instructions.

Both children had been doing exceptionally well. Mr. Palmer had been favorable in his explanations of Miss Amelia's growing skills and how much the young Lord Coventry had taken to General, his father's horse.

Nora was gratified that Edward's irritability had been tempered to a small degree. She wished his moodiness had disappeared altogether, but she would take her wins where she could find them. The fact that her son did not seize *every* opportunity to harass his sister but instead left her alone at every fifth or sixth opportunity was progress.

"But Bonnie is my horse," Lia exclaimed, drawing Nora's attention back to the little girl. "Shouldn't I be the one to decide whether or not I get to ride her?"

Those were the words of a young baroness trying to exert her authority. She was glad to see Lia strengthening herself. The girl's life would be hard enough, and it would do her some good to have the confidence to not be bullied at every turn.

But on the subject of the horse, Nora remained firm. "Bonnie *is* your horse; however, you must learn how to handle her first. That means you will have to work hard and listen very closely to everything Mr. Ellis teaches you."

"I *am* listening."

Nora smiled at Lia's pert response.

Edward entered the room, but unlike Lia, he brought with him a cloud of sullen gloom. He stumped toward the chair that he'd claimed as his, his shoulders slumped.

"I am very glad to hear that you *both* are doing so well in your riding lessons," Nora said, thinking the compliment might ease some of her son's tension.

But the compliment seemed to produce the opposite effect. He turned in the chair and swung his legs over the side so his back was to her.

Wanting to coax him out of his temper, she said, "I've heard glowing reports of your riding lessons with General."

"General's a stupid horse. I'll not ride that one ever again," her son retorted hotly.

"General's not stupid," Lia protested.

"Like you'd know. You're as stupid as General."

"I am not." Lia's eyebrows cinched together tightly as she frowned at her brother.

He leapt from the chair and dove at her with a raised fist. Lia scrambled back to escape the blow he surely meant to inflict on her, but Nora came between them and caught him by the shoulders before he could reach his sister. With Nora's arms in the way, the strength of his swing was diminished but not enough. She felt the vibrations of his wrist against her forearm and bit back a cry of pain.

Nora shot a glance to the door, worried Mr. Ashby, who was in the study with Mr. Palmer, might have heard.

Edward seemed startled to find that his blow had landed on his own mother—startled but not repentant.

"Edward!" she whispered harshly. "What has gotten into you?"

"He's unhappy because I'm a better rider than he is." Lia's voice was small, her earlier happiness drowned in the undertow of her brother's emotions.

"Shut it!" Edward snarled at her.

Lia shrank back further still.

"Who said you were a better rider?" Nora asked.

"Mr. Ellis said that if Edward practiced more, he'd become as good a rider as I am."

"I said shut it!" Edward likely would have lunged again, but, with Nora's hands on his shoulders, he was unable.

"Please keep your voices down." Nora hated how she felt like curling into a ball and weeping at her son's cruel reaction. "Needing practice does not make you unaccomplished, Edward. Everyone needs practice at everything they set their sights on. I must practice the pianoforte just as Lia must practice her letters. We all have things we are working to improve."

Edward jostled out of her grasp and turned his full glare on her. "Stop treating me like I'm a child. Father was right about you. You really are ridiculous."

The words stabbed painfully into Nora's heart. Lia gasped.

"You shouldn't speak like that to Mama," Lia said softly, defending Nora's honor even though Nora had been scarcely able to defend Lia against Edward for months.

Edward sneered at her. "I can speak to her however I wish. She's my mother, not yours. Your mother is dead."

Lia's eyes welled with fat tears, but instead of showing remorse, Edward seemed to feed off the response. "You two deserve each other. You're both ridiculous, just as Father said."

He stomped out of the room, a wave crashing over them and then pulling back to sea.

Tears rolled down Lia's face in steady streams, but her crying was silent except for the occasional sniffle. Nora would have gone after Edward, except she dared not risk him shouting again. Not with Mr. Ashby in the house.

"I'm sorry, Lia. I'm sorry he's so much like—" She stopped herself from saying "his father." Lia had so little happiness regarding her parentage. It would have been unfair to tell her that her father was capable of such unkindness.

Nora tucked the child into her arms again. She figured they both needed another embrace. She pressed a kiss atop Lia's head and said, "But I want you to know I'm proud of you, both for being such an excellent rider and for being such an excellent person. Your mama must have taught you very well for you to have such a kind heart. I am sure she is very proud of you as well." She glanced at the door again to make sure no one would hear her mention Lia's natural mother.

"Do you think so?" the girl sniffled out the question.

"I know so." She stood with Lia for several moments, then patted her on her shoulders. "Now, I believe it is time for you to meet your reading tutor."

Lia nodded and left, her sniffles having subsided even if her eyes were still wet.

Nora, alone and nearly drowning in her own sadness and apprehension, could not stand to be indoors for another moment, not with

Mr. Ashby intruding on the sanctuary of her home. She pushed out through the double doors that led to the back stone patio. With her eyes full of the tears, she fled down the path, hardly knowing where she was going.

When she realized she was near the stables, she veered off the path to head to the gardens where she was certain to be alone. As she turned the corner, she ran straight into someone. Strong hands caught her upper arms to keep her from stumbling back. She looked up in fear, terrified by the thought that it was Mr. Ashby coming to tell her he was taking her son because she was so clearly failing at raising him.

She met Mr. Ellis's widened eyes. The white scar at his chin clearly visible as his mouth opened.

He pulled his hands away and said in a tone so gentle that it could have been a feather falling, "Lady Coventry. I'm sorry to have startled you. Are you all right? Can I help you?"

For a moment, she thought to insist she was fine, to use the tone her husband had when he felt the servants had overstepped themselves. But she stopped the words from leaving her tongue.

She tucked her pride in her pocket. What had the pride her parents and husband had instilled in her done for her? And who was she to make herself out to be better than an honest-working stable master? Especially when compassion and kindness flowed from him. She needed help, and if he could offer that help, she was in no position to refuse it.

"I am not all right," she admitted, falling off the emotional edge she'd been teetering on since Mr. Ashby had shown up, a wave of panic and fear rising up inside of her. "Not at all. I hardly know myself. I am broken, shattered." The admission made her gasp aloud. She had thought the words so many times, but she had never said them aloud, not even to herself.

"A diamond cannot be shattered, my lady. And I've seen the strength of a diamond in you."

"How can you say such a thing? I'm failing—failing so miserably that I hardly know what I'm about any longer." With that, she began to cry in earnest, her body heaving with big, wracking sobs that were entirely shameful and inappropriate. She finally gave in to the tears she'd been holding since she'd been sixteen and newly married.

Mr. Ellis placed an arm around her shoulders, and she felt no desire to shrink away at his touch regardless of how improper such familiarity was. She leaned into him as he led her inside the stable to a small wooden seat. She felt safe for the first time in weeks. Mr. Ashby avoided the stables due to his allergies.

Mr. Ellis settled her down then crouched low so he could peer into her face. "Can I fetch someone for you?"

"Who would you send for? My housekeeper? My butler? What can they do for me? What power do they possess to help? I have no one, you see? Not unless you count my children who are, in fact, just children. And it is with them that I require help."

"Help, ma'am?"

"How is it that Edward is so horrible? Even to me? How can he be so much like his father?" There. She'd said it. Though her husband had not been cruel, neither had he been kind. His slicing words had been their own torture.

Mr. Ellis rocked back on his heels and looked around as if hoping to find someone else to bear the burden of the baroness giving in to histrionics. But there was no one. And so he turned his attention back to her. "Lady Coventry, I will not pretend to misunderstand your meaning, for I've seen enough in my life and in the last few weeks with the children that I know of what you speak. But you are not failing."

"How can you say such a thing?" Her tears subsided enough to allow her to speak without her voice catching.

"Quite easily. Young Lord Coventry is much improved since I've been working with him. I have seen a softening to him, a thawing if you will. He is not as quick to snap and bite when corrected."

"I only wish . . ."

"What do you wish?" His warm eyes fixed on her in such a way that she felt he truly was listening.

"I wish I knew what I was doing. I was married when I was sixteen years old, you know."

If the news confused or surprised him, he made no show of it.

"Sixteen, Mr. Ellis. My whole life spent training on how to curtsy and pour tea and play music at dinner parties. And then I married, thinking I could find myself in the work of being a wife. But do you know what the work of being a wife entails?"

He shook his head.

"The work of a wife, at least of being a wife to my particular husband, was curtsying to my husband's guests, pouring tea, and playing music at dinner parties. It was preparing menus and being lonely. How am I to teach my children how to be adults when I've scarcely had the chance to learn for myself? I *am* failing. And I cannot afford to fail."

"You cannot feel you are failing when things are improving." Mr. Ellis placed his hands on hers and squeezed.

His touch made her entire body spark as though she had been touched by lightning. She could not help but stare at where their hands connected.

He followed her gaze, and then immediately removed his hands. He jumped to his feet and backed up. "I'm sorry. I did not mean . . . I was only trying . . ."

She hurried to get her own feet under her. "Please!" she cried out when she realized he was retreating. "Don't leave. I am not angry. You offered me a kindness, not an insult. And I've seen so little of kindness of late that I can only be grateful. Please do not be uneasy. I promise you I am not uneasy. Only grateful."

"Ma'am, it is not for your sort to ever feel grateful toward my sort."

"I am most sincere, Mr. Ellis. What can I do to prove my gratitude?"

He stepped closer to her, and her heart thrummed. They were so alone and unseen, and she had asked a question that could result in any number of ill-conceived ramifications. She wondered at the fact that she did not feel afraid.

"There is something."

She raised her chin and held her breath.

"You can come to the stables more often. Watch Lord Coventry and Miss Amelia as they ride. Both children would dearly love to be praised and recognized by you."

"Oh." She felt a disappointment she didn't quite understand. "I do praise them. I do recognize them." She had not been insulted by his touch, though she should have been, but his insinuation that she did not give her children due credit for their achievements *was* insulting.

"If I may be so bold, Lady Coventry. You are not *here* giving that praise. Not in the moment. Come to the stables when they have their riding lessons. See them in this place. See them accomplishing their tasks and then applaud them in the moment. There is something about horses and people together that can heal and calm us if we let it. Will you come?"

Nora did not answer for several seconds. Instead, she inspected this man whom she had already declared she trusted and to whom she had confided far more than she'd confided to any other soul. *Who are you?* she thought.

She could not deny him his request. For one thing, it was perfectly reasonable. For another, it gave her an excuse to see him again under circumstances that were completely appropriate. No one would suspect . . . Well, she did not know what people might suspect. She did not know what she herself suspected. Except she did know, and it scared her.

"Yes. I will come." She forced a smile. "And I'll strive to make friends who will listen to me ramble on with ridiculous, silly thoughts, so that I might spare you such a task."

"I have heard nothing that could be called ridiculous or silly. I have simply heard the loving worry of a mother and the ponderings of a good person."

She felt as if she had become tangled in his gaze and hurried to look away. "Thank you for your kindness."

She turned and hurried away, wondering at the encounter, wondering at how like a friend Mr. Ellis seemed to her. Wondering at her own internal dilemma regarding this man.

Chapter Fourteen

Ridley spent a long time standing perfectly still in the stable. *What am I doing?* he thought. Lady Coventry was lovely, to be sure, and she seemed to grow more lovely with every encounter. But that did not mean he was free to place his arm around her as he had or take her hand as he had. Her tears were not his to dry. He needed to remember that.

Yet, she had trusted him enough to unburden her worries.

She had also not rejected his arm around her. She had allowed him to lead her to the stable and settle her on a chair. She had not pulled away when his rough hands covered the soft, almost silky, skin of her own hands. Touching her had been like touching the velvet of a rose petal.

He inhaled sharply at the memory. General snorted and stamped in response, pulling him back to himself. That it was the late Lord Coventry's horse fussing stood as further evidence that he had no business feeling so connected to this woman.

General snorted and stamped some more.

"I heard you the first time." Ridley broke free of the spell he'd been under and got back to work.

Don't think of her. Do not let your muddled feelings for her interfere with the freedom you have created for yourself.

He was determined to take his own advice.

When she showed up with the children for their riding lessons, a man was with her. Ridley drew back, intending to make himself scarce and let George take over, except Lady Coventry's eyes widened and she gave a small shake of her head.

"Mr. Ashby," she said, her tone stilted, "this is our stable master, Mr. Ellis. He's been furthering the children's riding education."

Ridley tensed at the introduction, but he remembered his promise to Lady Coventry to assume his proper title with this individual, and he stepped forward.

The staff had been whispering about Mr. Ashby's strange questioning and imposing demeanor, and now meeting the man himself, Ridley was unimpressed. Mr. Ashby was a short, sour-looking man. He had a slash for a mouth and heavy, thick eyebrows that were drawn together so closely that Ridley couldn't tell if the man had only one brow or two. Ridley had seen the solicitor when the late Lord Coventry had visited and had drawn the opinion then that the man was an oily sort of sycophant. Mr. Ashby seemed to sneer as he eyed Ridley, as if memorizing him.

Ridley did not like the scrutiny. Not at all.

He shouldn't have taken the position as stable master. What had he been thinking? He was on a baron's estate with a position that brought notice to him now that the estate was in regular use. How invisible did he really believe he could remain in such a situation?

Not invisible at all.

He nodded to Mr. Ashby while cutting a glance to Lady Coventry. The silence thickened the tension, so he greeted the children. "Lord Coventry. Miss Amelia. Let's begin and show Lady Coventry what you've learned so far."

He ran the children through several different situations until they were finally seated, guiding their horses through a walk to a canter. Their mother applauded and smiled broadly. She even called out a cheer until Mr. Ashby scowled at her, and her mouth snapped closed, her smile disappearing.

What was going on here?

In spite of the man's unwelcome company, Ridley was pleased

with how much Lady Coventry's presence improved the children's skills. They were eager to show off their abilities and obeyed his every instruction without fail.

Mr. Ashby released a series of sneezes that seemed to never end. He wiped a handkerchief under his nose. "Allergic to horses," he said, then headed toward the main house.

Everyone relaxed with Mr. Ashby gone. Lady Coventry finally allowed herself to show the children the praise he'd been hoping for when he'd requested her presence. She applauded. She smiled broadly. She encouraged loudly.

It bothered Ridley that the baroness had felt constrained in her admiration for the children's accomplishments with Mr. Ashby present.

After the lesson ended and the family returned to the house, Ridley returned to his cottage and packed a small bag so that it was ready in case he needed to leave quickly. Mr. Ashby had made a note of him, which did not sit well with Ridley.

The next time the children had a lesson, Lady Coventry was with them, but Mr. Ashby was not. Nor was he there for any of the several lessons that followed. Ridley relaxed. Perhaps he had overreacted. Perhaps there was no cause for worry.

Lady Coventry attended every lesson. The children beamed under her attention.

Not only did her presence help the children, it helped him as well. They were so eager to show her how well they were doing that they listened to his every word as if he were the most knowledgeable riding instructor in all of England. Though that had not been his intention, it was certainly a wonderful side effect and made his job so much easier.

Even young Lord Coventry improved.

He was not nearly so stubborn, and he no longer argued over every single direction given to him. He managed to stay in the saddle far more often, and his calmer temperament meant General took his lead with greater ease.

Not thinking of Lady Coventry the first few times she returned to the stables had been easy enough, but in the three weeks since she'd cried on his shoulder, so to speak, it had grown increasingly difficult with her every visit.

It didn't help that she'd begun to invite people to the house—and to the stables specifically—so she might take her guests out riding for entertainment rather than eating cakes with them in the drawing room. Mrs. Spencer and her daughter Mary had come several times, along with several new friends.

Lady Coventry always spoke directly to George when she was with her friends, careful to honor her side of the bargain to protect Ridley's privacy. Her respect for his request deepened the respect he felt for her.

It wasn't just her visits that brought Lady Coventry to his thoughts. Everywhere he went, he heard whispers about her. The whole of the neighborhood spoke of her. The tenants declared her kind and generous. They felt greater confidence in their situations now that she was settled at Windsong. The other members of society who came as her guests remarked on her elegance and grace. And the servants and grooms from neighboring households said their employers felt her to be a woman of gentle goodness with an informed mind.

He hated himself for listening to the gossip regarding her, but he felt keen to learn all he could from any source he could. Was it possible to become enamored with a woman over her reputation and his limited contact? No. Surely not. He wasn't enamored with her. He was simply grateful that she'd chosen to heed his advice and be more available to her children when they were at the stables. He was merely pleased in the marked improvement he'd witnessed in them.

At least, he *had* believed there was improvement.

But young Lord Coventry had taken a long slide backward in behavior.

"That girl's got a splat on her cheek redder than a tomato from the garden," George said while he was mucking out Angel's stall.

"What girl?" Ridley asked from where he was rubbing down

the individual saddles with neat's-foot oil and beeswax to soften the leather.

"Miss Amelia."

Ridley felt immediate outrage that anyone had dared to strike gentle Miss Amelia, especially hard enough to leave a mark. "What happened to her?"

"The new Lord Coventry is as mean as they come. Strange that one so small can carry so much anger all the time. You think it would exhaust him."

"When did this happen?"

"Not long ago. I heard the brawl just after breakfast. Cook made the most incredible marmalade. I don't think she's ever made it taste so good."

Ridley frowned at the irrelevant details of marmalade. "Is Miss Amelia all right?"

George shrugged and returned to his chores as if he had been gossiping about weather instead of real, breathing children. He filled his wheelbarrow with the old bedding and left the stables to dump it out in the fields.

Within moments, the stamping sounds of shoes running along the cobblestones sounded through the area. The stable door banged open.

"Saddle my horse!" young Lord Coventry bellowed. "I wish to ride."

Ridley pulled a rag from the drawer and wiped the oil from his hands. He took his time walking toward the boy, who looked like a full-on storm brewing in his stables. Lady Coventry had said she'd needed help with her children, and he had thought he had helped by bringing her out to see them ride, but clearly, he'd not done enough.

Ridley squared his shoulders and looked the boy in the eyes. "No."

"No?" The young man's hands balled into fists. If the boy had been a few years older, Ridley had no doubt that the young lord would have taken a swing at him the way he'd taken a swing at his sister.

"No."

"Did you forget you work for me? Mr. Ashby said it's important that I maintain discipline in my household. Did you forget that I am the master here?"

Who was Mr. Ashby to be giving such advice to the young baron? Was that man the reason the boy had hit his sister? "I did not forget. But neither did I forget that I am better educated. General has had a visit from the farrier and is walking with a limp. He cannot be ridden."

"Then one of the other horses."

"No."

Ridley did not believe the child could have darkened to a deeper shade of red. "No?"

"No. You're clearly unsettled and not in command of yourself. A horse cannot be led by one who has no control over his own self. So no. If you wish to enforce discipline, might I suggest you start with regulating yourself? You're not a stupid boy. It pains me to have to explain it to you."

Yes, he was goading a twelve-year-old child. No, such actions did not speak well of him. But the boy had hit Miss Amelia, and Ridley had no patience for a bully.

The two of them stared at one another. Ridley refused to look away. He'd had his own training as a child. Flinching first revealed vulnerability. When young Lord Coventry finally averted his eyes, Ridley felt triumph, but did not smile or gloat. Instead, he moved to General's stall, opened it, and rubbed the stallion's nose.

"How dare you call me stupid?" Lord Coventry snapped.

Ridley didn't hurry to answer. He clucked his tongue and tapped General's leg. General shifted his balance. "I did not call you stupid. I said the exact opposite, in fact. I said you were *not* a stupid boy. But your misunderstanding of my words makes me wonder if I spoke too quickly."

Ridley looked at the young man, who practically writhed with indignation, and pressed his lips together. How should he approach the wildness of this angry spirit? How could a child such as this be reined in?

"I'm very sorry for you," Ridley said after a moment. He didn't look up from the stallion, but the deep inhalation of air sucked in sharply was enough to tell him that his words had hit their mark.

"Sorry for me? You're a servant! You've no right to feel sorry for me."

"Any man in a situation superior to another's has the right to feel sorry. And if he's a good man, he *will* feel sorry. Only a monster rejoices in another's misery."

He propped General's leg on his own so he could inspect the hoof. He gently touched the red bruising of the sole. When the horse snorted in distress, he lowered the foot back to the ground and rubbed General's nose to comfort him. The poor thing must have stepped wrong on a stone when his shoe had cracked.

The young lord fumed throughout the whole of the process, clearly irritated to not have Ridley's total attention. "I'm not the one with a bruised cheek. If you want to feel sorry for someone, you can save your pity for my crybaby sister."

"I had heard you'd struck Miss Amelia. I had *not* heard you were gloating about it. Hitting your sister is an unfortunate sign of weakness in you. And that is the reason I feel so deeply sorry for you." He clucked his tongue in disappointment. "It's a shame really. I had thought you to be more promising."

"What do you mean? I'm not weak. To punish someone beneath you is strength."

Ridley laughed out loud, though he felt more alarmed than actually humored. What sort of man would this boy grow to be? "You think so, do you?" He shook his head. "What foolish teacher gave you such an ill-conceived lesson?"

The boy bristled, and his nostrils flared. "I could have you sacked for speaking to me the way you do."

"Yes. You could. And if you were the sort of man who would dismiss a hardworking and honest employee for speaking the truth, then

I would be glad to not work for you any longer. I'm an intelligent man with enough self-respect to not work for bullies and fools. A good employee is hard to come by. If you sack every person who vexes you, you will end up with worthless layabouts in your employ. Your lands and household will turn to ruin under their indolence. And you'll have only yourself to blame. So, are you going to dismiss me for speaking truth to you? Or are you going to be wise and listen to the counsel of one with more information than you currently possess on your own?" He fixed the child with a cold stare of challenge.

The young lord's fingers tightened into fists again, but after a deep breath, he relaxed his fingers. "I am wise." He jutted out his chin and squared his shoulders. The pride rolling off him could have supplied the entire country twice over.

Ridley waited, staying silent, forcing the boy to make the next move.

George returned to the stables but left again when Ridley gave a slight shake of his head. Ridley was glad George had moved silently—a skill he'd perfected in order to avoid Daw before the man had been let go.

"What do you mean by weak? How can I be strong?" The question, which had been long in coming, held an earnestness that gave Ridley hope.

"Hitting your sister was the move of a weak man. Striking out at anyone who is, by law or means, unable to reciprocate is the basest show of weakness. Anyone can immediately spot such frailty of character. A man not in control of himself can never hope to have control over others. Striking out shows a lack of control. A man who commands himself does not react to outside provocations."

Ridley picked up the broken bits of horseshoe that the farrier had left when he'd reshoed General. He wondered how the bruised sole had not been noticed at that time. He showed the broken metal to the boy.

"Consider yourself a horseshoe. A weak shoe cracks under slight and casual conditions. Everyone knows it's weak because it breaks so easily. A strong shoe can withstand all manner of abuse, all tests of pressure. Everyone knows it is strong because it does not surrender to its surroundings, no matter how difficult those surroundings might become."

He held out the bits of metal, and, to his surprise, the boy took them.

Ridley considered his own words, and then added, almost to himself, "Your mother is a fine example of strength."

"My mother?" the young lord scoffed.

Ridley blinked, realizing he'd unintentionally spoken aloud his esteem for Lady Coventry. But rather than back down from his stated opinion, he defended it. The child needed to learn respect for his mother if he were ever to overcome his other deficiencies. And Ridley did not want Lady Coventry crying in his stables again over the rot that infected her son's core.

Or maybe he did want her crying again if it meant he could place his arm around her and feel the warmth of her next to him, if it meant he could take her hand as he had done before. He blinked again and moved to place more bedding in General's stall so the horse had something soft to stand on while his sole healed, even though such a task should have been left to one of the undergrooms or stable boys.

"Yes. Your mother possesses a fierce strength. Everyone says so." The entire household had buzzed with admiration after she had fired Daw and brought Ridley back to the estate.

"And who is everyone to a stable hand?" Edward asked with a sneer as he gripped the broken horseshoe. "Do the horses share opinions with you?"

Ridley fixed the boy with another stare. "*Everyone* is everyone. All those in your household's employ. All those who work the lands you own. All those who are in the shops in town. All those who have come to your home as guests and who've ridden your horses over the last few weeks. All the ladies and gentlemen. Everyone."

The young lord was the first to look away again.

Ridley pitched more straw over the cobbled floor of General's stall and waited. He'd learned that his conversations with the boy were chess games of words, and any phrase could put a player in check.

"What did everyone say about my father?" The whispered words came out with a fragility that reminded Ridley of just how small the boy really was.

"I don't think you want to know." Ridley pitched another forkful of straw.

The young lord went quiet again, and for the first time, the silence did not feel like a pawn being pushed around a game board. "I suppose by warning me that I don't want to know, you're giving me the answer I seek."

"Yes. And by understanding that nuance, you prove to have something your father did not have."

"And what is that?" It wasn't a challenge. The young boy truly wanted to understand.

Ridley leaned on his pitchfork, glad he'd sent away the stable hands so he had this time with the boy. "It means you've enough awareness to choose."

"And what is it I'm meant to choose?"

"You can choose to be weak metal like that in your hand, like everyone knew your father to be. Or you can choose to be something substantial, something that lasts against adversity, something strong. Something like your mother."

The young lord stepped forward, his words tumbling out of him. "How will people know what my choice is? How will people know if I'm strong?"

"People will know that you contain strength of character when you are strong enough to hold in your rage. Not everyone is capable of such strength. And others respect the person who is."

The boy nodded and then dropped the broken pieces of horseshoe to the flagstones beneath his feet. The clattering echoed through the barn, making the horses shift uneasily.

"I will not hit her, or anyone, again."

Ridley bowed his head in respect. "See that you do not."

The young lord bowed his own head before realizing he'd paid such deference to one of his servants. His mouth tightened into a line, but he gave a second, sharp nod as if he meant for the show of respect to stand.

In a single swift movement, the boy swept up the broken bits of metal again, and then he was gone.

The young lord did not return to the stables the next day, nor the day after that. Miss Amelia did not miss her lessons even though her brother's handiwork had turned purple on her cheek. Lady Coventry did not join her daughter for lessons. On the third day, both children missed lessons, and Ridley began to believe he had overstepped his mark.

On the fourth day, when Lady Coventry arrived alone in the stables in a dress instead of her riding clothes, he was certain he was going to be relieved of duty. He would have expected her to send Mr. Palmer to handle him, but then, she was a woman who'd surprised him before by handling matters on her own.

"Mr. Ellis," she said.

"Lady Coventry." He felt wariness down to his bones. He did not wish to leave Windsong. He did not wish to leave her.

"I came to thank you."

"Thank me, ma'am?" The words tumbled out in his surprise.

"Edward has been much improved these last few days, and I know it's your doing."

She wasn't angry with him. She was coming to thank him. Unbidden, and unable to help himself, he stepped in her direction. "What makes you think this is my doing?"

She did not retreat from him. "He returned to the house with broken bits of horseshoe in his hand, then went straightaway to his sister's room. He apologized, Mr. Ellis." Lady Coventry's face erupted into a smile as bright as the sun. "He actually apologized." She took a step closer to him. She looked up into his face and whispered, "What sort of magic are you working, Mr. Ellis?"

Her whispered breath swept over his lips. He almost bent his head. He almost leaned closer. He stepped back abruptly, breaking whatever spell had woven around the two of them.

"No magic, Lady Coventry. I simply spoke to him."

She had not retreated from his moving closer, but she did at his moving farther away. "I've spoken to him for months, yet my words have never generated such a transformation as this. So whatever you have done, I thank you for the magic it has produced." She turned and left the stables.

He stared at the place where she'd stood so close to him, her mouth close enough to feel her breath on his lips. How had she made his heart race and stop all at once? How had she elicited a leap of joy in him he had sworn to never give in to?

"I am not the magician here, my lady," he said out loud.

Chapter Fifteen

"Why do I continually return to those stables?" Nora whispered to herself as she made her way across the path. She straggled behind her children, who were racing to arrive at the stable door first. Whoever did so would get to ride first.

She had not realized how unorthodox Mr. Ellis's methods were until she'd witnessed them firsthand. If her children had not seemed so much improved by the time she had seen for herself, she'd have likely had the man run off for his impropriety.

She was glad Mr. Ashby hadn't been around for lessons beyond his first visit to the stables. If she objected to Mr. Ellis's methods, Mr. Ashby would certainly do much worse. But the solicitor's return to London a few days prior had flooded her with relief, easing the tension she'd been carrying in her shoulders for weeks. He'd said he would return soon, but any break was welcome no matter how brief. She took it as a good sign that he'd left without taking Edward with him. Was it possible they were safe from that threat? She let herself hope.

Mr. Ellis had the children doing small chores for the horses. He called them "services," but it seemed like work to her. A baron and a baroness were not meant for such work, and she'd have objected to the idea entirely except as she was about to raise a protest and scold Mr. Ellis severely—no matter how well he looked in his leather riding breeches and gaiters—she saw how happy her children were.

Lia did not mope or cower or cry. She beamed and smiled and talked excitedly. Edward did not snap or bite, but laughed good-naturedly at something Lia said to him, almost as if he enjoyed his sister's company.

Edward beat Lia to the stable door and slapped his hand on the wood with triumph. Nora felt surprised the little girl had come in at such a close second. With her shorter legs, she should have been much farther behind.

She refused to hurry after the children. Someone in the family had to maintain propriety at the stables, or they would all descend into chaos.

Except as she entered, there was no chaos to be found. Lia rubbed Bonnie's nose and cooed at the horse. Edward helped cinch up a saddle on General.

"Good. You're getting better at that," Mr. Ellis murmured to her son. "Have you noticed how much more General trusts you, how much more he responds to you?"

"I have," Edward replied.

"You're doing very well, Lord Coventry. A gentleman should always be able to saddle his own horse,"

"Why?" Edward asked, echoing Nora's own silent sentiment. "If I know how to do it, won't you be out of a job?" Her boy smiled at his riding instructor.

Mr. Ellis laughed. "Knowing how and planning to do it all the time on your own are not the same thing at all, m'lord." Mr. Ellis's voice lowered, and Nora strained to hear. His tone took on a near-mystical air. "Knowing how allows you the luxury to come and go as you please. It allows you to be a ghost when you need invisibility most desperately." He cleared his throat and said in a louder voice. "Sorry. Never mind that. I don't know where my head is sometimes. This practice allows your horse to feel complete trust for you. Naturally, sir, I would not ask, or want, you to perform such duties on a regular basis. You need not worry on that score. You are very near to graduating from this particular task."

"I did not mean to imply that I minded this task," Edward rushed to say. "I quite enjoy my time with General."

"Very good, sir."

Edward mounted and instructed General to head outside where he then instructed the horse to stop. Horse and rider seemed to be in an easy agreement with one another. As Mr. Ellis had said, they trusted one another through the service Edward had shown the horse.

She'd never seen such a method of teaching used before. Her own riding instructor from her youth had never allowed her to do anything but get on the horse and become its master. She was not to garner trust but to command and control.

She often felt that many people of society were trained to handle other people the same way she'd been taught to handle a horse.

Mr. Ashby reminded her of her first riding instructor. When the solicitor had first arrived, Edward had reverted to his previous behavior. The fact that Mr. Ashby nodded his approval when Edward was at his worst made her realize how little control she had over her child. Anything she said to contradict Mr. Ashby quickly turned to her disadvantage.

The man made her second-guess every syllable she uttered to her children. He questioned her handling of the staff and criticized any perceived lenience in her. He seemed particularly obsessed with Mr. Daw's removal from the estate and asked everyone how they had perceived the events from their point of view. Mr. Ashby didn't hide that he was not overly fond of Mr. Ellis. Nora thought she understood why. Mr. Ashby had held Edward in some sort of thrall. She had felt her son slipping further and further away. But it had all changed when Edward had returned from the stables with the bits of broken horseshoe. She was no longer alone. Mr. Ellis was on her side.

Mr. Ashby did not like losing his grip on her son.

Nora glanced up, realizing everyone was following Edward into the pasture where he waited for further instruction.

"Is Bonnie ready yet?" Lia asked Mr. Ellis.

"Not yet. But she stands still whenever her lead is tied to a fence post or a tree, and she is beginning to stand still when her lead is merely dropped. She's getting closer, Miss Amelia. Much closer."

Lia sighed happily at the prospect of riding her horse.

Mr. Ellis returned his attention to Edward. "We're going to try a canter again today. I know it feels fast and might be a little unnerving, but I assure you, it's actually quite comfortable once you master following the flow of movement. It is important for you to be relaxed. Can you be relaxed, Lord Coventry?"

"Yes. I can."

Nora raised an eyebrow. She wasn't sure she had ever seen her son truly relaxed. How could he have been with a father who demanded perfection in every step and syllable?

Mr. Ellis did not mention how very tense and awkward Edward seemed at the moment but instead said, "You may bounce at first if you hold yourself too stiffly, but I assure you that you'll bounce far less than you do when General is trotting. And you'll hardly bounce at all if you relax your hips and sit as deep into your saddle as you can."

"How do I ask him to canter? I don't remember."

Nora's heart warmed at watching her son admit to a flaw of memory. As Mr. Ellis continued his instruction, Lia's hand slipped into Nora's. Nora glanced down, surprised once again by the familiarity and comfortable manner Lia had begun showing her.

"I like Mr. Ellis. He reminds me of my grandpapa," Lia said, watching as the riding lesson continued.

"What? Mr. Ellis?"

Lia nodded. "He's gentle. Mama once told me that a gentle man was the kind I should search for when it came time to wed." Lia wrinkled her nose to let Nora know what she thought of the idea of being wed.

Nora never chastised Lia for mentioning her real mother when it was just the two of them. Lia needed to be able to speak of her past experiences with someone. If Nora didn't allow it with her, then those memories might accidentally slip out with someone who would not forgive the girl for her past.

"Yes. I can imagine she would want you to find a gentleman. Most mothers have such hopes for their daughters."

"No," Lia said with a slight frown crossing her pale features. "Not a *gentleman*. But a man who is *gentle*. I do not think they are the same thing, are they?"

Lia tore her gaze away from Mr. Ellis and fixed it on Nora as if to see if she might be right in her assessment of men.

"No, Lia, they are not the same thing." She looked to where Mr. Ellis stepped away and called out instructions to Edward. She felt her own frown forming. "They're not the same thing at all. They can be. But, apparently, not always."

When the children finished their lessons, they scurried back to the house so they could wash up before their maths lessons.

Nora lingered, watching Mr. Ellis as he patiently gave directions to George. She wanted to interrupt, but it felt rude to step into the middle of his instructions to the groom. She found herself mesmerized. She'd never seen a man who acted with such calm fortitude while explaining the details of a job that needed to be done. He did not bellow. He did not snort in derision when a particular instruction required repeating.

She continued watching from her corner in the stables as she waited for an opportunity to make her presence known. George finally left, and Mr. Ellis removed his waistcoat, which made her feel uncomfortable for not announcing her presence sooner. But she didn't know how to do so now with any form of delicacy.

Mr. Ellis worked with an efficiency and confidence that she admired. The only skill she had where she felt even a tenth of that confidence was at the pianoforte. She had good tutors, and she practiced diligently, but she knew she was still not as proficient as she would have liked. She thought she might be accomplished at singing, but it felt so personal that she had rarely performed in front of others, except her children.

Before her moved a man with grace and agility and complete confidence in his work. The idea mystified her.

"Does your work give you satisfaction?" she asked, no longer able to contain herself.

He whirled on her, his eyes wide. She smiled at the thought of her being capable of startling him.

"My lady." He let out a long breath of relief.

A flutter of something she could only call happiness stirred inside her at the way he had called her "my" lady, as if he'd claimed her as his, which was ridiculous. Such a thing could not be, but it didn't stop her heart from lifting at the idea.

"I'd assumed you'd gone with the children." His hands fumbled with a tool she did not recognize. He caught it before it hit the ground, and he settled it on a table. "Forgive me. You asked a question, and, in my surprise, I cannot recall it."

"I am sorry to have caught you unawares. I only wondered if your work gives you satisfaction."

That pale spot along his jaw disappeared as he smiled. "My work gives me great satisfaction. Does yours?"

"I don't work," she said, feeling a little less happy at the idea that he might be mocking her.

"You're a mother. And you do your mothering without the benefit of a governess. Plus, you have the responsibilities of being a baroness while raising a baron to be a good man and a baroness to be a good lady. I would say your work is vastly important."

She hadn't thought of it that way. His point of view explained why she felt so exhausted all the time. And it also helped her feel *seen*. Someone understood her worries and the burden she felt to do the right thing with her children.

"With your definition in mind, I would have to say that, yes, I do find satisfaction in my endeavors, most of the time. More especially lately." At least she did when Mr. Ashby wasn't immediately before her, criticizing her every move.

"The children are doing well then?"

"Yes. And as I have said, I believe I owe that to you. I can never thank you enough."

"Not at all. You've only yourself to thank. You should see how Miss Amelia shines when she speaks of her mother."

Nora winced and leaned against the outer stone walls of the birthing stall. "You should know that when she speaks so lovingly of her mother, she does not refer to me." She didn't know why she'd told him the truth; she had vowed never to tell anyone. It would be a violation of the late Lord Coventry's demands.

Mr. Ellis moved closer to her, peering down into her face. His voice lowered to a deep thrum. "You are mistaken, ma'am. I know for a fact that she is referring to you."

His nearness scattered her thoughts and opened wide her vulnerabilities. She hurried to speak, but it only served to open them wider.

"You cannot know that. You see, I'm not the girl's natural mother. Our circumstances are complicated and impossible to explain. When she speaks of her love for her mother, she means the woman who was there for most of her life."

Regret instantly filled her as soon as she stopped talking. She breathed deeply and closed her eyes in shame that she'd revealed something that could open Lia to censure. When she opened them again, she saw Mr. Ellis shaking his head.

"You are wrong, ma'am. I hate to contradict a lady and my employer besides, but the truth cannot be helped. You are wrong. When Miss Amelia says she loves you, she references things that have occurred since her arrival at Windsong. Am I correct in assuming her other mother did not visit her grandfather on their way to Windsong?"

Nora tried to make sense of his words. "No. Yes. I mean to say that you are correct. That was my doing."

"And am I correct in assuming there is no other woman interceding on those occasions when Miss Amelia's brother behaves horribly?"

"Her mother has never even seen Edward."

"Quite right," Mr. Ellis said. "Further, I must conjecture that there was no other person who took great pains to find me so that Miss Amelia could have riding lessons from someone she trusted. Nor did anyone else give Bonnie to Miss Amelia as her very own horse.

Nor is her other mother the one who shows up to riding lessons and applauds enthusiastically or plays the pianoforte so beautifully that it brings tears to Miss Amelia's eyes just to mention it."

Nora did not know what to say. Tears blurred her vision. Had Lia really said all those lovely things about *her*?

As if eavesdropping on Nora's thoughts, Mr. Ellis said, "She spoke of you, Lady Coventry. She sometimes missteps and calls you 'Nora,' but that is rare and she is quick to correct herself." Mr. Ellis's voice lowered further; Nora had to lean toward him to hear. "And when she says 'Nora,' it is said with the same affection and warmth as when she says, 'Mama.' And before you try to correct me again, I do know the difference from when she speaks of her other mother and of you. She has also confided in me regarding her other mother."

Nora felt the sting of that statement until he followed it with, "But that is a topic that seems to cause her pain. When she speaks of her past or of her other mother, she always sounds as though she is wounded. I believe the young lady is conflicted regarding her feelings between her past, present, and future. But when I say she shines when she speaks of you, I mean she shines when she speaks of *you*."

"Thank you for saying so, Mr. Ellis. It means a great deal to me to hear that she cares for me in the same manner that I care for her."

She stared in open wonder at Mr. Ellis. How did he always manage make her feel so valued? His words cradled her like something cherished and admired. Nora could not deny that she felt an attraction to him, but her feelings were so much more than that. His kindness was a thing of mystery to her. The way he served the stable boys and undergrooms and her children—the way he had served *her*—wound him more tightly in her thoughts. She took a deep breath; he was so close. She kept her eyes on his face because his broad shoulders were quite distracting. But looking at his mouth was equally problematic. Heat flooded her cheeks. His eyes made her want to draw even closer to him. Watching for the pale scar to appear and disappear made her want to reach up and smooth her fingers over it.

Did the fire that burned in her belly also burn in his? But no, that was impossible. What qualities could she possibly possess that he would find attractive?

"What can I do for you, ma'am?" he asked.

"Do for me?"

"Your reason for remaining in the stables? Surely there is something I can do for you."

"Oh. Yes. Of course." Nora was sure the crimson roses in the hothouse would pale in comparison to her own cheeks. She couldn't remember why she'd held back to speak to him alone. Did she even have a valid reason other than a recurring need to be near him?

"I . . . merely wanted . . . It's only that . . . I should really go now."

She stepped back and felt like she'd been released from some invisible prison that had held her captive when he was right before her.

He visibly slumped as she moved away and left the stable. Had he been captured by the same invisible trap? Was it possible he felt it too? That attraction. Could he want to be near her as much as she wanted to be near him?

She did not think herself improper for wanting to be near him. Lia had declared him to be a "gentle man." If Nora knew anything after her years with her husband it was that a man who was gentle was a man worth knowing.

"I will tell him," she whispered to herself as she entered the house. "The next time I see him, I will tell him how he is becoming dear to me."

She wasn't sure if the brazen thought came because Mr. Ashby was not there, but with or without the specter of the man's disapproving stare, try as she might, she could not begin to think of how such a conversation would go. A servant knew his place. And while she'd heard of the odd scandal of a woman entertaining dalliances with a man beneath her rank, it certainly didn't happen often, and certainly not publicly and permanently like one would expect from a marriage. That was what she wanted from Mr. Ellis. She wanted something permanent and lasting and gentlemanly in the best sense of the word.

"Mama?" Edward called down from the landing on the stairs.

"Mr. Palmer is taking me out tomorrow to visit the tenants. You needn't worry about coming out to see me ride because I won't be there."

Edward. The young baron of Windsong. She'd allowed herself to forget that she could not think of men who were gentle, not when her job was to be raising a gentleman. Not when Mr. Ashby was paying attention.

She thought of the things she wanted to say to Mr. Ellis and swallowed them back down.

"I will not tell him," she whispered under her breath, feeling her heart strangle itself on her words.

Chapter Sixteen

Ridley sat at the dinner table with the rest of the servants. Lady Coventry had made him feel like he was a child's spinning toy. He wondered at the life choices that had led him to spending the whole of his days with horses instead of people. If he had chosen differently, would he have found himself happily situated with a woman he respected in the way he respected and admired Lady Coventry?

No. Had he married, it would not have been to a woman he admired. Such options had not been placed before him. And now that he was his own man, he found he couldn't form attachments that would lead to marriage. He had changed his stars, rewritten his future, and he could never hope to make a woman understand his choices, let alone live with them.

He listened to the others at the table laugh and joke and commiserate over the workday and smiled at how happy they all seemed in their positions.

Feeling regretful about his life was absurd. No one could dispute that he had truly made the best decisions for himself.

Nathaniel, the young lord's valet, spoke up, bringing Ridley's attention back to the table and his companions. "You'll like this one, Ridley. Lord Coventry dismissed his maths tutor today."

Ridley tensed, unsure of how the young lord's newest tantrum would be a cause of diversion for himself.

"Any guess as to why?" Nathaniel asked.

"If you'd just get on with it, 'e wouldn't have to be makin' guesses, now would 'e?" Alison, the kitchen maid, said.

"Right enough," Nathaniel said. "He had the man sacked because the man told Miss Amelia she wasn't none too bright and that she'd never learn her numbers. Miss Amelia said that you, Ridley, had told her that she *was* very bright, and the tutor scoffed at the idea. He told her that a man who tended to beasts all day would not be able to measure the intelligence of a human. That was when Lord Coventry stepped in. He abused the man quite thoroughly, though he's barely out of his leading strings, and he did it all while speaking high praise of you and of his sister."

"He defended Miss Amelia?" A swell of pride in the young man swept through Ridley.

"He did. Which was impressive enough, but that he included you? The devil take me, but I thought he might duel the man over your honor!"

Everyone laughed at the notion of a twelve-year-old baron counting the paces to defend a stable hand's honor, and a few jokes were made about Ridley being worthy of such attention.

"I doubted the young lord could possibly do anything that could be considered 'kind,'" Nathaniel said.

"It's likely his mother's doing," Cook said. "Lady Coventry is one of the most genteel ladies I have ever worked for. And more generous than I could have imagined. She gave me time off to go and visit me ailing mum—and I hadn't even asked for it. Mrs. Cole merely mentioned that me mum was feeling poorly, and the next thing I knew, I'd been bundled in a carriage and was off to see to her."

"Aye," Rebecca, Lady Coventry's maid, said. "And she is always so grateful—since the first day I arrived to work for her. She thanks me and thanks me. No matter how small a task I might be doing, she's quick to praise me for it. It's why I've no intention of finding employment elsewhere. I often felt invisible to the ladies I worked for prior to Lady Coventry. And though the rest of you wouldn't know to see the difference, she is much happier here than she ever was in London."

"More is the pity that we scarcely saw her face while the old baron was alive," Cook said. "Maybe she could have helped him keep his temper."

"Would that I could say she had such power over him," Rebecca said sadly. "The old baron never let her forget he was master of his household. He could say the most unkind things."

Ridley couldn't understand how any man could act in such a manner to members of his own family. He rubbed at his jaw and thought of his own past experiences. He might not understand it, but he knew firsthand that it happened.

"That man was a mean 'un," Alison agreed. "Lady Coventry 'as been a delight compared to the old baron. She 'asn't once sent back Cook's meals and insisted they be done all over again on account of not liking the way a garnish sat on the tray. Mercy, but I don't miss that!"

"Nor I!" cried Mrs. Cole, the housekeeper. "I am sorry, Cook. It was hard to know how he preferred to have his trays dressed when he changed his mind so often about them."

Cook lifted her glass as if to agree.

Murmurs of agreement came from every person at the table except Nash. "You all forget yourselves," he said. "It is not our place to criticize the dead, especially when the dead kept us in our jobs."

The servants' apologies weren't exactly as heartfelt as had been their complaints, but Nash seemed satisfied. He was a good sort of butler and managed to keep everyone in line. But he wasn't fooling any of them. Everyone at the table knew of his particular relief at no longer being caught in the storm that made up their previous employer. And Ridley knew they all wondered if the son would grow to be like the father.

Well, Ridley used to wonder, but he didn't any longer. The young baron was not at all like the old one. Ridley felt certain of that now that he'd spent time with the boy. The fact that he'd rushed to Miss Amelia's defense proved the young baron would grow to be his own man.

He had only needed a little coaxing.

Though Ridley would've loved to take the credit for young Lord Coventry's improvement, such credit belonged to the goodness of the mother who had worked tirelessly to set her son on a gentleman's path. Ridley had not been exaggerating when he'd told Lady Coventry all that Miss Amelia had said of her. Every time the girl spoke of her mother, Ridley's interest grew. He wanted to hear Lady Coventry play the pianoforte and sing to her children but could not imagine why he would ever have reason to be in the house to do so.

He was a stable hand, and she was a baroness.

He remembered that she'd asked him if they'd met before, and he felt a wave of worry pass through him. Did she know him? She'd certainly looked at him as if she did. Now though, he wished that she did know him. He wished . . . Well, what did it matter? They were what they were to each other, and he was happy to have her acquaintance only.

He reassured himself of his current happiness all the way out to the stable and while he did the evening chores.

George tossed him curious glances every now and again until he finally said, "What's eating you? You look right miserable."

Fine. Devil take him, maybe he wasn't happy. But he certainly wasn't miserable. "I am perfectly content, thank you."

George guffawed. "If you are so content, why do you look like a mouse ate your last crumbs of bread?"

"Do I?"

George nodded emphatically. "And maybe the mouse chewed a hole in your best shirt besides. Is this got something to do with that man poking around here the other day?"

That got Ridley's full attention. He set down the saddle he'd been repairing. "What man?"

George shrugged and picked up a bag of oats. "Clean, nice clothes. The man kept a kerchief to his nose as if the stables smelled like a chamber pot. And you know they don't. We keep a clean stable with fresh hay and everything. No one complains about the smells in our stables." George frowned as though he'd never been so offended by anyone before.

"What did he want?"

"Said he wanted to talk to the stable master. Since you told me you never wanted to deal with the fancy folk, I told him that was me." George finished spreading the oats and put the empty sack on the peg.

"What did he say to that?"

"Looked at me like I was dirt under his boot. Nothing I could do to convince him of my position, at least not until I started telling about the way we ran things. You taught me right, you did. Only, he seemed disappointed to think I was the stable master."

"Did he say what it was he wanted?"

George shook his head. "I'm pretty sure he wanted you specifically, but he didn't say so, did he? It's not like I lied. Isn't my fault the man wasn't clear in his words. But why do you think he wanted you? And why do you look so sick now? You're not in trouble, are you?"

"No, no," Ridley lied, a pit opening in his stomach. "Of course not."

George nodded easily. "Also, I need to say I'm sorry."

Thinking of the stranger who had come looking for him, Ridley said, "Sorry for what?"

"You told me to not let Bonnie out to pasture with Jericho since he's been trying his luck with the ladies, and I thought it wouldn't hurt since it was only for a minute, but now we might need to keep a watch on Bonnie since she could be in the motherly way."

Ridley let out a huff of exasperation.

"I'm sorry. I really am."

Of course George was sorry, and what was done could not be undone, but it changed how long it would take to train Bonnie, which would delay Miss Amelia from riding her horse. The child would be quite disappointed.

Ridley would need to make Lady Coventry aware of the new circumstances so Miss Amelia could shift her expectations. With George handling the feeding of the horses, Ridley crossed over to the stable doors and settled his gaze on the house. Lights spilled from the back windows, making the scene appear peaceful and welcoming. His news could wait until morning when Mr. Palmer could be informed, but even before Ridley knew what he was about, he was on the path toward the servants' entrance.

He tried to talk himself out of his foolishness. Hadn't he already told himself he had no reason to be in the house? This news was not of such importance as to earn him an invitation. Wasn't there trouble enough at his door without him seeking further disturbance?

The man who had come looking for him should have been enough to occupy his mind for the evening, but Ridley's desire to see the lady of the house, to see a smile lift her pretty lips, proved far greater than the common sense that should have driven him away.

Ridley found the kitchen empty, as were the hallway and the stairs leading to the main floor. Neither Nash nor Mrs. Cole were anywhere to be seen, and therefore not in a position to stop him and take his message to the lady for him.

He heard music from deeper in the house, bright and alive, and he followed the melody drawing him forward. He had wanted this, to hear her play, to hear her sing. Her notes were clear and perfect, the tune haunting in its melody. It was only a few moments before he realized that, while he did not recognize the tune, he *did* recognize the words. They were from one of William Wordsworth's poems.

She sang, "The world is too much with us; late and soon. Getting and spending, we lay waste our powers. Little we see in nature that is ours."

He turned a corner, losing the thread of her words, but when he came to the closed doors of the drawing room, he heard her finish her song.

"So might I, standing on this pleasant lea, have glimpses that would make me less forlorn. Have sight of Proteus rising from the sea, or hear old Triton blow his wreathed horn."

The notes from both her voice and the pianoforte seemed to linger in the air around him, then fade.

Silence fell on him like a heavy weight. He glanced around. This was a mistake. Surely, he would be sacked immediately if anyone were to see him in the hall, let alone inside the drawing room with the baroness.

And was she even alone? What if someone was in there with her—one of her children, or perhaps a friend or acquaintance? What would he possibly say to explain such an intrusion? How could he possibly excuse himself?

No. I will not be foolish today. He turned to leave, but the wooden floorboards creaked underneath his feet, heralding his presence as easily as if Nash had opened the door and announced him.

"Lia? Is that you, darling?"

He cursed under his breath. Did he make a hasty retreat or did he admit to his intrusion? He sucked in a deep breath and straightened. He would not lose his honesty along with his good sense. He rapped lightly on the door to announce that it was a servant and not a member of her household outside.

"It is I, ma'am. Mr. Ellis from the stables."

A sudden flurry of noise came from the other side before she called out, "You may enter."

She was not at the pianoforte as he'd expected, but she instead stood by the fireplace. Her hair was plaited into a single golden braid hanging over her shoulder and tied with a pale green ribbon. She did not appear angry that he'd intruded so magnificently on her privacy. If anything, she seemed almost afraid.

He glanced around the room and found they were alone, which might account for her wide eyes and tightly pressed-together lips.

Devil take him, she was more beautiful every time he saw her. He hated that he'd made her nervous.

"What's the matter, Mr. Ellis?" she asked when he failed to speak.

He opened his mouth and then closed it again. The ridiculousness of his errand struck him full force.

"Well?"

"It's Miss Amelia's horse. But it's nothing urgent, I now realize. I apologize for my intrusion, ma'am. I don't know what I was thinking, coming all the way here without an invitation over a matter that seems wholly unimportant now that I'm here. I have no excuse for my poor behavior or lack of judgment. If you'll excuse me, ma'am."

"Is something wrong with Miss Amelia's horse?"

His body felt painfully stiff as he stood before his employer. He didn't dare so much as roll a shoulder to ease the tension lest he breach propriety altogether. "There's a good possibility that Miss Amelia's horse is . . . in the motherly way and is therefore not able to be ridden, at least not until she's much further along. She could lose the foal if she is worked too hard in her current state. As I said, it is not an urgent matter, and I can make no excuses for myself."

"I see," Lady Coventry said. "But you are inaccurate. Miss Amelia will find this information to be the most important news in all of England and will desire it to be brought to her attention immediately. So telling me immediately was clearly the only appropriate course of action." She smiled, and he relaxed enough to offer her a bow.

He was eager to retreat to the stables where he could spend the rest of his days feeling the fool for *being* the fool.

"Would you care for some refreshment?" She motioned to the tray of pastries. "Cook makes enough for a house full of guests, yet there is only me to enjoy them."

She was inviting him to take refreshment with her? The poor woman must have been unspeakably lonely to make such an offer, and he was unable to refuse. Everything about her drew him in. He nodded his agreement.

She sat and poured him tea as if he were an esteemed guest. He should have stopped her, should have insisted on waiting on her and not the other way around. What if Mrs. Cole came to speak with her and found him in the drawing room? What scolding would Nash give him?

"I have not heard the song you were playing, though I believe the lyrics are taken from the poem 'The World Is Too Much with Us' by William Wordsworth."

She looked surprised as she handed him his saucer and teacup. "You read poetry, Mr. Ellis?"

"I was afforded a rather extensive education, ma'am." He silently berated himself for bringing up a topic that would likely lead to questions he felt no inclination to answer. But the coziness of the room, the warmth of the tea, and the way he felt around her made him forget himself and the privacy he wanted.

"It is Wordsworth's poem." She motioned for him to sit.

He took the chair across from her. "I did not recognize the arrangement."

She sipped her tea. "You would not. It is my own, you see. When I was a young girl, I found it easier to memorize the poetry my tutors assigned to me if I put them to a tune in my head. I've never really outgrown the habit."

Her answer was charming and innocent and intriguing all at once. "The habit has served you well. I don't believe I've heard anything half so lovely in many years. One can only imagine you like the poem."

She laughed. "Yes, I do. Goodness, that makes me seem brooding and sad, doesn't it?"

"Not at all. I quite like it as well. I prefer the sonnet form. Something about that meter and rhythm speaks to me. That particular poem speaks to the cacophony of my soul in my youth. 'For everything we are out of tune.'"

Her lips parted, and a small breath escaped her as she stared at him in wonder. "Yes. That's it exactly. I did not realize how completely out of tune with nature I'd become until I left London and came to Windsong. I was such a sleeping flower and only now feel like I am waking."

"I know that awakening all too well. I was only too glad to trade in that sordid boon of my past life for the one in which I currently reside. Nature gives us hope in the future. Would you not agree, ma'am?"

She nodded. "Oh, please do not call me that. It makes me feel so old when I am barely nine-and-twenty."

He smiled apologetically. "Lady Coventry, then."

"You could always call me N—" She stopped herself and set her teacup back on the serving tray. "I'm sorry. I should not—I apologize if I've made you uncomfortable. It's only that I have not heard my own name from another's mouth in quite a long time. I fear you will think me quite pathetic when I admit to you that I'm in need of a friend."

"You often have people from the neighborhood over. Have you no friends among them?"

She frowned, her eyebrows drawing together and a slight crease appearing in her otherwise smooth forehead. "My neighbors, I fear, are people for whom I must perform. They expect a certain air of dignity from a baroness. Mrs. Spencer is delightful, and I think perhaps we might form a true friendship in time, but it's too soon to tell."

He didn't remind her that her acquaintance with him wasn't any longer than her acquaintance with Mrs. Spencer. He didn't know what to think or say, only that he wanted to be in her company. He hoped she would not remember that he was an interloper in her home.

Her frown deepened as she picked up her teacup again and stared into it. "To be free to speak my mind would be something. To speak to an adult who is not always peering over my shoulder to find some perceived fault with me or hired to wait on me and serve me but who can converse with me about things like poetry would be a gift. Might we do that?"

"Speak about poetry?"

"Be friends."

What could he say to such a request? How would such a relationship be managed? Did she even know what she was asking? He worked in the stables, but regardless of where he chose to labor, he knew in his core that he was not inferior to any member of the household he served. He knew what societal expectations dictated, but did she? Did she believe him to be inferior?

Or was she different somehow from the rest of them? From that society he so loathed.

"I would like that very much," he said. "And I will call you whatever you ask, but only while we are as we are now, away from eyes who would judge you."

"You are a true gentleman, as my Lia has stated." She set down her teacup again and stood.

Ridley immediately scrambled to his feet.

She held out her small hand to him. When he took it, she gave a curtsy, and he bowed. *What is this dance I am in?* he thought as he met her blue gaze.

"Please call me Nora."

"Then you may call me Ridley." He brought her hand closer, intending to press a kiss to her knuckles as if he was making some declaration to court her. He stopped himself barely a breath away from her skin. It took all his energy to straighten and release her hand.

"Friends then, Ridley?"

"Friends then, Nora."

Chapter Seventeen

Nora smiled as she slipped beneath her bedcovers. How fortuitous that she had told Mrs. Cole she would not need anything further for the night. It had allowed her to enjoy a meeting that felt like a warm fire on a bitter cold night. How long had she been lonely? Since she was a child, really. And here was a man with kindness in his eyes and poetry on his lips. She'd watched him reassure her children, comfort horses, evoke changes for good in her household. She had confessed to him that she needed help with Lia and Edward, and then he had quietly and humbly given her that help.

He'd changed them all for the better.

He carried himself so differently from any other member of her staff. His manners were as fine as any gentleman she had ever met, yet his hands had the rough calluses of one who knew what it meant to work.

The juxtaposition of those characteristics made him someone she wanted to know better.

She shouldn't have invited him into the drawing room. She shouldn't have served him tea or curtsied to him. Mr. Ashby could never discover what she'd done. Her behavior was nothing short of foolish and shocking. If she was discovered . . . All of her training screamed at her that she was making mistake after mistake. But with him standing before her, she could not have acted any other way. She was not his better. He was at the very least her equal and more likely *her* better.

Even now, as she lay in her bed, staring up at the ceiling, she remembered him bowing over her hand and lightly tracing his thumb over her fingers. She could not regret her actions. She would not. Did she not deserve some happiness too?

The fact of her situation was that Ridley—she smiled in the darkness at the mere thought of his name—cared for her. He treated her as if she were a great treasure. And she knew him to be of worth greater than any treasure. What difference did it make if she'd found that treasure in the stable rather than a ballroom? Worth was worth. Value was value. And his friendship was valuable to her.

Unlike all the times she'd chanted to herself that she was a baroness or even a mother, something new came to her.

"I am a woman."

When she finally closed her eyes, she was sure she was still smiling.

Nora woke the next morning well before the sun had even considered crawling out of its own bed. Her heart hammered loudly from inside the confines of her ribs, like a bird beating its wings against a cage, eager to escape. She hurried to tuck her chemisette into her skirt and fumbled with fastening up her favorite green riding jacket, her fingers clumsy at a task usually done by her maid.

Nora and Ridley had settled on this clandestine ride just before he'd left the drawing room. She wanted to speak with him again without fearing another member of her staff overhearing or catching them unawares. And though it was not unusual for a lady to have her stable master ride with her for protection, she worried people would see through her and correctly ascertain that her feelings for the stable master went beyond society's expectations. What if word got to Mr. Ashby? So she'd agreed to this secret method instead.

She did not light a candle but felt her way down the stairs while listening for sounds that might indicate someone else was up and about. All she heard was the steady tick of a longcase Mora clock her late husband had inherited from his father, who had inherited it from his father, who had imported it from Sweden. She normally loved the clock's charmingly cheerful design, as out of place in the imposing house as she herself often felt, but the moonlight from the windows shone on the face of the clock, which seemed to glare down at her.

Go ahead and glare, she thought. She slipped through the back doors off the drawing room to the gardens and hurried her steps, her riding boots crunching loudly on the graveled path. She darted furtive glances all about her before she slipped between the stable doors that Ridley had left open for her.

Ridley stood alongside Opal, the black Friesian that had become her horse, and the large quarter horse she recognized but did not know.

She opened her mouth to speak, but he placed his finger over his lips and pointed toward the ceiling. How could she have forgotten? The other stable hands slept in the rooms above the stable.

He led her to the mounting block and quietly helped her onto her saddle.

He then threw a leg over his own horse and led them out of the stable. There was no way to muffle the sound of the hooves clopping along the stone floor, but once they were out to pasture, they were off, traveling down a well-worn path. The cool wind exhilarated her almost as much as the company.

"Won't the grooms question hearing the sounds of the horses as we were leaving?" she asked.

"I often take the horses for rides in the early hours, so the noise would not cause alarm to anyone. If there had been voices . . . Well, that *would* have provoked curiosity."

She was glad he'd held his finger to his lips so quickly when she'd first arrived.

She glanced at him from time to time as they rode and wished she had more than the moonlight. She wanted to see him clearly, to study his features.

"Tell me about the scar on your face," she said when they had moved from a gallop to a walk.

"My scar?"

"Yes, the one near your chin."

He rubbed a gloved hand over his jaw. "Ah that. Well. Let us just say that I did not always get along with my older brothers."

"Is this why you and Lia get along so well? Similar pains?"

Ridley laughed, a low and rumbling sound that made her feel absurdly happy. Had she ever brought anyone enough joy to laugh like that? She didn't think so.

"Perhaps. Though my brothers were both much older than I, and their personalities a thing of staggering cruelty. Young Lord Coventry is not cruel by nature. He's misguided at times but has enough of your goodness in him to keep him from running too far astray. I've seen how much he's changed over the time you've been at Windsong."

"I worried I was making a mistake leaving London for Windsong— almost everyone advised me against the move—but it has been for the better in so many ways. Lia and Edward are entirely different children here."

She was glad of her gloves and warm riding jacket. Though the cool summer air had been enlivening at the beginning of the ride, she now felt the damp settling into her clothing, making her shiver. Even with that discomfort, she would not wish to be anywhere else for the world. The branches of trees lit by the moon and the smell of rich earth and life fueled her euphoria.

"And what of you, Nora?"

"Me?"

"Are you an entirely different woman here?"

She pulled her horse to a stop and met his gaze. "I am profoundly changed."

His smile was soft and warm. "So you are."

"Let us not talk of me," she said. Her past was too sad and her future too uneasy. "Tell me about you. When did you first know you loved horses?"

His laugh rumbled again. "I can hardly say. I do not recall a time in my life where horses were not part of my world. I often went riding in order to escape my regular life. After a while, I recognized that horses were, for me, a connection to an uncorrupted beauty. They brought me closer to nature and offered me calm instead of chaos. Serenity instead of agitation. I knew I could never be happier anywhere else than while racing across a perfect landscape with a perfect creature of majesty."

"Was your father a stable master?"

"My father?" Ridley appeared startled by the question. "No. Not at all. Why do you ask?"

"How were you afforded the means of riding so extensively?"

His face paled, and his body stiffened as if frozen by an icy wind.

"I'm sorry," she said quickly. "I did not mean to demean your station. I was simply curious."

"No. Your question is perfectly reasonable." He fiddled with the reins as if searching for an answer. "There were many horses on the estate where I grew up. I was given access to many of them."

"I am very glad for that." Nora rubbed her horse behind her ears. "And it would seem Opal here agrees with me. As do all the horses. You are a benefit to everyone within your reach."

"You flatter me. Especially when the same could be said of you."

She laughed and wished she had not brought them to a stop; she suddenly felt quite vulnerable under his gaze. "Hardly."

"I am sincere. Many people look to you for their care, and you meet those needs completely. You make a simple stable master feel useful."

"As if you need me for that, not with all the demands placed upon your shoulders each day." She wished they could be closer, but the horses created a necessary distance. "The river is not too far off. Should we allow our valiant steeds to have some refreshment before we return?"

"Of course. They do enjoy the water straight from the source versus from a bucket." He clicked his tongue against his teeth and led the way to where the path met the river. He slid from his horse and then held out his hands to her.

She put her hands on his shoulders. He placed his hands at her waist and gently lowered her. They were nearly embracing as her feet touched the ground. He smelled like the stables—like leather and honey from the beeswax he used to clean the saddles. She had not properly thought through her plan, for, though she'd desired him to be close enough to converse with easily, they were now much closer than was appropriate for a woman alone with a man under the moon.

He stepped back quickly, creating the necessary space between them. There were no witnesses who might later gossip, and she wished very much to keep it that way. She could not afford even a whisper of impropriety.

Yet, she had sneaked out of her rooms in the middle of the night for a secret meeting with a man. What had she been thinking?

"You're frowning," Ridley said.

"No. Yes. Well, I wasn't meaning to frown."

He stood perfectly still, as if waiting for her to continue. When she didn't speak, he took the reins of both horses and led them closer to the river. "May I ask—what kind of girl were you when you were accepting callers?"

"Timid," she answered immediately.

"Hmm." He tied the reins to a tree branch. "Only one word to describe a fully realized person?"

"It is enough. My timidity made me a moldable daughter. It made me, as much as I was allowed, into a respectable wife. I do not know that I have ever been a fully realized person. My parents and my husband were every inch the society they belonged to. But I never felt as though I belonged. Does that make sense?"

"It makes a great deal of sense." He returned to her side and leaned against a tree.

She did not lean against anything. It would be hard enough to explain to her maid why her boots were muddy and why her riding clothing required cleaning. If she caught her clothing on a tree branch and ripped something, it would be so much worse. While Rebecca was a marvel with needle and thread, there was no reason to force extra work upon her.

Nora breathed in the night air, heavy with summer and life and growth. "I went from my father's home to my husband's. I went from a situation that required my obedience to another situation that required even more of my obedience. What would it say about me if I were to fit comfortably into either of those places?" She shuddered.

"Are you cold?"

"No." It was not a lie, but it was also not the truth. Her skin might be cold, but everything inside her felt warm.

"It speaks very well of you that you do not fit *there* but that you fit *here*."

He took off his jacket and moved slowly toward her, his eyes asking for permission. It was as if he knew no one had ever bothered to consider her feelings before pushing her forward into a thing. It was as if he could sense her emotions rising in her the way he sensed it in his horses.

She nodded her permission, and his fingers grazed her neck as he placed the jacket over her shoulders.

Nervous at the way his touch thrilled through her, she allowed a scoffing laugh. "I belong right here—in the woods, in the dark?"

A small smile played over his lips; she would have missed it had he not been so close. "'She walks in beauty, like the night. Of cloudless climes and starry skies; and all that's best of dark and bright meet in her aspect and her eyes.'"

Was he calling her beautiful? "Are you a fan of Lord Byron?"

"Not exactly, no. But I do quite like that particular poem. I find the night quite beautiful. *Exempli gratia*, there are stars burning brightly against the darkest cloak of sky and a moon lighting our path. The night offers a cool reprieve from the heat of day."

How did a stable hand have such refined speech? From poetry to Latin? He never ceased to amaze her.

He kept his gaze on her while he spoke, and warmth wove through her insides into an incomprehensible heat.

"The night is beautiful." She agreed. "But it will not be night for very much longer. The sky is brightening."

"You're quite right. We should return. The household shall be up soon." He held his arm out to her.

She placed her hand in the crook of his arm for support. "Ridley?"

"Yes?"

"I am glad you accepted my request for you to return to Windsong."

"I am glad you are the sort of woman to champion someone of humbler means. It is an action that speaks highly of you."

She felt herself blush at the compliment.

As they rode back to the house, they talked of various newspapers. She confessed to being uncomfortable when she read the gossip columns that seemed to delight in overturning reputations. She learned that they both preferred London's *The Examiner* for being bold in speaking inconvenient truths. He was remarkably well-informed when it came to Parliament and current happenings. And the way he peppered his speech with bits of both Latin and French proved his education to be beyond exemplary.

She wanted to ask him how such a thing was possible given his station, but she had already shamed herself by making insinuations regarding his access to horses. She was willing to afford him his privacy on that topic.

After a while, the conversation turned to child rearing and the difficulty Nora felt of raising up a boy to become a baron.

She was grateful to have someone to discuss her reservations and concerns regarding Edward with. She couldn't talk to Mrs. Spencer about her son; though Mrs. Spencer was an interesting conversationalist, it wasn't the sort of thing a mother discussed with the neighbors. Especially when that son was the heir to the barony. Especially when any gossip of her struggles could result in her losing that son. She appreciated Ridley's insights and observations. She trusted him to not allow rumor to stain his tongue. And though she couldn't explain why, she believed Ridley would help her keep Edward safe from Mr. Ashby's grasping hands.

By the time they had drawn close enough to the house for their conversation to end out of necessity, she'd discovered his taste in literature and art and life to be far superior to that of many other gentlemen she knew. She did not wish to stop talking, but continued conversation was impossible even though the stables, carriage house, and manor were still dark and quiet. No one else was yet up.

Ridley helped her off her horse, bringing her in close to him again. After their ride, he smelled like the woods, green and alive and wonderful.

He bowed over her hand but did not speak. He lifted his head and met her gaze.

She lowered herself in a curtsy as deeply as she had when she'd been presented at court and hoped he felt all the meaning the gesture contained. She mouthed the words, "Thank you." He nodded to accept her gratitude.

Breaking eye contact with him caused her physical pain, but the sun was stretching into the sky, and she did not want to be caught out of doors. She left the stables and nearly floated all the way back to the house and to her rooms. She'd never felt happiness so deeply and with such earnestness in all her life.

"I am a baroness. I am a mother. I am a woman." She whispered her new mantra, but she added something more. "I deserve happiness."

She was still happy when Lia joined her for breakfast. Though seeing the girl reminded Nora that she had important information to share.

"You mean I can't ride my own horse for a whole year?" Lia exclaimed.

"That is how long she will be with child, approximately. But I don't really know. Mr. Ellis will have to make that decision. He knows best, and we must trust his judgment."

Lia's bottom lip jutted out. "This is the worst news I've ever received."

The overdramatic sentiment might have been amusing if Nora was not painfully aware of how much distressing news Lia had received in her young life.

"I'm sorry, Lia. I truly am. But Bonnie's situation is delicate. You would not want her to lose her baby, would you?"

Lia put her elbows on the table, rested her chin in her hands, and sighed loudly.

"Is that where a lady's elbows belong, Lia?"

Lia hurried to correct her posture, but her pouty lower lip remained. After a few moments, she asked, "Will her baby be mine, too, since she's my horse?"

"That will have to be a future discussion. Let us eat our breakfast in peace."

"Then we should eat before Edward comes down," Lia said with a wry grin.

"Be nice to your brother. He has been much improved of late, and we would not want to poke the bear, now would we?"

Lia shook her head emphatically. "Especially not when he can be such an angry bear."

Nora hid her smile. She found herself doing that more and more—smiling. She wondered if any of the London staff would recognize her with such an expression. She doubted it, and that thought pricked at her happiness. London society would be horrified to know she had taken a long ride alone with her stable master that morning, and the gossip of such disgraceful behavior would be on every tongue and announced in every paper. They would declare her folly to be incomprehensible.

How could they not?

But she could not see herself in the same way. How could finding happiness be folly?

"Mama?" Lia looked up with bright, inquisitive eyes.

She had wandered off mentally. Another of her faults. "Yes, darling?"

"When will we have this future discussion?"

"A discussion about what?" Edward asked, finally joining the family for breakfast.

"Bonnie is having a baby, and I think her baby should also be my horse because it is my horse who is having her."

Not too long before, Lia would never have dared answer her brother's question with such determination. To declare herself the owner of something that her brother might wish to claim was a new level of confidence.

"You don't know that the new horse will also be a girl. It might just as easily be a boy. In which case, perhaps the new horse should be mine."

Edward settled himself on his chair and selected several Bath buns from the tray that the footman held out to him.

He was about to pluck the dried fruit off the top to eat only that and not the rest of the bun, but Nora stopped him. "Please eat all of it, dearest."

He sighed but did as asked.

She would thank Ridley again for helping to instill confidence in her little girl and gentleness in her little boy when she took the children to their riding lessons. And just like that, her smile was back. She was excited to see Ridley again, to tell him about the children and the way they were so delightful, to hear him tell her about the horses he cared for and to hear how his morning had fared after they had parted.

She thought of how familiar he seemed to her, and a sudden memory came to her, an odd image of the sea and a boy's face full of mischief and fun. She reached for it but couldn't grasp hold before it dove back into the depths of her mind.

Nash entered the room. "Ma'am, I am sorry to interrupt, but Mr. Ashby has returned."

Nora dropped her spoon, the clatter of the silver on the plate echoing the sudden clatter in her soul. So soon? She cast a glance at Edward, who looked as disconcerted by the news as she felt, though not for the same reason. Edward didn't know what was at stake if they failed to meet Mr. Ashby's expectations. His worry was only because Mr. Ashby heightened the tension in the house and undermined his confidence. She gave him what she hoped was a comforting smile. If he only knew what power Mr. Ashby could truly wield.

"Please have him wait in the library until we have finished breakfast."

"Of course, ma'am." Nash bowed and left.

Nora's appetite was gone, her stomach tangled into knots. Though she quietly pushed her plate aside, she stayed with her children until they had both finished. She would not hurry to meet Mr. Ashby. She was the baroness. Though her husband had given Mr. Ashby some control in the management of her affairs, she could control her notice of him.

After breakfast, she hurriedly spoke to Cook to solidify the dinner menu for the week. She'd invited Mrs. Spencer and her family to dine with them so that Mary Spencer could spend more time with Lia, and she wanted the menu to be perfect—and she wanted to do it without Mr. Ashby looking over her shoulder.

She finally entered the library, congratulating herself for not allowing Mr. Ashby to dictate her schedule to her while also feeling a prick of panic because she'd not rushed to meet him. Had that been a mistake?

He stood as she entered. She sat but took a few moments longer to lift her hand to invite him to be seated. He narrowed his eyes as he settled into the chair. It was an insignificant triumph, making him dance on a few strings since she had her dancing as if on hot coals, but she was tired of being ordered about. Ridley had made her feel stronger than she'd ever felt before. She didn't want to give that up.

Ridley.

Ridley believed she had value. More, he made her believe it as well. *I am a baroness,* she thought. *I am a mother.*

"Lady Coventry, I hope you and the children are well."

"Never better. We have adapted to life here quite nicely. We're all better for it."

"I'm pleased to hear it. I've made inquiries regarding Miss Amelia—to make certain the late Lord Coventry's wishes are being honored, you understand—and was glad to hear reports of you claiming the girl as your own in every particular. You're wise to be attentive to those details. They'll protect your own claim in your children's futures."

He'd been spying on her? She said nothing. She would not give him the satisfaction of twitching even a muscle. She didn't know why she felt such sudden surprise. Hadn't she expected he would investigate the details of her life?

"How long do you intend to be in town this time?" she asked.

"Long enough to make certain my client's needs are being met."

She smiled patiently as if tending to a rather slow-witted dog, though her stomach lurched. What if he never left? What if her life was never her own? "Should you not be more concerned with your future clients than with clients who can no longer benefit you?"

"My clients take care of me because they're secure in the knowledge that I will continue to keep their good names free from rumor or scandal long after they are gone. Have a care, Lady Coventry. We have no reason to be enemies, do we?" His insipid smile frightened her even more than his words did.

She did not answer, feeling a sudden chill. But his warning did not fall on deaf ears. He was her enemy. And her life was in his hands.

Chapter Eighteen

Ridley pulled his horse to a stop and looked over the countryside. The rains had deepened the grass to an exceptional shade of green. Had the countryside ever looked so beautiful?

He turned to young Lord Coventry. "Your improvement is truly excellent. At this rate, I daresay few gentlemen in this county will be able to keep up with you during the hunts."

The young lord grinned and let out a huge breath of obvious relief.

"Shall we continue on, my lord?"

Another sigh escaped the boy, this one of regret. "Would that I could. Mr. Ashby is quite insistent that he join me and Mr. Palmer to visit the tenants."

Mr. Ashby. That man had been lurking about the estate for several days like some awful specter. He had never seen Nora so on edge. She was even more uncomfortable than when the man had first come to Windsong.

"Why is that, do you think?" He hoped to discover some information from the young lord as Nora had been entirely unavailable since the man's arrival.

"It was a requirement of my father's will that he record my progress as lord over this land. But I honestly don't see what he has to do with any of this. Mr. Palmer and I have things well in hand."

"If you have things well in hand, why worry?"

"Because Mr. Palmer and I have made changes I don't think Mr. Ashby will like. He'll put it in his report and then, oh, I don't know. Then anything can happen." The boy flicked his reins absently and suddenly looked his true age.

He really was just a child playing at being a grown man. Ridley felt immensely sorry for the boy. He understood all too well the pressure the child must be under.

"I see. But if your visit to your tenants is focused on their welfare and your commitment to keeping the property in good repair, then Mr. Ashby's report can only reflect good things. And if not, you will have your tenants' trust without needing to worry over what some ridiculous man, trumped up with his own self-importance, might think."

The boy sighed again. Ridley would have worried that the child was becoming asthmatic if he hadn't known better. "I just don't understand why everything falls to me. Why must I be the one to survey crops and to make repairs for them? Why is that not their job?"

Ridley wanted to sigh too. "The world does not work that way. With your privilege, the people of your lands are under your care. They look to you for protection. It is a grand thing to be in a position of power and to use that power for the good of others. You, sir, have an opportunity to be a fierce protector, a prudent investor, a fair landlord. You have the opportunity to choose to be so much better than those peers who are twice or three times your age. And I believe you're up to the task."

"But why must I do it with Mr. Ashby? He's such a severe man. He reminds of a less-important version of my father."

The boy showed incredible bravery to admit such a thing. "What you must remember is that Mr. Ashby has no right to tell you what to do. If he gives instruction today that feels contrary to what your own instinct tells you, then you are to firmly give your position."

The boy looked at him and rolled his shoulders as if the idea of such a confrontation made him uncomfortable. "But how do I explain my position?"

Ridley's horse flicked his ears and sidestepped, clearly eager to race the wind over the grasses. He pulled the horse under control and said, "You are Lord Coventry. You are a baron. You do not need to explain your position. You need only give it with the authority of one who will not be shoved about."

The boy snickered. "Didn't you tell me that a wise lord listened to his lessers and took advice from servants who were well-informed?"

"I did. And my position has not changed. However, from all I know of Mr. Ashby, he is not one I would considered to be well-informed. You are ten times the man he is, and you need not bend to him."

The young lord said nothing for a time. The two of them sat on their mounts and listened to the wind rustle the grasses.

"You would make a good baron," the boy said after a while.

Ridley laughed. "Why? Because I am so overbearing?"

"You *are* imperious. I give you that."

Ridley laughed again, noting that the young lord had avoided answering the question directly. Not that it mattered to Ridley. He enjoyed teaching the boy how to manage his own business. Not because Ridley was imperious, but because the boy was scared, and it pained Ridley to see such fear. He'd already given advice on how to choose which people to hire for various projects, how not to cheat or be cheated, and how to listen to the tenants' concerns.

He was pleased the young lord paid attention and asked questions and tried to understand. It was a marked change from the angry boy he'd been when he'd first arrived at Windsong. Though Nora often tried to give Ridley credit for the change, he believed the credit was all hers. He liked that the children told him how they took their meals with their mother rather than taking them with a governess. Children learned best how to behave by watching their parents. That she allowed her children access to her showed how much she loved them.

He loved that about her.

He found himself thinking of the things he loved about her more and more often. She wasn't afraid to take control over situations that most women would have delegated to the steward or another member of the staff. He smiled thinking of his surprise when he'd entered the inn's common room to see her waiting for him. Of her willingness to pour tea for him. And how she'd curtsied as if he was worth her notice. He'd thought of the things he loved about her so often that they blurred into one definitive thought.

He loved her.

Their ride together the other morning had revealed his true feelings completely. He'd been waiting for her to ask to go riding again, not daring or trusting himself to initiate such a request. What if she did not feel the same? But how *could* she feel the same? Women of society did not fall in love with their stable masters. And what would she say when she learned he hadn't been fully honest with her? No matter what his circumstances, he had no chance of a romantic relationship with her. Disclosing the truth could result in a hangman's noose for him.

"What are you thinking that has you frowning so fiercely?"

Ridley had almost forgotten the boy. "Nothing, sir. Shall we return and tend to your tasks with the solicitor and steward?"

The boy slumped in his saddle. "Can we not? We could say the horse stumbled and broke an ankle."

"I apologize, sir, but that would be a hard story to tell when the horses show no sign of a limp."

"Fair enough. I suppose I should get it over with then." He clucked his tongue and turned his horse toward home.

General obeyed his rider as readily as if Ridley were the one issuing the commands. The young lord had indeed come a long way.

When they returned to the stables, Mr. Ashby was waiting for them with a handkerchief tied around his nose and mouth and ledgers in his hand.

Mr. Palmer didn't look happy about the prospect of spending his day with the solicitor. A horse was saddled for Mr. Palmer while a gig was prepared for Mr. Ashby to keep him from having to come in direct contact with the horse. Ridley apprised George's work in preparing the men's horses and the gig, satisfied with what he saw.

Ridley smiled to himself as he watched the young lord swing down from his horse and stand before the two men. Though the child was shorter than either man, he towered over them in presence. Gone was his derisive sneer and sharp-as-a-blade tongue. Instead, he held an air of confidence—in his position, if not exactly in himself yet.

Ridley gathered General's reins as Mr. Ashby stepped in front of him.

"I hear Lord Coventry spends a great deal of time with you."

His nasally voice made Ridley wonder if the man had broken his nose as a child and it had never mended properly or if it was just his allergies. For reasons Ridley could not fathom, the solicitor's words sounded like an accusation.

"Yes, he's become quite a master at riding. His father would be proud." Ridley turned his attention to the young Lord Coventry, effectively turning his back on the solicitor. The only men present to whom he owed deference were Mr. Palmer and the young lord. "Sir, would you like a fresh horse for the day's activities?"

"No. I believe General has it in him to last the rest of the day. I'll see to his care. Thank you, Mr. Ellis."

Ridley handed the reins back to the young lord, gave a short bow, and left with his own horse. He smiled to himself as he entered the stable. He felt certain the young baron would meet the challenges of the day and prove himself superior to a silly solicitor.

He almost felt sorry for Mr. Ashby.

Almost.

Ridley was checking carriages and noting some minor repairs in need of attention, when he heard someone enter the carriage house.

"There you are, Mr. Ellis," Nora said.

He stood from where he'd been surveying the buggy's wheels, his entire person feeling lighter in an instant. "Yes, Lady Coventry?"

Addressing her properly in places where others might hear, though they were alone at the moment, amused him more than vexed him. How it changed things to have her permission to use her Christian name.

"Have you seen my son?" She drew much closer to him than she ever had before their morning ride. Close enough he caught the scent of orange blossoms in her hair. He found it was a fragrance he quite liked.

He breathed her in before remembering she had asked him a question. "No, ma'am. Not since he left with Mr. Palmer and Mr. Ashby."

"They've been gone for hours. Should they not be returned by now?"

No one else would have noticed the change, but he saw her worry in the slight widening of her eyes.

"Mr. Palmer will not let anything happen to the young lord, ma'am."

"Sadly," a man's voice said, "Mr. Palmer was not able to do a thing to protect Mr. Ashby *from* the young lord."

They turned to see Mr. Palmer standing by the doors, a smirk on his face.

"What happened?" Nora asked.

"Mr. Ashby had quite a few ideas on ways to avoid spending money on repairs for the tenants and was perturbed to find Lord Coventry to be formidable rather than malleable." Mr. Palmer seemed pleased to share this information; clearly he spared no love on the man either.

Nora had opened her mouth to speak when Mr. Ashby appeared behind Mr. Palmer. Nora immediately stepped away from Ridley as though she'd been caught doing something inappropriate. How could a mere solicitor hold such sway over a baroness?

"So here you all are. I thought I heard voices from this direction." Mr. Ashby's nasally voice sounded more petulant than before. He was apparently still stinging from discovering that the new Lord Coventry was not as enamored with him as the old one had been.

"Lady Coventry, I wish to speak with you this evening if it is convenient."

"I'm afraid it is not convenient this evening," Nora said. "Perhaps tomorrow afternoon or the day after?"

The man's simpering smile showed teeth that had not been properly looked after. "As you see fit, Lady Coventry." He bowed, though he appeared pained to have to do so.

"If I may be so bold, ma'am, why do you tolerate that odious man?" Ridley asked once Mr. Ashby had gone.

"The late Lord Coventry left many stipulations in his will. Mr. Ashby checks in on me from time to time to make certain I am adhering to those wishes."

"He acts quite lofty for a mere tradesman," Ridley said.

"The late baron kept him fed on a steady diet of self-importance." She blinked her large eyes, as if realizing she'd spoken aloud. She glanced at Mr. Palmer in horror.

Mr. Palmer grinned. "Do not worry yourself, Lady Coventry. No one here shall admit to having heard you say such a thing, though it is true enough."

"I appreciate your discretion." She took a step toward the door, then stopped and said, "Mr. Ellis?"

"Yes, ma'am?"

"I have felt a desire to ride my horse. A little practice would enable me to go riding with my children when they are ready for such adventures. Would you accompany me this evening?"

Ridley nearly swelled with happiness at such a prospect. He was glad she had asked in front of Mr. Palmer, which was proper. Though their ride the other morning had been an unexpected delight, he preferred to not have the baroness skulk about on her own estate.

"Of course, ma'am. I'll ready your horse immediately so that we're sure to have you back before dark."

"Wonderful. I'll return shortly."

She left with Mr. Palmer, and Ridley jumped into action to prepare their horses. He hurried through the task and then looked down
at his boots, dirty from a full day of work. He cleaned them with an
oiled rag, then washed his face and hands. He ran his fingers through
his hair. It was the best he could do on such short notice.

He heard Nora's footfalls on the path outside the stables. She arrived dressed for riding and looking lovelier than ever. "I apologize it
took me so long to return. I wanted to check on Edward to verify he
was all right after spending a day with that loathsome man."

"And was he?" Ridley asked as he helped her onto Opal. He knew
Nora had grown fond of the Friesian.

Nora settled onto Opal's saddle and smiled with what seemed to
be deep satisfaction. "Yes. He is becoming his own man. I daresay Mr.
Ashby is at the inn, tending a bruised ego."

"It's cause for a celebration," he said from atop his own horse.

She seemed lighter and freer than he had ever seen her. "And what
shall we do to celebrate?"

"I will leave that to the lady to decide."

"I propose a race."

"A race?"

"To the river."

She clucked her tongue and was gone in an instant. As he hurried
to follow, he decided he would tell her he loved her today. His heart
could not bear holding such a secret any longer. If his hope was all
one-sided, it would be best for him to know sooner rather than later.

He would tell her.

As soon as they were at the river.

And then, at some point, he would tell her his secret and trust her
to keep it, and his life, safe.

Chapter Nineteen

The laughter that erupted from Nora's mouth in a most unlady-like way was one her parents would have frowned over. She flew down the path. The trees blurred with her speed. How had she allowed herself to forget this part of her soul? The part that loved riding free and fast, that loved the wind on her face and the pounding of hooves beneath her? She had traded the pounding of hooves for the pounding of piano keys because her mother had told her that was the way things had to be for a lady. How else was a lady to catch the attention of a baron?

She had been so afraid of Mr. Ashby, but her fear was now balanced by the hope she felt at seeing how Edward had grown. Her son was proving himself to be his own man, to take charge as a leader. He had shown Mr. Ashby the improvements he'd made for the tenants. He'd pointed out the areas where he'd found wasteful expense that he'd done away with and where he'd found more efficient means of working the lands to make them profitable. Surely that was proof his training as baron was satisfactory and would require no intercession from the solicitor. Her son would remain safely under her roof and in her care. She felt such delirious joy that she could scarcely contain it.

She reached the river first, though Ridley was not far behind, and he was laughing as he approached.

She blinked.

She had the strangest sensation, one that had tickled her mind before on several occasions but was now something stronger and more pressing. She knew that laugh, that smiling face from atop a horse. But the memory didn't exactly match the scene in front of her. There were no cliffs overlooking an azure sea here at the river. There was no cove where children splashed and played together. There was no great stone arch over the water where the governesses refused to let her and the other children go because the water was too deep and dangerous.

"Is something the matter?" Ridley asked. He'd already dismounted and was reaching up, offering his help.

"No. Not at all. I just had the strangest memory—something I haven't thought about in years. It was a happy memory, and here and now, everything is truly perfect."

She did not move her hands from his shoulders when her feet touched the ground. It was brazen, but she finally felt she might be free from her late husband's reach. Her son had given her that gift by choosing to be his own sort of baron. He would not follow in his father's footsteps of cruelty and indifference. She dared to allow herself to feel real hope for her own future happiness and for the happiness of her children.

"Happy memories are things worth treasuring." His hands remained on her waist, the warmth of his energy mingling with hers.

"What happy memories do you treasure, Ridley?" she asked.

His eyes searched her face. "Honestly, Nora? Every moment I have shared with you has given me a memory to treasure."

She could scarcely breathe with him so near, knowing how little it would take to close the distance between them, knowing how much she wanted to close that distance—to forget what was proper.

"Every moment?" she asked with a nervous laugh. "Even when I stood aside and allowed you to be upbraided by Mr. Daw?"

He smiled, the pale scar disappearing. "Every story requires some sort of beginning, doesn't it?"

"I suppose it does." She couldn't help it. She reached up and touched the spot along his jaw where his scar was. She cursed her gloves for coming between her fingers and his face.

His breath hitched, and his hands tightened around her waist. "I must speak. I must tell you how I feel before I lose my nerve entirely. May I have your permission to speak?"

"You never need my permission."

"I should want it just the same." His dark eyes felt like fire on her skin.

She loved the consideration he always showed her. "Then it is yours."

"I am mostly certain that I have come to love you." He closed his eyes and growled low in exasperation. "No. That came out badly. Let me try again." He opened his eyes and lowered his head nearer to her. "I *am* in love with you. Not *almost*. Not *possibly*. But for a certainty. I understand this is far from conventional. I understand society dictates that I am not the sort of man you should ever think to look at with any degree of interest. I understand I am overstepping all boundaries in every way."

He took a deep breath. "I do not tell you this with any agenda to lift myself in society's eyes. Indeed, I strive to blind society to my presence in every regard. The words must be said because I cannot live in an emotional falsehood." His eyes held hers, pleading for her to understand.

What had she done to earn such a moment? To earn Ridley's voice, low and clear and beautiful, speaking such kindness to her as his warm breath washed over her lips and his warm words washed over heart?

He waited as she formed her response, always patient.

"That you could brave such honesty when the repercussions could be so severe for you is a mark of your character," she said slowly. "I have never been in love, despite my years in marriage, but I did allow myself to dream of such a thing, to imagine what it would be like. However, I imagined it all wrong, for not even in my most fervent fantasy did I ever imagine it to be as wonderful as this."

He tilted his head, as if by viewing her from a different angle he might better ascertain her meaning. "Are you saying . . . ?"

She could scarcely breathe with him so near, knowing it would take very little movement to close the distance between them.

Before she could consider the propriety of her decision, she answered by tilting her face to his and pushing up on her toes until there was no longer any distance between them at all.

His lips were softer than she'd imagined. And heaven help her, she *had* imagined them. He kissed her gently, his soft lips on hers as if they were made to be together.

She wrapped her arms around his neck and pressed him more tightly to her. Her kiss to him was fervent and not gentle at all. She had waited a lifetime to be kissed by someone who loved her, and she was determined to feel the moment in its entirety. She no longer knew where her breath ended and his began. She was enveloped by the scent of beeswax and leather. With him so close to her, she felt warm and protected and cherished.

He pulled away and cradled her face, his fingers tracing her jawline as his eyes stayed fastened to hers.

"How are we to proceed with all of this?" she asked.

"I do not believe it would be wise to make our emotional agreement public," he said.

I deserve happiness. "My feelings for you outweigh any pain that may come from the society column." She meant it. Who were those people to her? What could their words do to hurt her?

"Especially since neither of us read the society columns in any of the papers. However, my dearest Nora, let us be patient and prudent. I do not wish to see you hurt by hasty actions. Let us remain as we are for a while yet."

Mr. Ashby's face flashed in her mind. He was right. The repercussions that would surely come from such an announcement would be swift and without mercy. For herself, she hardly cared. But her children. What would Edward and Lia think of such news? How would it affect them? Yes. She would be willing to remain as they were for a while longer.

But she could still have a secret happiness. Her cage might still exist around her, but she wasn't in it alone.

She melted into his arms, and he kissed her again. She never wanted to leave. Had any river in all the world ever flowed so beautifully? Had any woods ever been so green and vibrant? Had any man been more perfect?

She was sure none had.

"Will you unbutton my glove for me?" she asked after a moment.

He laughed. "I'm sorry?"

"My glove. I can do it myself, but it's difficult and takes me a good deal longer than if someone does it for me." She held out her hand, her wrist upturned to him.

Holding her eyes with his, he did as she asked. His fingers worked slowly as he undid the three buttons. She could feel the callouses on his palms through the fabric of her gloves and suddenly longed to feel them on her bare skin.

She inhaled a sharp breath and held it as the last button came undone.

Still holding her gaze, Ridley lowered his mouth and pressed his lips to where her heartbeat pulsed beneath her skin at her wrist. He slowly eased the glove from her hand, first revealing her wrist, then her palm, and then her fingertips. As his lips trailed the path of the glove, her eyes fluttered closed.

Cherished. She felt cherished with his every touch.

"Your glove, my lady."

She opened her eyes to find him holding her glove in his hands like an offering.

Instead of taking it, she reached up and touched the pale scar on his jaw, letting her fingers run over the scruff of his skin. "How exactly did you get this? No vague answer this time," she whispered.

"A gift from my brothers. Well, my eldest brother anyway," he said with a rueful twist to his mouth. "My other brother never hurt me outright, but neither did he intervene to save me. This was a horseshoe thrown at my jaw. The shoe had a jagged edge that ripped flesh and bone both. I was glad it healed so well."

"Did it?"

"You don't think so? I think it makes me look daring." He smiled and the pale scar disappeared.

"It does make you look adventurous. But you speak of it in a way that makes me wonder if you are not still wounded."

"Dearest Nora," he said, slowly taking her hand from his cheek and holding it to his heart. "You have uncovered an inconvenient truth."

"Would you like to talk about it? Sometimes that helps."

"I would. But not today. Today, we should return you to the house and the children."

He was not wrong. It was past time that she return, but she could not resist kissing him once again, with greater fervor than before.

Once they were back in the stables, Ridley helped Nora from Opal's saddle.

"I will leave the back doors to the drawing room open so that you might listen while I play for the children tonight," she whispered. "I would invite you to join us, but you have already made your position clear on that point."

"I will be certain to go walking this evening so that I might enjoy the music in the night air," he whispered back.

George walked past them, preventing her from saying what was in her heart. She wanted to tell Ridley again that she loved him. She wanted to kiss him again. She wanted so many things. Instead, she smiled, inclined her head in his direction, and returned to the house.

Despite being gone for much longer than she had intended, Nora was able to be properly dressed for dinner and downstairs in time to meet the children in the dining room. She worried they would notice the change in her—she felt her happiness was shining from every part of her—but Edward was too busy regaling her with tales from his visit to the tenants with Mr. Ashby.

"He was most surprised to hear that I already knew and understood the reports from the previous year's crops and harvests as well as the supplies needed for this year's harvests. He seemed to think he would be taking me on a tour of his knowledge and did not expect to be forced into a tour of mine. I do not know why my father ever hired such a stupid man."

"We shouldn't call people stupid, Edward," Lia said.

Edward smirked at his sister. "So you would rather I lie then?"

Lia blinked, clearly torn between allowing her brother to speak ill of others or allowing him to lie.

Nora intervened before Edward could further create a moral quandary in his sister. "I am glad you've learned so much from Mr. Palmer. He is a very good steward."

"I didn't learn it from Mr. Palmer. Well, I did learn some of it from him, but much of it I learned from Mr. Ellis."

"Mr. Ellis?" A tremor ran through her, and she forced her hands to be still as she said his name. "He taught you what exactly?" She knew he'd helped smooth her son's rough edges and taught him to control his temper, but she had not been aware he'd been giving lessons on the finer points of being a good baron.

Edward finished chewing the bite of pheasant in his mouth before he responded. "He has been helping me understand how to make sense of the reports I read by understanding their practical applications."

She smiled at his use of the term *practical applications*. Eton could not have provided him with a better education than the one he'd clearly been receiving here from Ridley and Mr. Palmer. "I am glad to hear of it. It is fortuitous that we have Mr. Ellis in our lives. He is a good man." She made the comment, hoping to ascertain what her children thought of Ridley, not only as a riding instructor but also as a person.

"Yes, he is," Lia agreed, her tone almost worshipful.

Edward nodded in agreement.

Yes he is.

She and the children retired to the drawing room where she mentioned the fine evening and how nice it would be to feel the breeze to temper some of the summer heat. Nash opened the back doors, then drew the sheer curtains to discourage the mosquitos and June bugs from entering the house.

Nora sat at the pianoforte, awash with sudden nerves. She'd been playing for the children for months, but now she had a third audience member. Did he really enjoy listening to her play and sing? He'd said he'd never heard anything that gave him greater pleasure. Had he meant it? What if she played horridly or sang like a screeching cat?

"Mama," Lia said. "Play me the lullaby."

Nora looked at Edward to confirm he wouldn't mind hearing that song again. He nodded, which eased her out of her paralysis. Her fingers pressed the keys while she sang, "Can you hear the sleepy bird? He's singing you a song. He's calling. You're falling . . ."

She'd written the lullaby for Edward when he was a baby. And though she was no great poet, she had loved singing it during those first few months when her husband had allowed her the greatest access to her son. She'd begun singing it again when she'd brought Lia home and Lia had cried so much at night.

Lia always smiled at the line, "Off you go on wings of love to explore the stars above." She would sometimes ask Nora to speculate with her the things that might be found among the stars. On occasion, Edward would join them. Those were the nights Nora enjoyed the most—just the three of them, dreaming up possibilities out of silliness and wonder.

When Nora finished the song, Lia asked, "Do you think Asteria is the goddess of falling stars because she knocks them down to earth when she thinks no one is looking?"

Edward snickered. "You think Asteria is a mischievous child?"

"She might not be mischievous," Lia said. "Maybe Zeus locks the stars in cages in the sky, and she waits for their jailers to look the other way and then sets them free by knocking them down to earth."

"I quite like that idea, Lia." Nora glanced to the curtains rippling in the faint breeze. She knew about cages. And she was only now discovering what wonders lay in freedom.

She sang more songs for the children, taking their requests as they came and enjoying the time she had with them. As she thought of Ridley listening outside, she smiled. Her earlier nervousness had been forgotten in the intimacy of love and music.

After her maid readied her for bed and Nora was alone and staring up at the canopy above her, she remembered Ridley racing up on his horse and his smile so filled with apparent delight, and again, she felt the tug of something familiar.

Devon. The cove. The children. The boy.

She frowned. Why would Ridley make her think of a boy from her childhood when she'd been barely five or six years of age?

She also remembered dancing lessons, but not with the boy she remembered on the horse. She had danced with a much older boy who had been surly and who had made her cry when she hadn't gotten the steps right.

But she *had* danced with the boy from the horse as well, hadn't she?

She turned onto her side as if that could shove her strange recollections away. A ridiculous fancy, the late baron would have said.

And for a change, she was inclined to agree with him.

Chapter Twenty

Ridley could not contain his happiness to have found a woman so perfect—and so perfect for him. After listening to Nora sing to her children and listening to the imaginative and charming conversations that had followed, he'd returned to his cottage. The night had been magical, and he fell asleep feeling a peace he had never known.

After breakfast the next morning, Mr. Palmer walked with him to the stables. "A new farrier has just arrived in Lancaster. I was heading there today to conduct some business and wondered if you might want to join me."

"How long will you be in Lancaster?"

"I plan on returning tomorrow morning. What do you say?"

Ridley mentally ticked off the day's duties and realized there wasn't anything George couldn't handle until he returned. He nodded and said, "I'd be glad to meet this new farrier."

Mr. Palmer clapped him on the back. "And I'd be glad to have intelligent company for the journey. I'd like to leave in an hour's time."

"I'll have the horses ready for us both."

"Excellent." Mr. Palmer set off toward his own house on the other side of the property.

Ridley found George in the exercise yard with Opal and gave him a list of tasks that required attention. As he was about to leave, George said, "Would you buy me a bottle of gin while you're there? From St. Martha's Pub?"

"Such spirits are the ruin of good men, George."

George ignored the lecture as he fished out a few coins from his pocket. "St. Martha's Pub. Mind you don't go anywhere else. The other pubs water it down till it's barely better than a weak grog."

"It's a reckless waste of money, George."

George grinned. "What's the point of having money if you can't be reckless with it now and again?"

Ridley rolled his eyes but agreed to make the purchase. Ridley owed him for taking on all the work for the day.

Packing was easy and quick work. Ridley included a few shoes to show the new farrier in order to gauge the man's knowledge. Mr. Palmer arrived, and they climbed onto their horses to leave.

"St. Martha's Pub!" George called out in farewell.

"What was that all about?" Mr. Palmer asked, their horses turned toward Lancaster.

"Just George. One would imagine that is explanation enough."

Mr. Palmer laughed. "True enough. The young man is coming along quite nicely. I daresay he'll make an excellent stable master someday."

"I am counting on it. It would be nice to see him lift himself above his station and settle into a good and respectable life."

Mr. Palmer gave him a sideways glance. "Do you think it is wise to encourage a dream of lifting himself above his station?"

"Oh, Palmer. Please tell me you've not been hiding snobbery behind that beard of yours for all these years."

"Not snobbery. Merely caution. Ours is a complicated world. I would hate to see his hopes dashed on the rocks of disappointment."

"How can he be disappointed when you said yourself he would make a fine stable master someday?"

Mr. Palmer laughed again. "So I did. I do believe I spent too much time with Mr. Ashby yesterday. It was nice to see that the young lord would not submit to his will. The boy has changed into a man nearly overnight."

"It was hardly overnight. But he is much improved and continues to improve because he has chosen to become a man worthy of his title and comfort. And his sister is also much improved. It has been a delight to watch them grow into themselves."

"You sound like a proud papa."

It was Ridley's turn to laugh, though he felt he had revealed too much of his affection when it came to the children of the woman he had come to love.

"I am proud of both of them. With no children of my own, or nieces or nephews, it is pleasant to see the children's accomplishments and feel gratified in the small part I play in their daily lives. It might be the closest I will come to fatherhood. Vicarious living has its own amusements."

Mr. Palmer did not reply beyond a murmur of agreement.

Ridley wondered if he had spoken the truth. Nora was still a young woman, and he was still a young man. Should they marry, there would likely be more children. He could still be a father. He shifted his shoulders uncomfortably. What was he thinking? He couldn't marry, not without her knowing the truth about him. But if she knew the truth, she likely wouldn't want him. Telling her might mean losing her. He could not live in an emotional falsehood.

He and Mr. Palmer crossed over the canal and made their way through the bustling streets to the King's Arms, the inn where they would be staying the night. Mr. Palmer paid the stable boy, but Ridley insisted on accompanying the animals to their stalls, saying he wanted to be certain they would be under good care. Mr. Palmer nodded his appreciation for Ridley's dedication to the animals.

The horses settled, Ridley and Mr. Palmer enjoyed their evening meal, then the steward retired to his room for the night. Ridley took the opportunity to go walking in town. He'd promised George a bottle from St. Martha's Pub, and he wanted to know where the new farrier had set up shop, as he planned to visit the man first thing in the morning.

While out and about, he found a shop with musical instruments in the display window. On a whim, he ducked inside and began to

look around. When he saw several small books of musical arrange-
ments for the pianoforte, an idea struck him.

"Pardon me," he said to the shopkeeper. "Do you happen to have
manuscript paper specifically for music?"

The shopkeeper nodded, then fumbled around in a few drawers
behind the front counter. He then placed a modest stack of parch-
ment on his counter. "Here you are. It's preprinted with staffs ready
for musical notation."

"That's perfect. I'll take the lot of it."

Ridley grinned as he looked at the parcel in his hand, imagining
Nora's face when she unwrapped it. By the evening's end, he'd found
small gifts for the children as well: a small wooden horse figurine for
Miss Amelia, and a pair of battledores and a shuttlecock for the young
lord.

Knowing the late baron's temperament, Ridley suspected there
had been little time for such frivolous games for the young lord. But
Ridley felt the children would enjoy batting about the brightly feathered shuttlecock; it might even help the pair build deeper camara-
derie. He often felt that if his own father had allowed some degree
of levity in his household, Ridley would not have had to leave. He
might've had relationships there, love there, something of value there.

He balanced the gifts in his arms and made his way back to the
inn. He had relationships, love, and so much to be content with right
where he was. What did he care that his past held nothing but pain
for him? His present and future were wrapped up as brightly as the
packages he held.

He made his way to St. Martha's Pub for George's requested gin.

After requesting the bottle, Ridley felt as though someone was
staring at him from behind. He turned slightly to cast a glance over
his shoulder. A man watched him intently.

The man stood, moving as if to approach Ridley, when another
man clapped him on the shoulder and engaged him in conversation.
The first man tried looking around the second man's shoulder, but
Ridley quickly tucked himself into an alcove while he waited for his

purchase to be wrapped. He hid himself out of many years of habit. When he left the pub, he checked for any sign of the stranger, but the man had gone.

"Stop being paranoid, Ridlington," he said to himself as he made his way back to the inn. He pushed aside all thoughts of the man at the pub and fell asleep thinking of Nora and her children.

He awoke the next morning to an incredible banging in his head. No. Not in his head, but on the door to his room. It took him a moment to remember he was not in his cottage at Windsong. The knocking at his door had stopped, but he hurried to dress anyway. When he opened the door, no one was there. He poked his head into the hallway and peered in both directions. A shadow flitted from view in the stairwell, which indicated someone had recently descended that way.

Whoever it was, they were gone, which meant their knocking couldn't have been anything too urgent.

He ducked back into his room and quickly washed and shaved. He wanted to meet the farrier early so as to be finished when Mr. Palmer had concluded his own business. Mr. Palmer wanted to be on the road early enough to be in their own beds come nightfall. Ridley was in full agreement. He wanted to be home early enough to catch a glimpse of his beloved Nora or perhaps listen as she played and sang for her children.

Seeing no sign of Mr. Palmer at breakfast, Ridley set off for the farrier's shop. He ducked inside and felt the immediate surge of heat within its walls. A young boy greeted him. His leather apron and leather gloves were both far too large for his small frame. Before Ridley could ask to be directed to someone older, a man opened the door in the back and stepped out. A wave of hot air billowed into the room. The man thrust a bit of iron into a water barrel that sent sizzling steam into the air. He ran his sleeve over his sweat-drenched forehead before he noticed Ridley.

He turned to the boy. "Why aren't you tellin' me we 'ad customers?"

"Not my fault. Just got here, didn't 'e?"

Ridley held out the horseshoes he'd brought with him. "I heard you were new here, and I was hoping we might do business together."

"Always grateful for new business," the man said, taking the offered horseshoes. "My name's Matt."

"I'm Ridley. I hoped you could look at these and tell me what you see."

Matt sniffed. "I can tell you that your horses' hooves weren't balanced and trimmed proper before they were shod."

Ridley smiled. That had been the work of one of the first farriers he'd worked with when he'd arrived at Windsong. He'd kept the shoes and used them to judge what a farrier knew or didn't know.

They discussed the details of work and what it would cost to bring Matt to Windsong and struck a deal that pleased Ridley. Ridley took his horseshoes back and returned to the inn.

Mr. Palmer found him soon after. "There you are, Ellis. I thought maybe you'd gone with that man who was looking for you."

Ridley's blood froze in his veins. "What man?"

"The one who had your watch. Did he return it?"

"Return my watch?"

"He mentioned running into you last night at the pub and said you'd dropped your pocket watch. Said he wanted to return it to you before you left town."

Dread welled up in Ridley's chest. Sweat slicked between his shoulder blades. "What did you tell him, this man?"

"I told him I hadn't seen you today but that you had business with the farrier."

"Did you tell him anything else?"

"No. I didn't have time. He hurried away to find you. So did you get the watch?" Mr. Palmer peered at Ridley as if trying to see if the watch was in one of Ridley's pockets.

"Yes. I have my watch." Ridley turned toward the inn's stairs. "Is your work finished, Mr. Palmer?"

"Yes."

"Good. Have your belongings packed. I'm anxious to be for home immediately. I'll meet you in the stable."

Ridley barely heard Mr. Palmer's promise to hurry as he took the stairs two at a time. In his own room, he quickly shoved his belongings into the saddlebag and fled down to the stables where he helped the stable boys saddle their horses so they might be out of Lancaster that much faster.

He handed them each enough money to buy their silence if anyone came asking about him. He was waiting on his horse when Mr. Palmer finally arrived.

Once they were on the road and away from the town, Mr. Palmer laughed. "Goodness, man! You're acting as if you're trying to outrun a ghost."

Ridley offered a tight smile.

And so I am, he thought.

Chapter Twenty-One

Mrs. Spencer walked through the gardens with Nora while Mary and Lia looked for ladybugs among the flowers. Mary had been the only thing to pull Lia out of her sulking over Ridley being gone. Nora perfectly understood the child's feelings.

"There are rumors about you in town," Mrs. Spencer said as easily as if remarking on the warm weather.

"Rumors?" Nora's pulse raced. Had someone seen her with Ridley?

"Oh, do not look so worried!" Mrs. Spencer waved her fan energetically. "It's regarding your previous stable master. The man is attempting to stir up trouble by saying he was wrongfully let go."

Nora waved her own fan, only not because of the heat, but because she felt relieved to hear such a silly rumor. "How did you hear of such a report?"

"Oh, my, my! I have the most talkative maid. She tells me everything that reaches her ears. I truly treasure my relationship with her and pay her well to keep from losing her to another household. Where else would I learn such news but for her? But though the report may be harmless, I felt it necessary to inform you of it. You have become dear to me, Nora, and I would not want you to be ignorant of any gossip regarding your household."

They sat on a stone bench, enjoying the shade provided by the beech tree.

"I'm surprised Mr. Daw stayed in the county," Mrs. Spencer

continued. "He isn't well-liked, and without references, it is hard to say what he hopes to gain."

Nora absently murmured her agreement. Now that she knew the reports in town were not about her specifically, she found it difficult to feel concerned. A scorned servant who didn't have claim to a legitimate work contract and who had been dismissed for good reason was the very least of her worries.

Ridley would be returning from Lancaster that night. Her excitement at the thought of possibly seeing him when he returned filled her thoughts enough to crowd out anything else. Including the current conversation with Mrs. Spencer.

"I'm sorry. What was that?" Nora asked, feeling foolish to have been caught not paying attention.

"The girls. I'm delighted they've become such good friends. My nephew will be coming to spend the rest of the summer with us. He's about the same age as Lord Coventry. I think the children will all get along quite well; do you not agree?"

Nora agreed. A friend would be good for Edward in the same way it had been good for Lia. Edward had been racing to learn all he needed to know in order to take up his father's mantle, but he was still just a child and deserved the luxury of childish things every now and again—at least once Mr. Ashby completed his review.

She spent a long time talking with Mrs. Spencer before the woman called her daughter, saying it was to leave for home.

Nora was both sad and not sad to see them leave. She enjoyed Mrs. Spencer's company, but her departure meant Nora could focus on Ridley's return.

He did not return that afternoon, which meant Nora could no longer keep her watch over the stable. She joined her children inside the house so they could dress for dinner, eat, and then retire to the drawing room for music and reading and art.

From the drawing room, she could not verify if the light in the stable master's cottage had been turned on. She left the drawing room doors open to the outside, just in case, and sang as if Ridley were her only audience.

Once the children had retired to their rooms and she had dismissed Nash and Mrs. Cole for the night, she picked up her wrap and crept out of doors, making her way down the path until she could see the stable master's cottage. It was still and dark.

Deeply disappointed, she grumbled her way back to the house. She slipped through the drawing room doors before closing them and turning back to the room with a general feeling of dissatisfaction.

"Your mutterings are a thing of fascination. But I am glad you're back. I didn't think you were ever going to return." The low voice came from the shadows by the pianoforte.

Nora jumped, stifling a small shriek by covering her mouth with her hand. "Ridley!" As much as she had wanted to see him a moment ago, she could not help but glare at him now. "You frightened me half out of my wits!"

His rich, low chuckle made her skin tingle. She could not stay furious when he was so close and when the timbre of his voice beckoned her near. She joined him by the pianoforte. "What are you doing here in the dark?"

She moved to light the lamp, but his hand caught hers and he pulled her into his arms. "Perhaps we remain here in the dark."

"That's hardly proper," she said with a smile.

"My lady, it is hardly proper for us to be together regardless of light or dark. But the dark will discourage visitors to this room as they will think you have already gone to bed."

He made an excellent point. And his lips trailing over her hand left her no breath to argue.

"I missed you," he said.

"And I you," she whispered. "I think you should not be allowed to leave the estate without my express permission."

"Ah, but I have secured a new farrier, and at a price that will save the estate money. Do I still need your permission?"

She thought of Mr. Ashby and Edward and how every small

efficiency that could be gained in the estate would be another reason
for her to be able to keep her son. "No. Never. But you must know
how your absence was felt by the whole of this family. Lia sulked and
barely ate a thing today even though she had her friend visiting. You've
never seen a more mournful little creature than my Lia when she feels
all is not well with her world."

"I brought her a present. I hope it will earn her forgiveness for
leaving her for such a short period of time."

Nora grinned, glad for the darkness that hid any hint of devious-
ness. She pulled him over to the sofa. "And what might you do to earn
my forgiveness?"

If her brazenness shocked him, he hid it well. "I brought you a
present as well," he said, settling next to her.

"You must know that your presence is all the present I shall ever
need."

He leaned close enough that she could feel his warm breath
against her ear as he whispered, "It would seem we have that in common." He pressed a kiss just behind her ear and then straightened as
he took both of her hands in his. "How was your day, dear Nora?"

She loved how he said her name with such reverence. "My day
was fine. I had a small moment of worry when Mrs. Spencer informed
me of rumors in town regarding members of my staff."

He tensed. "Rumors?"

"Don't worry. They are not regarding us. They are regarding Mr.
Daw, of all people. It seems he feels rather put out by his dismissal."

"Oh." Ridley's laugh was tight. "I suppose he would at that."

"I'm glad I moved us out here to the country, Ridley." She leaned
against him.

"For entirely selfish reasons, I am glad as well. But I am also glad
for you and the children."

Nora let her head drop softly to his shoulder. She hadn't realized
how tired she felt. "It has been good for us all. But I believe I have
found myself here."

"Were you lost?"

"In some ways, yes. When I was a girl, I was my father's daughter. When I married, I became my husband's wife, though that experience was not at all as I had imagined it would be. And in London, I was my children's mother and a widow in society's eyes. But I've never known who I was as just a woman. Just me. Here, I am Nora. I am my own person, making decisions for my children, and for this estate, and for myself. Here, I am no one's possession."

"The titles you bore previously do not make you a possession, Nora."

He was a stable master, so he could not know about the intricate web society could weave around a person to bind them into a life. She shook her head. "I *was* a possession. To my father and husband, I may as well have been a plate or a handkerchief. And society could praise or break my good name as they saw fit." She felt her thoughts start to blur and her head hum with sleep. Her tongue felt thicker as she kept talking. "No more. Now, I will be in control of my own life. I will do what I want. No one will take the people I love from me. You'll help me, won't you?"

As she drifted off to sleep, she felt Ridley's lips against the top of her head and heard him whisper, "I'll help you. We are the same in this. We know what it means to be ourselves. And to defend our right to be such. And that is why I love you so very much."

She awoke to the sound of her maid entering her room. It was morning, and she was in her own bed. She felt wonderfully relaxed, even though she had no memory of walking to her room or climbing into her bed. She was still fully dressed.

"I'm so sorry, ma'am," Rebecca said, settling the morning tray onto the bed next to Nora. "You said you would dress yourself last night, but I should have stayed up and helped you." Rebecca cast a meaningful look to Nora's wrinkled and very slept-in dress.

"Nonsense. I had every intention of caring for myself but was much too tired to be bothered with it once I came to my room. I would have been much too tired to have let you bother with it as well."

Rebecca's creased brow eased slightly. "Still, I should have—"

"Done as I asked and tended to your own affairs for the evening. Thank you for doing so." Her maid's obvious guilt only served to stab Nora with her own guilt for not being entirely truthful.

Rebecca nodded and went about setting out clothes for the day. "Mr. Ashby is waiting in the study."

Nora's wonderful mood vanished; she wanted to bury her head under her covers. That man! She could not wait for him to be gone— gone *without* her son.

Rebecca helped her dress, though Nora forced herself not to hurry through her morning routine. *I am a baroness. I am a mother.* She'd told Ridley she wanted to be her own woman. With Edward having behaved as a respectable baron, she felt true confidence. Her son was thriving. Anyone could see it. Surely Mr. Ashby could see it as well.

She went to breakfast and tried to listen to Lia chatter excitedly regarding her plans with Mary Spencer. Listening proved very hard, however, since Lia finally said, "Mama, I don't believe you've heard a word I've said."

"You're right, dearest. I'm afraid I am preoccupied. I'm meeting Mr. Ashby as soon as breakfast is over."

"I don't like him," Lia said.

"Nor do I." But like him or not, Nora could not delay the odious task any longer. She made her way to the study.

When she opened the door, she saw Mr. Palmer and Mr. Ashby in a heated discussion.

"Mr. Palmer," Nora said in surprise. "I hadn't realized you were also waiting. I would have made a greater effort to hurry if I had known." Her heart ticked faster with her insolence. She didn't have to look at Mr. Ashby to know that her words infuriated him.

"Lady Coventry." Mr. Palmer hurried to stand and bow. Mr. Ashby was slow to stand, and his bow was short and irritated.

I am a baroness.

"Nor do I," she muttered under her breath as she thought of Lia declaring not to like the man.

"Ma'am?" Mr. Palmer looked confused.

"Oh. I was merely saying, '*my, my*' as it appears I've interrupted something." She moved to sit in her late husband's chair behind the desk. She did it to remind Mr. Ashby of his station—and to remind her of hers. She outranked everyone in the room; why didn't she feel like it?

Mr. Palmer sat but seemed so agitated, Nora suspected he might leap up again at any provocation. Nora shot him a look of confusion and then turned her attention to Mr. Ashby, fixing him with a stare icy enough that she hoped it would make him shiver inwardly. This man threatened to take her son from her. *I am a mother.*

"What is going on, gentlemen?"

"Lady Coventry, my presence here is to verify that you were keeping the conditions of the late Lord Coventry's expectations. I hope you realize that I mean no disrespect but am only doing the bidding of my employer and repeating words he, himself, had said to me, as well as what he wrote before he passed." Mr. Ashby shuffled through several papers and placed a pair of spectacles low on his nose.

Nora felt as though a fist gripped her stomach. Something was wrong. She could feel it in the tense way Mr. Palmer held himself, in the triumphant way Mr. Ashby sat and read through his papers. Something was horribly wrong.

"Ah. There we are. The late Lord Coventry worried that you would not be up to the task of creating a baron out of the young Lord Coventry. As you're aware, he stipulated that I was to keep tabs on events as they unfolded so that I might assess his heir's abilities. Naturally, I chose to be respectful while you were in mourning, but now I fear I am unable to overlook the gross neglect that has occurred regarding your son's education." He paused as if waiting for her to react.

She kept her hands still in front of her on the desk, though she wanted to make fists, to pound the desk and shout at the man before her. "Gross neglect? Where have you found such neglect?"

His simpering smile made her clench her teeth.

"The late baron expected his heir would handle his tenants and land with the same strictures he had used. He worried the young lord would be too soft and be taken advantage of due to his youth and his inexperience. And it would seem the late baron was right to worry."

"Don't be ridiculous, man," Mr. Palmer all but shouted. "You know that no one is taking advantage of that boy. You've seen for yourself that he manages in his own way and under his own will. There's not a soul who would call him soft."

"*I* would call him soft." Mr. Ashby peered over his glasses at Mr. Palmer. "He's spending absurd amounts of money on repairs for the tenants. He's making allowances that cost the estate considerably in terms of profit. He—"

"Is being moral and just and creating changes within the estate that will foster greater prosperity long-term," Nora interrupted. "For this you call him soft? I call him cunning and wise."

Mr. Ashby's heavy-lidded eyes fixed on her in a way that made her want to squirm with discomfort. "Lady Coventry, with all due respect, I've found nothing to convince me that your husband's heir is being trained appropriately, so, as is my direction and my right, I am removing the young lord from your care and placing him under my own care." Mr. Ashby slid his entire stack of papers into a leather satchel and stood even though she had not excused him to leave.

No. This wasn't happening. It could *not* be happening. Edward had proven himself efficient and careful and capable. This threat was supposed to be over, not made into reality. Nora's stomach clenched. She felt her blood drain into her feet. She was going to faint.

No.

She would not faint. She would not lose her son.

I am a mother!

She stood and crossed to the front of the desk, cutting off his path to the door. "Your own care? What do you know of the business of being a baron? You're nothing but a solicitor."

Mr. Ashby smiled his oily grin again. "As you've been allowing him to take lessons from the stable hand, certainly I am a considerable improvement. Though in truth, he will not be in my care specifically. He will be with Lord Francis Grimes, the Viscount of Millburn."

Nora shook as furious energy surged through her. "What? That horrible man?" He'd been friends with her late husband, and she'd heard he'd gambled away his family fortune and been forced to sell off parcels of land to pay his debts.

"He is a superior choice to your stable boy. Don't think I don't know about your inappropriate fraternization there. People talk, Lady Coventry. There are those in town who feel you are far too familiar with that man. That you dined with him at the Goose and Crown, that you spend more time in the stables than anywhere else on the estate. Your actions point to a shocking lack of propriety. How is such a mother to raise a respectable man?" His mouth curled up in a satisfied grin, and she fell back a step, as if he'd physically struck her.

He knew.

How?

But the how didn't matter. *He knew.* She'd allowed herself to get lost in the newness of love, to believe she could escape her cage, and now she had lost.

Lost my Edward.

She was supposed to protect him. She was his mother. Ache filled her. She had done this to them.

It took all of her power to keep from wringing her hands in her desperation to prove all was not as Mr. Ashby painted, to prove she had behaved properly at all times in regard to her children and their upbringing and with her interactions with her stable master. "The only lessons the stable master is giving my son are riding instructions."

Mr. Ashby's smile became a leer. "And what lessons, pray tell, has the stable hand been giving your ladyship, I wonder?"

Mr. Palmer rocked forward with his fists clenched. "You, sir, are treading on very dangerous ground."

Mr. Ashby seemed not to hear the threat. "The Court of Chancery has already heard of this situation with the young baron's unfit upbringing, and they agree with my assessment. Good day, Lady Coventry. Mr. Palmer." He continued to the door.

"I will fight you on this!" Nora cried as the door opened.

"And you will lose."

She cast wild eyes at Mr. Palmer. "Can he do this?"

Mr. Palmer's clenched fists dropped in defeat. "He has a writ from the Court of Chancery."

She launched herself after the solicitor. "I will bring the entire House of Lords upon you!" she cried. "Every misfortune will fall on your head! I will see you drown in the agonies of your own making." She knew her words were meaningless.

Mr. Ashby didn't even bother to turn around when he said, "Such dramatics are terribly unbecoming of a lady. I will collect the boy in the morning. Do try to prove yourself fit in some motherly fashion and see that he's ready." Then the man was gone.

Nora stared after him, her breathing coming in erratic, ragged gasps. She whirled on Mr. Palmer. "How can he do this?"

"Your husband's will was quite specific. Why he left such judgment and power to his solicitor I cannot say. The writ from the Chancery means he can, legally, take your son to be raised by a member of the peerage until the young lord reaches his majority. Or until he turns fourteen, when the court will hear his opinion on the matter if he chooses to make a request for such a change."

I am a baroness. I am a mother. I am—

Her shoulders slumped. She couldn't save her own son.

I am nothing.

Nora fled to the drawing room to find Edward, as if she could will him to stay simply by laying eyes on him. She flung open the door to find it empty. She let out a wail, then forced herself to calm down. He wasn't gone forever; he was simply with Mrs. Spencer's nephew.

Then she saw the sheet music Ridley had purchased for her. Ridley. He would help her. He had *promised* to help her protect her family. He knew so much, surely he would have some idea of what she could do. She had to see him immediately.

Chapter Twenty-Two

Ridley had spent the entire night, and most of the morning, pacing. If someone was looking for him and found Daw instead, the old stable master would most certainly point the searcher toward the Windsong stables.

He needed to tell Nora.

He needed to confess himself to her as soon as possible, for if she heard the truth from someone else, Nora might not understand.

"You're being paranoid, man," he chastised himself. The chances of someone finding him at Windsong were so absurdly small as to not exist at all. He picked up the saddle for General. The horses needed to be exercised. He had neglected his routine long enough.

Besides, whoever was looking for him was in Lancaster. Palmer had mentioned to the man that Ridley had met with the farrier, but Ridley was sure the farrier wouldn't give out his information.

"It is not enough for anyone to tie to me," he said aloud.

"What's not enough?"

"George!" Ridley said the boy's name like a curse and nearly dropped the saddle. "What are you doing sneaking in here on cat paws and listening in on other people's private conversations?"

George's eyebrows shot up. "A private conversation with yerself? And that doesn't seem . . ."

"Seem what?"

George shrugged. "A bit dodgy?"

Ridley laughed, though knots tightened his stomach. "Don't you have work to do? Troughs to fill? Hay to stack? Something?"

George chuckled and left to do his work. The boy was getting cheekier by the day.

Ridley shook his head. The shadows of his past were biting at his heels, and he could not seem to run away fast enough or far enough.

The man in Lancaster had shaken him. Looking to return a pocket watch? He hadn't even been subtle.

If Ridley was found, he could die for his perceived crimes. There would be no way to stop the onslaught of anger and pain that would follow.

He itched to go to his cottage, pack his belongings, and put distance between him and Windsong.

He would have done so but for three faces that had taken up residence in his mind: Nora, Edward, and Lia. They had all taken root in his heart, and he couldn't leave them no matter how his past ghosts compelled him forward. He took a great breath that seemed insufficient to fill his lungs and finished saddling General. He would not run. Not yet. Not until he was sure he had no other choice.

The storm would pass. Then he would be free to tell Nora everything, on his own terms.

"Ridley?" One of the footmen suddenly appeared, startling Ridley as he was cinching General's saddle.

Devil take him! He was jumping at everything. "Yes, Sam?"

"Lady Coventry wants her horse readied. And be warned. The lady's in a mood like I've never seen before. I heard shouting. No—it was screaming really."

Ridley's hands stilled on the saddle's leather straps and buckle. "Over what?"

"Dunno. The house is quiet as a tomb now. It's scarier than the screaming had been."

"Are the children well?" It was a stupid question. Of course they were well, or Nora wouldn't be wanting a horse to ease her emotions. If there had been a problem with the children, she would have been right there in the middle of everything and coming up with a solution. He loved her fierce protection of those she loved.

He quickly finished with General and hurried to prepare Opal.

Nora swept into the stable a moment later, tugging on her gloves without bothering to button them. She barely glanced at him, thunder and fire burning in her eyes. She climbed the mounting block and launched herself onto Opal's back. She didn't even wait for him to get into his own saddle before she urged Opal out to the yard.

He scrambled up onto General and followed. Out in the yard, Nora had already disappeared into the tree line.

He urged General into a gallop. There was no time to ease him into exercise. Today, they would be running.

He caught up with her at the river. She was already sliding off Opal's back. She didn't seem to want his help. He wasn't entirely sure she wanted his company at all. He hopped to the ground and cautiously approached.

She wrapped her arms around herself and began to weep. Explosive sobs shook her shoulders. Tears flowed down her cheeks in steady streams.

"Nora?" he whispered. "What's happened?"

"He's taking him. He's taking Edward, and there is nothing I can do to stop it. I am . . . I am so . . ." Turning away, she doubled over and sicked up.

He waited until she was through, until she was on her knees at the river, cleaning off her mouth. "I'm sorry," she said after a moment.

He took this as her permission to approach. He knelt by her and pulled her in close. "I cannot think of anything you need to apologize for. You've had a shock. It's natural for your body to react to that shock. What exactly happened?"

Her explanation tore through him. Mr. Ashby would be taking her son in the morning. He'd said she wasn't a good mother, that she hadn't trained the boy properly. And Mr. Ashby knew about *them*—about her and Ridley. He'd said people had talked. But which people?

She and Ridley had never shown any indication of preference for one another while in any other company.

"It's all my fault," she said over and over.

It was not her fault. It was his. He was the one who had given the boy so much advice. He had been the one to encourage the relationship with Nora. He had selfishly thought he could interfere in their lives, and now he had hurt them.

When she was done speaking, she seemed to have been emptied emotionally. She had no more words, no more tears. She knelt in the grasses at the side of the river, skirts muddied and water seeping into the cloth. She stared into the current with wide, vacant eyes.

His heart ached for her, for Edward, for the whole of the situation.

"Oh, Nora. I wish I knew how to help you."

His words seemed to startle her out of her thoughts, as if just remembering that he was there with her. "No one can help me." She hung her head in her hands.

"Did he say who told him about us?" he asked.

"Does it matter? What difference does it make? We were fools to think—no. *I* was a fool. What could either of us do now to remedy our mistake? *I* have no power here. I am nothing—helpless. And you? Who will listen to a powerless stable boy?"

He tried not to flinch at her words. She was angry and hurt. She didn't mean it. She couldn't mean it. He opened his mouth to say that he would do everything in his power to assist her but stopped before he could utter a syllable. What right did he have to offer hope when he was certain he could be of no assistance?

So he said nothing and stayed by her side until she stood. Her dress was covered in mud and green stains from the grasses and moss, but she didn't seem to care.

She faced him and said, "I should go to Edward now. I was on my way to him when I realized he is with Mrs. Spencer's nephew today. I couldn't bear to pull him away from a happy time. Nor could I bear to be alone with my thoughts until he returned. But he might be home by now. He doesn't even know. I have to tell him. And then I have to plan."

He wanted to reach for her, but she gave no indication she would welcome his touch. "Of course." He felt the severity of her pain and wished there was something more he could do than stand there helplessly.

"I'm sorry," he said. He scrubbed his fingers through his hair. "I wish I knew what to do."

"Mr. Ashby might not have taken him if I had behaved like a lady. If I had been a *baroness*." She said the words slowly, her tone confused. "I shouldn't have come out here with you. I don't know what I was thinking. We've done enough damage, haven't we? Last night, you said you would help me protect my family. Perhaps you can best protect my family by staying away."

Her final glance to him was not one of warmth and love, but of pain.

And he suspected his own face mirrored hers.

She refused his help to get back onto her horse and instead used a large rock to climb into the saddle. Then she sped to the house as quickly as she'd left it. He followed, not knowing what to say. He'd gone against all good judgment by encouraging their friendship. Who had discovered them? Who had told?

"George?" he called out to the stables. When the boy's head popped out of the back room, he added, "Will you and the boys see to the horses? I need to return something to Lady Coventry."

Ridley rushed after Nora, determined to tell her the truth. He would not leave it like this. There would be expectations of him once he told her everything—expectations he would not be able to meet. She might not understand. Her own circumstances had become so desperate, she might not see reason. But at least he would have told her everything. Maybe then, she would allow him to offer comfort and help her come up with a plan.

He had nearly reached the gate when a man stepped out in front of him.

"Lord Ridlington Devonshire."

It was not a question. The man was not looking *for* Ridlington Devonshire, because he knew he was looking *at* Ridlington Devonshire.

Ridley did not know how to respond.

"You've not been an easy man to find," the man said. He had a blue coat and a scarlet waistcoat—a runner from London. "You slipped away from me in Lancaster. But not here."

This was the man Ridley had glimpsed going down the stairs back at the inn. Ridley finally found his tongue. "You're a long way from home."

"True, but the pay has made it worth it."

"How long have you been searching for me?"

The man grinned. "Long enough that I despaired of ever finding you. Some of us runners said you were dead, but I knew better. Luckily for me, this estate's previous stable master has a loose tongue and strong inclination to drink. He's been most beneficial."

"You'll forgive me if I do not join you in praise of his many benefits." Ridley looked past the man's shoulders to the house where Nora had fled, lamenting the coming loss of her son. Then he glanced to the woods to the right of the man.

The man noted the shift in Ridley and shook his head. "It's not wise to make such a move, sir. I am faster and stronger than I look. Please come with me, now. Quietly would be best. There's no reason to upset this household with the details of your crimes."

"What do you know of my crimes?"

"They're enough to hang for. You're now in my custody." He slipped a club into his hand. "As I said, quietly would be best."

Ridley shot a desperate glance to the house. He was too late to confess the truth to Nora. *"Powerless stable boy."*

She wasn't wrong. At least not about him being powerless.

And she would certainly never forgive him.

Chapter Twenty-Three

Nora had expected Ridley to steal into the house, to find her, to offer comfort, to actually help by coming up with a plan instead of saying he wished he could help but then doing nothing. She had yet to talk to Edward regarding his new situation. How long would she have to wait for her son? How long would she have to wait for Ridley?

When Mr. Palmer entered the drawing room, Nora felt keen disappointment. She wanted to hold her son. She wanted Ridley to hold her, even though she had abandoned him earlier.

"I have news of a troubling nature," Mr. Palmer said.

She gaped at him. "More troubling than what we already have sitting in our laps?"

"Ma'am," Mr. Palmer said softly, "truly nothing is more troubling than Edward being taken, but this news cannot wait."

Nora did not believe she could bear any more bad news, but she invited him to sit.

"It's regarding the stable master."

She drew a breath. "I know what you're going to say."

Mr. Palmer frowned. "You do?"

"Yes. And I know my behavior was not what it ought to be. I know this is my fault."

Mr. Palmer sat very still for a moment. "Forgive me, ma'am. But what have you to do with Mr. Ellis's crimes?"

"Crimes?"

"Yes. He's been taken by a runner from London."

Nora's heart stopped. "Wait. What are you talking about?"

Mr. Palmer frowned. "I fear we were greatly misled by Mr. Ellis. He is not Ridley Ellis from nowhere in particular. He is Lord Ridlington Devonshire from Devon, son of the late Duke of Devon, younger brother to the current Duke of Devon. He has apparently been missing for thirteen years."

Devon. She'd been to Devon when she'd been a small child nearly twenty years ago. She'd played in the ocean with several other children. The memories that kept tugging at her were real. He didn't simply remind her of that boy from the oceanside. He *was* that boy.

"You're saying we've had a duke shoveling after horses in our stables?" The words made no sense. Nothing made sense. First Mr. Ashby taking Edward and now Ridley being a duke? It was entirely impossible. How many ways could her mind and heart be broken in one day? How many times could she be betrayed? She worried she might be sick again.

"His brother is technically the duke, but yes, the man we hired to be your stable master is secretly a lord." Mr. Palmer grimaced. "There's more."

"More? How could there possibly be more?"

"His brother, the duke, had accused him of stealing a horse—"

Nora scoffed at such nonsense. More likely, the horse had been a gift from his father or some such thing. Misunderstandings between siblings on such points happened often.

"Though horse theft is bad enough, there is also the weightier matter of him attempting to murder his eldest brother."

"That's preposterous!" she blurted even as she pictured the scar on his jaw, the way he'd spoken of his brother's cruelty. Could there be some truth to the accusation? Could some altercation have happened? Was this why he wouldn't even try to help her? Was he worried he'd be found out? Had he been saving his own skin no matter the cost to her?

"As I said, he's been detained by a runner from London. Chances are they will want to interview all of us. I wanted you to be prepared as we are not in a position to say no to such interviews."

Before Nora could reply, the door opened, and Edward entered.

"Mama?" he said, looking concerned. "Nash said you wanted to speak to me right away."

"I'll leave you to your privacy." Mr. Palmer stood and crossed the room to the door. He placed a hand on Edward's shoulder as he passed him, which served to further furrow Edward's brow.

"Something *is* wrong, then?"

"Yes." Nora patted the spot next to her on the sofa, inviting him to sit with her. She put her arm around him as she relayed all the details from Mr. Ashby, though her voice cracked and shattered on nearly every word she spoke.

"I'll not go!" he shouted, as angry as he had been when they had first arrived at Windsong. "They cannot make me!"

"Yes, they can, dearest."

"But I'm a baron."

She let out a shuddering breath. "Laws must be obeyed. Even by—no. *Especially* by people in unique positions in society."

He sank deeper against her side, a boy seeking refuge and security that was not to be found. "How can he just take me away?"

"Your father's stipulations for his heir left me very little control. You will be living with a viscount who will help train you to be a baron. But I need you to do something for me, something very important. I need you to not let this viscount change who you are at your center. Can you do that for me?"

Edward sat up and peered at her in a way that reminded her of when he was very small and still enthralled by the snails in the garden. "I can do that. I can be like you, Mama."

"Like me?"

He nodded. "Mr. Ellis told me that you were an example of strength and that if I wanted to be respected, I should try to be like you. I will not forget that while I am away from you."

Tears blurred her vision as she looked down at her precious little boy. That Ridley had been the one to help her son find his way while he was apparently so lost himself struck her as a sad sort of irony.

He let her hold him for a long time. When Lia entered the drawing room, she must have sensed something was wrong because she climbed up beside Edward and leaned her head on his shoulder. Edward, for once, placed an arm around his sister and pulled her close.

Nora had many thoughts running through her head regarding both her little family and the man who had captured her heart, but who had not been what he'd said. She would need to examine her emotions in order to understand them, but she couldn't let the betrayal she felt from Ridley take away from her last moments with her boy.

Nora told Lia about Edward's new situation, and tears rolled down her pale cheeks in steady streams. She cried all through dinner and continued to cry once they'd all returned to the drawing room.

"Will you play for me, Mama, one more time?" Edward asked.

"What would you like to hear?"

"My song. The sleepy bird."

Lia nodded her emphatic agreement even while she sniffled and drew her pictures.

Nora placed her fingers on the keys and played the song she'd written for her infant son all those years ago. Every note and word conjured up memories of him. Of his eyelids drooping while she rocked him to sleep as an infant, of his tiny fingers, and the way he giggled when she tickled his pink toes, of his determined scowl when he'd decided he wanted to learn to walk, of the many times he'd picked wildflowers for her and left them in front of her door.

She'd finally had her sweet boy back, and now they were taking him from her again. The ache in her swelled with the chorus, but she kept her voice strong so that her son might hear it clearly in his memory later.

The next morning, Edward was in a mood that would have made a tempest feel like a slight breeze. He'd stormed and ranted and flatly refused to leave, which had been a relief. What would she have done if he had not cared and declared himself glad to go?

She would have died.

As it was, she felt she might die anyway, now that he had kissed her cheek and solemnly sworn to return quickly. She wrapped her arms around him and whispered in his ear, "Please know, Edward, I will be working with all of my might to bring you home again."

He nodded.

Lia thrust a paper and a satchel into his hand. "I drew a picture of us, so you'll remember who loves you best in all the world." She lowered her voice so Mr. Ashby could not overhear. "And I've given you my doll. I put her in your bag. You can talk to her instead of me. She's very good at listening."

He smiled at her. "Thank you, Lia," he whispered. "I am glad you are my sister. I will talk to her every day." Edward squared his shoulders, tossed Mr. Ashby the coldest, darkest look Nora had ever seen on her son, and stepped up into the carriage.

Then the carriage was gone.

Nora covered her mouth to stifle the wail of her soul that tore free from her throat. She felt like someone had hollowed out her body. How could she still have breath and a pulse when surely her lungs and heart were missing?

She wanted to run away, to flee the feeling, but the stables were no longer a safe haven. There was no Ridley to offer solace or guidance. She took several fortifying breaths, then took Lia's hand and solemnly went back into the house.

They went straight to the drawing room. Nora did not allow herself to glance at the chair usually occupied by Edward. She sat at the pianoforte, intending to hurl out her emotions in the music. The sheet music Ridley had bought her in Lancaster was still there. She ignored the pages and sat down to play, plunking at the keys. One soulless tone after another.

Lia rested her small hand on hers. "Mama?" her soft, sad voice brought Nora back from the abyss, if only just. "What will we do?"

What would they do?

"You will bring him back, won't you? Promise me." The little girl's eyes were full of fear. Just a few short months before, Lia's fear would have come from her brother's presence, not his absence.

"I promise we will get him back, dearest." She pulled the little girl to her chest and rested her chin on Lia's soft, warm head as they both wept.

They stayed in the drawing room the whole day, writing letters. Lia wrote to her brother while Nora wrote to anyone with enough power to right this terrible wrong in her life. They took their meals there together, and, at the end of the worst day of Nora's life, she walked Lia to her bed and tucked her in before returning alone to the drawing room.

She opened the doors at the back of the room and looked out into the darkness. Her son no longer belonged to her to raise. Ridley had lied to her. He was not a stable master. He was not her friend. He was Lord Ridlington of Devon—a criminal hiding from his own family. No one would come in through those doors to offer her comfort for the loss of either son or friend.

Nora finally allowed herself to look at the chair Edward had claimed as his own. With a great shout, she shoved hard at the chair, upending it with a crash.

Nash hurried in. "Ma'am, are you all right?"

She heaved in great gulping breaths. "No." She glanced at the double doors leading out to the garden. "No, I'm not."

Chapter Twenty-Four

Ridley sat atop his horse, escorted by two other London runners. The three men kept a close watch over him to ensure he didn't try to escape. When he asked where they were headed, the short, burly one said, "Lancaster." The man who had caught Ridley had Ridley's horse tied to his and didn't speak to him once. He merely stared menacingly at Ridley as if daring him to try to leap from his horse and flee to the woods. The urge to do so was considerable.

They made good time on horseback and arrived at the Black Lion Inn in Lancaster before midnight. The runner herded him upstairs to a room. Ridley felt apprehension in every bone and muscle in his body. His oldest brother had sent the law after him long ago. After so many years of separation, Ridley hoped his brother might have softened or at least grown less vengeful. Otherwise, he would not fare well. At best, he could hope for dueling pistols. At the worst?

The runner opened the door and shoved Ridley inside.

The person sitting in the chair before him *was* Ridley's brother. But not the one he had expected.

"Typical," Ridley said. "You have always been Alexander's hound, catching his prey for him. He never could do anything on his own."

Peter ran a critical eye over Ridley. "What is it you're wearing? Had I passed you on the street, I would have assumed you to be a pauper."

Ridley huffed out a breath of exasperation. "A stable master is hardly a pauper. It's a respectable position. There is no shame in the life of a pauper either. When did you become such an incredible snob? And what does it matter what I wear to the hangman's noose?"

Peter flapped his hand, indicating Ridley should sit. "If I've become a snob, you've become dramatic. Would you like something to drink? Eat? They must feed you at that stable of yours—you don't look like you're starving."

Ridley raised an eyebrow at his brother.

"No, then. Perhaps you can tell me why I would send my only living brother to the hangman's noose."

Ridley blinked in surprise. "Alexander's dead?"

"Yes."

"So, you are the Duke of Devon."

"So it would seem." Peter lifted a small glass from the table next to him and took a sip.

"Congratulations."

Peter smiled and lowered his glass back to the table. "Is that the proper thing to say when one's brother has died? Wouldn't 'my condolences' be better?"

When Ridley didn't answer, Peter grinned. "It is good to see you, Ridlington. I have spent a considerable amount of time and money searching for you. Not to hang you, as you supposed, but to apologize. I should never have believed Alexander. But when he was found beaten in the stable and saying you'd tried to kill him over Father's pocket watch, it seemed plausible. There was no love lost between the two of you. He could have easily pushed you to a limit. That watch had been a source of contention from the moment Mother had handed it to you in front of our brother. Alexander made for a sympathetic victim." He paused. "And there was an awful lot of blood."

Ridley shook his head. "I didn't try to kill him. He cornered me. Demanded the watch back. Said it was his property. When I refused, he came at me. He was so drunk. We exchanged punches, but on the last one that connected with his jaw, he fell back and hit his head. Yes, he was bleeding when I left, but he was also breathing."

"But you still ran."

"Of course I ran. I knew how it looked. I knew the cost of that fight. With Mother gone, there was no one to stand up for me or the truth." Ridley fixed his brother with an even look. "With Alexander dead, why bother to find me? Do you want justice for his perceived damage?"

Peter took another drink. "Certainly not. A few years after you left, Alexander confessed to me that he'd lied about you trying to kill him. His drunken confessions of guilt were almost worse than his drunken tantrums. I set out to find you immediately after that. You proved to be a hard man to find." Peter smiled. "When Alexander died and I became duke, I had to redouble my efforts to find you. It turns out my wife is unable to bear children. It is a source of heartbreak for us. She often tells me I should have married another, but that would never do. My wife is perfection on every count, and I would be quite miserable without her. But Devon will, someday, require an heir, and I have gone far too long without my family. I had hoped we could reconcile, and you would let me be your brother again."

"Alexander tortured me throughout my entire childhood. How many broken bones did I suffer through while *you* stood aside and listened to them snap? I have a scar the length of my hand on my side. *Scars*, Peter. Permanent. Do you know how many nightmares I've had since leaving Devon? And now you want to reconcile? Pretend none of it ever occurred?" Ridley stood up and turned toward the door. "I'm leaving."

Peter jumped to his feet and hurried to stand in front of Ridley.

"Move aside, Peter. I am not a quivering child fearing for my life any longer."

"I know," Peter said. "I know. But I *am* sorry. I am sorry I didn't stop him. But you must remember, Ridley. I was a child, too. I could not have stopped him without his temper falling upon me as much as it fell on you. So before you run from me, please give me a chance to be the brother to you that we both wish he had been to us."

Ridley's emotions clashed within him. He'd hated his old life so much. There was so much pain in those memories, but was it only pain? His memories of his mother were mostly pleasant. He had loved the stables and being on the oceanside with cliffs that seemed to have overlooked the entire world. But Alexander lurked in even those memories, casting his shadow over the whole of it.

Ridley had seen a lot of the way the world worked since leaving Devon. He'd seen men do good things and bad things, great things and terrible things. He'd also seen unexpected forgiveness. As he held Peter's gaze, he saw only sincerity and fervent hope in his eyes.

He thought of Nora, of his hope that she would forgive him for not telling her the truth of his past. How could he deny his brother the mercy he hoped to gain for himself? He moved away from the door and settled back in his chair.

Peter sighed in obvious relief. He also sat back down.

Then he brought out an antique silver pocket watch. "This is for you." He handed it to Ridley.

Ridley's breath caught in his throat at the weight of the watch in his palm again. "Father's watch. He would have wanted it to be given to Alexander, and then to you."

Peter shrugged. "Alexander is gone, and we both know Mama always meant for you to have it."

Ridley found a brief peace in the weight of the pocket watch, not because it had belonged to his father but because his mother had valued him enough to give him such a gift.

And then the two brothers did something Ridley never believed would be possible—they talked.

They talked well into the night, sharing nearly a decade of experiences until their throats became dry and their eyes became wet. And somehow, through it all, they found a reprieve from the years of pain. Their relationship wasn't entirely healed—Ridley wasn't certain a single night's work was capable of total absolution—but it was a start.

He awoke with a start, feeling like he'd dreamed it all, but Peter snoring in the bed across from his proved he hadn't. Ridley couldn't remember the last time he felt like he'd truly slept. He was rested in a way he hadn't been in years. What would Nora think when he told her?

Ridley bolted upright. Nora!

He yanked back the draperies to see the sun high in the sky. Devil take him! How had he slept through half a day? He opened his pocket watch. It was almost three in the afternoon. Nora had been distraught when he'd last seen her. By this point, Edward would surely have already been taken. She was alone. He had to return.

He tugged on his clothes and shoes. He tossed a pillow at his brother. "Peter! Wake up. I have to go."

"What? Now?" Peter glanced out the window.

"It has to be now. I should have left hours ago."

When Peter hesitated, Ridley simply said, "Nora. I love her, Peter."

His brother hurried to his feet. "I'll go with you."

They were off within the hour.

Ridley had traveled the road between Lancaster and Windsong dozens of times, but it was much longer traveling in a carriage than on horseback. He hadn't considered that when they'd left. His mind had been so frenzied with panic that he hadn't thought to insist he ride on horseback. It was far too late to make such a demand now that they were already on the road. His only option was to stay the course. His leg bounced up and down in a frenzied fashion until Peter put a hand on it and said, "You need to relax. I cannot tolerate the tension rolling off you for another moment."

"I told you what she means to me. To know she is enduring such pain alone is more than I can bear."

"We'll travel through the night. My driver will push the horses as much as he can without killing the poor creatures. We'll be there soon."

But soon was not soon enough for Ridley. He checked his pocket watch. What must Nora think of him after he'd disappeared entirely? Had she already heard rumors regarding his whereabouts? He wished he knew what she'd heard and what she thought and how she felt and if Edward was safe.

I'm coming Nora, he thought as the carriage inched forward.

He checked his watch again and again, keeping diligent track of the minutes as they crept past. Peter had urged his driver to make haste and there was no doubt that the driver had done as asked. But a team of horses pulling a carriage could not make the same time as a single horse and rider.

By the time they arrived at Windsong, it was midmorning the next day.

Ridley hopped from the carriage almost before it had come to a complete stop. He should have waited for Peter, but he had no time to waste. Not when Nora was somewhere in the house, needing him.

He stopped at the stairs and looked up at the large imposing door. Did he knock and have Nash announce him as if he were truly the ranked man of society he'd once been? Or did he go around back as the servant he currently was?

He went around back.

The kitchens were in the full force of morning preparations: Cook shouting orders to scullery maids. Nash giving directions to the foot-men. Rebecca, working on mending a dress. Nathan, Edward's valet, was notably absent. George sat at the table, peering mournfully at a plate of food that looked like it hadn't been touched.

Everything came to a halt when Ridley appeared. Even Cook stopped stirring whatever boiled in her pot and gaped at his arrival. George's head snapped up, and the look that crossed his face seemed to be at war between fury and joy.

"Hello," Ridley said, realizing how wretched his standing must be if their expressions were any indication.

"Hello," Nash said, taking the lead. He approached Ridley care-fully, as if stalking a wolf. "We've heard rumors, sir."

Sir. So they knew of his birth then. "Yes. I suppose you would have."

"Are they true?" Alison asked. The plates she was carrying made a slight tinkling noise as she shifted her weight and added a hurried, "Sir."

"I'm sure some, if not all, are true. Let me be quick so I might continue with my errand here. My brother is the Duke of Devon. I am now, apparently, his only heir. I ran away from my home when

I was sixteen and have been working for my living in stables. Until now."

"Did you really steal a horse? Did you really kill your oldest brother?" George asked the questions that were clearly on everyone's minds.

Ridley shook his head that the rumors were so far from the truth. "No. The horse was mine, a gift to me from a much-loved aunt. And I assure you, I left my brother quite alive, if a little worse for wear. I'm sorry I came to you under false pretenses, but I am still Ridley. I am still your friend. And I would stay, but I must speak with N—with Lady Coventry. The matter is urgent."

"I would imagine so," Nash said before waving his hand to the rest of the staff to get back to work. "You should know, they took the young lord. They had a writ from the Chancery. If there's anything you can do, then do it. Please. I will announce you, sir."

Ridley had wanted to avoid being announced, but he followed Nash up the stairs, feeling the eyes of everyone on his back. Nothing could be as it was now that his heritage had been revealed. He could never be just Ridley to these people whom he had counted as friends. George, who had always looked at him with trust, now viewed him with suspicion and confusion. The loss of those easy friendships weighed heavy on him as he mounted the stairs. He kept his eyes forward with the hope that there was not more loss to come.

Nash showed Ridley to the drawing room as if Ridley did not know exactly where it was, then withdrew, no doubt to speak to Lady Coventry.

Ridley noted an overturned chair and wondered why Nash or one of the footmen had not righted it. He considered doing so himself but felt incredibly unsure of any action he should take in this situation where he straddled two worlds.

The door opened, and Nora appeared. He felt immediate relief, realizing he'd been uncertain if she would even agree to see him.

She approached him, and he bowed as low and as deferentially as ever before. If possible, her curtsy to him sank deeper than his bow had.

"My lord duke," she said, her tone painfully neutral.

"No. My brother is the duke. I'm . . . Well, I'm his brother."

"I was told you stole a horse and tried to kill someone."

"Those are falsehoods." He shifted uneasily. Her face showed the weight she had borne over the last two days. Edward was clearly gone and had taken her heart and soul with him.

"Then you are not in trouble with the law?"

"No."

Her jaw tightened as her chin lifted. Fire bloomed in her eyes. "How long have you known you were not in trouble?"

He frowned, unsure of her meaning. "As soon as I arrived in Lancaster and was reunited with my brother. The night before last, I suppose."

Her blue eyes widened. "The night before last? So you knew immediately." Her voice rose until she was shouting. "You knew in time to have turned around and stopped that man from taking my son yesterday morning! As a duke, you could have stopped him, yet you did not return for me, to help me, to help my son!"

Understanding dawned on Ridley far too late. As a high-ranking member of society, he could have been the hero she had hoped for, and he had failed her. He shook his head, trying to think of how he could rectify his mistake.

"We traveled all through the night, Nora. We came as fast as we could." He frowned, knowing he wasn't being entirely honest. If he had turned around and left on horseback as soon as he'd realized Peter was no danger to him, he could have returned before Edward had been taken. "I don't know that I could have stopped him. He had a writ allowing him to take the boy. I was in a stable master's uniform. Who would have listened to me?"

Her eyes narrowed, and her mouth hung open in disbelief. "*Everyone* would have listened! You're a duke! You have authority over everyone except the royal family."

He knew he should not argue his point, but his emotions were frayed and twisted from seeing his brother and having his past catch up to him. He could not seem to stop himself from saying, "No, I am *not* a duke. That title went to my eldest brother."

"To whom you are related!" Nora began pacing around the overturned chair, occasionally brushing it with her fingertips. "Do you know the first thing that happened to me when I discovered they were stealing my son? I went to the drawing room to find Edward, and there on the piano was the sheet music you had purchased for me. And I thought to myself, 'Ridley will help me. He'll know what to say—what advice to give on how to stop this madness.' But you didn't. You apologized. You claimed you did not know how you could offer me aid. You didn't even tell me the truth about yourself." Her face twisted in pain, and she wrapped her arms around her chest as if to hold herself together. "You lied to me."

"I was going to tell you—"

"When?" she interrupted. "When my son reaches his majority and becomes a member of the House of Lords? Or maybe when you are on your deathbed. That seems a place to drop inconvenient truths."

"Nora, please—"

"Please? Please what? What could you possibly dare ask of me? You're a complete stranger to me. I do not know you."

"Please just listen to me. I love you."

"Love me?" She laughed, but the sound was cold and came with a wrenching sob as she covered her face with her hands. When she removed her hands, her anguish had shifted again to fury. "What is love to you? Do you even understand the meaning of such a word? Love is not music sheets and poetry!"

She picked up the music sheets he had given her and threw them to the air, a flock of startled starlings taking flight and then fluttering to the ground.

"I want you to leave Windsong." Nora's tone left no room for argument, but Ridley could not stop himself from trying.

"We can fix this, Nora."

"Fix this? He took my son! You could have stopped him, but you didn't even try. And do not ever call me by my name again. You'll refer to me as Lady Coventry. I am a baroness, and unlike some, I do not shirk the duties that come with such a title. Leave, Lord Ridlington or whoever you are. Go home. Tend to your own stables. I have no need of you in mine."

"Nora, please."

"Do not use my name!" she shouted. "You no longer have the right to my name. You have not earned the right to my heart. I do not want your pathetic excuses. When I needed you the most, you were not there. Love is dependable. You could have depended on me. I would have married you as a stable master—even as the stable hand. I would have endured the scorn and censure such a choice would have brought from society, and I would have done it happily. But I have learned I cannot depend on you. You are a coward. I want nothing to do with this duke you are." She turned and left the drawing room, her head erect, her shoulders squared.

Ridley stood alone, unsure of what to do next. He stared at the doorway where Nora had walked out of his life, for good, it seemed.

"I'm *not* a duke," he whispered to himself.

He exited the drawing room through the double doors that led to the back gardens. He took the path to the stables where the boys watched him warily.

"I wanted to say goodbye and to thank you all for being such wonderful friends."

They wished him well on his journeys, but they did not wish him—Ridley—well. They wished a member of society well. It broke his heart. He continued to his cottage and packed up his belongings. He could no longer run from his past.

And he no longer had a future to look forward to.

Chapter Twenty-Five

Nora spent days furiously writing letters to anyone who could help her recover her son. She spent days, well . . . *furious.*

And anguished.

And lost.

"Foolish, fanciful wanderings of my mind," she said out loud. She was in the conservatory despite the heat. She'd placed a chair exactly where her son had been watching the frog all those months ago. She wished she could go back to that time, even though she was fairly certain he'd hated her in that moment. At least he had still been with her.

"When was the last time you've eaten?"

Mrs. Spencer's voice startled her. She'd entered the conservatory, followed by Mrs. Cole, who directed several footmen carrying trays to set up a luncheon with the efficiency Nora had come to expect and depend on from her household staff.

Depend on.

How many people had she thought she could depend on only to learn she'd been wrong? She'd thought she could depend on her father to choose a husband who would be kind and generous to her. She'd thought she could depend on having the luxury of raising her own son. She'd thought she could depend on Ridley—or Lord Ridlington or whatever he wanted to call himself—to be there for her. She'd been so wrong on all those counts and many others besides.

She shook herself, realizing she could not look askance at every other human in the world, expecting them to disappoint her.

"I appreciate your concern, Mrs. Spencer, but I find myself lacking an appetite. But do please sit and eat your fill. I will find pleasure in your company."

"Nonsense," Mrs. Spencer said. "I will have no pleasure at all if you do not take at least three bites of food. The strawberries are red and plump and perfect. And your cook's sandwiches are sublime. The cheeses are rich. Surely there is something here to tempt you to three bites."

The footmen had set the table and other chairs around Nora as if she was the centerpiece of the scene. She was grateful for that since she didn't think she could have lifted herself up if she'd wanted to. And she didn't want to.

"The girls will join us for a moment if you don't mind." Mrs. Spencer waited for an answer, so Nora agreed. She didn't mind, did she?

Mrs. Spencer's arranging of such details was bold to say the least, but it was also incredibly thoughtful. Nora could not find fault with her friend.

"If you wish to talk," Mrs. Spencer continued softly, "I am happy to listen. If you wish to shout, I am happy to listen to that as well. If you wish to sit in silence, I hope you will allow me to keep you company as you do so."

Nora only blinked, too exhausted to even know what she wished for herself.

Mrs. Spencer sat at the table and busied herself with pouring tea and preparing plates of food. "I want you to know that, as I've watched you over the time you've been residing here, I have noted what an excellent mother you are. Such excellence is not a common trait among our sort, is it? My, my! If you knew of the rumors that are whispered regarding my own methods, you'd be quite shocked. You would perhaps want to quit your connection with me altogether."

Mrs. Spencer paused, looking at Nora with gentle eyes. "But no. You would not, for you understand what it means to be the protector over a child's entire world. It isn't that other mothers don't love their children—my, my, no, of course they do—but they seem to do their loving from a distance, don't they? Not us. We love up close. We love intimately. So our pain is that much more acute when something goes wrong. I say all this, not to try to make you feel better. My, no. I know such relief will only come from the return of your son. I say this because I want you to know you do not walk this dark path alone. You are seen and understood."

Nora's throat tightened, and her breath hitched when she said, "Thank you, Mrs. Spencer."

Mrs. Spencer offered a wobbly smile, and her eyes shined with her own unshed tears.

The topic turned to gossip found in town, and Mrs. Spencer informed Nora that not only had Mr. Daw been the one to draw Mr. Ashby's attention to the state of the barony but he had also revealed Ridley's whereabouts to his brother.

"I should have had that horrible man hanged when the chance had been mine," Nora muttered, glad that Mrs. Spencer merely smiled patiently at the sentiment rather than admonishing her for it.

Lia and Mary entered the conservatory, though Lia was somber and subdued. The little girl still wept occasionally at night, and she did not ask to go riding, nor did she mention the riding lessons that had ended so abruptly. She had not given her daughter the details of Ridley's departure, only the simple truth that he had to return home.

"Good afternoon, Mama." Lia kissed Nora's cheek before seating herself at the table.

Nora acknowledged the girls with a smile, the act requiring so much more energy than she could have imagined. She gratefully allowed Mrs. Spencer to carry the conversation with the girls. And just as Mrs. Spencer had offered to walk the dark path with Nora, so it seemed that Mary had decided to do the same for Lia.

The kindness spooned over Nora's heart did not heal it, but she found it was slightly easier to breathe knowing she was not alone.

After a while, Lia invited Mary to go look at the new kittens

George had found in an alcove in the carriage house. Nora had promoted George to stable master. She doubted anyone knew as much as George did, and she had no desire or energy to hire someone older.

"Thank you," Nora said to Mrs. Spencer after a few moments.

Mrs. Spencer smiled. "A bit of food and a spot of tea might not repair what's wrong in the world, but it allows us to put another foot forward. Sometimes that is enough."

"It isn't just the food," Nora said, though she did feel marginally better in physical terms. Having something in her stomach had eased the nausea. "Thank you for sitting here with me. I feel as though my entire existence has become one of waiting for the mail and praying for a letter that might change my situation."

"Would that I had the power to do more. But I can sit here and wait with you whenever you like."

And she did. Mrs. Spencer sat and waited with her for the mail. She stayed while Nora read letters. She did not pass judgment when Nora tore a few of them up.

Mrs. Spencer returned the next day. And the next. Lia seemed to have improved with Mary's constant company, and Nora felt both guilty and grateful. Grateful that Mary had the power to lift her daughter's spirits, and guilty because Nora could not seem to pull herself out of her own melancholy.

After Mrs. Spencer and Mary left on the fourth day, and Lia had gone to her lessons with her new maths tutor, Nora went to the stables. She couldn't have said why she wandered to a place that held such complicated memories, but eventually her feet carried her to Opal's stall. The Friesian sniffed at Nora's arm.

"I know. You likely don't even remember me since I haven't been here in a while," she said softly.

As if to contradict her, Opal nudged at Nora's hand.

Nora obliged the horse and rubbed her nose.

"Oh! Lady Coventry. I didn't see you there." George sounded startled. His eyes darted about, as though he contemplated scurrying away again. "Want me to saddle her for you, ma'am?"

Nora opened her mouth, for a moment forgetting her loss, her bone-deep sadness, but then it returned in full force. "No. Thank you."

"Right. Well, if you change your mind, let me know."

He began to scurry off, but before he could leave, she called out, "George?"

He made a *tch* sound, clearly sorry to have been stopped. "Yes'm?"

"Did you know?"

"Know what?"

"That Ridley was not who he claimed to be."

George scratched at his face and crept closer. "I didn't know. But then, he didn't act like the rest of us. Didn't talk like the rest of us. Didn't even stand like the rest of us. But . . . Ma'am, can I speak freely?"

She nodded.

"At first, I was mad that he'd lied. But the longer I think on it, the more I think he didn't ever lie. He didn't ever say, 'George, I'm not a lord or some such.' He didn't ever say, 'I was born in a hovel and have been poor like you my whole life.' What he did say was 'I'm here to work.' And then he worked. So, no, I didn't know. But he never said himself to be something he wasn't. I feel awful low that I didn't say a proper goodbye when he left. He tried to wish me well, but I was too bruised in my feelings to give him the time of day."

"I understand how you feel," she murmured.

George nodded, and she left him. Her anger regarding Ridley was mostly tempered, but the hurt remained a barbed point in her soul. She could not so much as reach into her memories of her time with him without pricking a finger on those barbs.

That evening, she sat at the pianoforte and plunked listlessly at the keys. Lia didn't complain, though the poor child had to be weary of the disconnected tune.

"I think I will go to bed," Lia said, her voice as flat and toneless as the music Nora had tortured all night.

"I think I should do the same." But she didn't. She did not walk Lia to her room. The energy to climb the stairs felt too much. She did not even rise from the bench she sat on.

Lia also seemed weighed down by the same heavy sorrow and desolation that had wrapped itself around the whole household. She all but dragged herself across the floor and out of the room.

Nora stayed at the pianoforte until a boom of thunder startled her to her feet. She hurried to the open doors leading to the back gardens, but instead of closing them, she stood and stared at the incoming storm.

After a few flashes of lightning, followed by the roll of thunder, the sprinkles of rain turned into a deluge. "Rain on me, will you? Haven't you heard? I'm a baroness!" Nora shouted and stepped onto the stone terrace and was about to walk down the steps when Lia called out above the storm.

"Mama! Where are you going?"

Nora stopped and blinked into the rain-soaked night. What had she been about to do? Where *had* she been going? She truly didn't know. She turned to her daughter standing in the open doorway.

"What are you doing up? I thought you'd gone to bed."

"The thunder was loud." Lia ran to her and hugged her with a ferocity that ached. "Were you going to leave me?" she asked.

Nora pulled away and dropped to her knees to draw Lia close to her. *I'm a mother.* "I'm not going anywhere," she said. "I'm staying here with you, my darling girl."

They stayed in the rain for several moments before Nora stood and took Lia into the house.

She didn't wake any of the staff to help get Lia warmed up and into dry clothes. She could not think of a suitable explanation for why she had been out of doors, and the thought of waking anyone embarrassed her. Besides, she found some sort of relief and happiness in drying Lia's chattering face and tangled hair. Nora bundled the girl into her arms and sat in the rocking chair in the nursery. She sang and rocked and pressed kisses atop Lia's head.

"I love you, Mama," the small, tired voice said from her arms.

"I love you, too, Lia. I am so glad you have come to be mine."

Nora fell asleep in the chair and awoke with her arms numb and tingling from Lia's weight. She gently eased Lia onto her bed, then stretched deeply to bring feeling back to her arms and legs, gritting her teeth against the pricking sensation as blood returned to her limbs. She rolled her neck to relieve the cramping. Pale light came from the windows; it was morning, if only just.

With Lia sleeping soundly, Nora headed to her own rooms but met Rebecca in the hall.

"Ma'am!" Her maid appeared rather frantic. "I was worried when I saw your bed had not been slept in." Rebecca's eyes trailed down Nora's dress. "Are you all right?"

Nora followed Rebecca's gaze. She had changed her clothes hastily after the rainstorm, eager to have warm, dry cloth next to her skin, but she saw now that she hadn't fastened anything correctly.

"I am well, thank you."

Rebecca sighed out the breath Nora was certain all the household still held. None of them knew quite what to do with Nora, which made sense since Nora didn't know quite what to do with herself. She barely even knew who she was anymore.

That wasn't true. *I am a baroness,* she thought. *I am a mother.*

Those identifying reminders no longer gave her the strength she needed. She remembered Ridley telling her that titles didn't make her a possession. What title was her strength now?

She lifted her chin when the answer came to her.

I am Eleanora Coventry.

Eleanora Coventry was a woman who happened to be a baroness, but more importantly, she was a mother who loved her children with her whole soul, a woman who would never give up. She was done waiting for anyone to answer her letters. She would travel to London herself and do what needed to be done.

"Rebecca, I will need to have my bags packed."

"You're going somewhere, ma'am?"

"Yes. We'll be returning to London for a while."

"What's the occasion?"

Nora squared her shoulders. "I am going to fight for my son."

Chapter Twenty-Six

Traveling with Peter was not the happiest of ways for Ridley to pass the time. Though he could hardly fault his brother for his own misery. The fire in Nora's eyes when she'd said her final goodbye had been his undoing.

Peter began to ramble to fill the silence between them. "Now that I understand where you've been this whole time, it's rather obvious. I truly do not know why I did not look in every stable from here to Devon in the first place."

Ridley stared out the window and said nothing. The English countryside rolled past, each turn of the carriage wheels putting distance between him and Nora. He felt like it was tearing him apart.

"I apologize I am not better company, but I do not expect you to understand why I left home," he said.

"No. That is something we can agree on. You left a comfortable home to live among livestock. To smell like manure. To work and labor with your hands each day. No. I do not understand."

"Our home was not as comfortable for me as it was for you, you'll remember."

Peter grunted. "Right. Quite right. I am sorry about that. And I've already said as much, but I will continue to say it if it makes you feel better."

"It does not make me feel better," Ridley said.

They traveled on in silence for several minutes. Ridley turned back to the window, glad for the respite from conversation. He needed to untangle his thoughts.

When his brother began talking again, Ridley wondered if Peter had any ability to withstand the quiet. "You are not unhappy with me, but you are unhappy. Has this something to do with the baroness?"

Ridley jerked his head sharply back to his brother. "No. That is done. She will not have me."

"Ah, so it has *everything* to do with the baroness." Peter seemed to enjoy getting a small rise out of Ridley. "How interesting. She would have a stable boy but not the son of a duke."

"Yes. She is a woman of good sense—one of the few true members of human society who has more *humanity* than *society* in her. I have never respected her more than I do at this moment."

"And yet, she rejected you for it." Peter shrugged, his forehead furrowing in confusion.

"No. She rejected me for my lack of humanity. I could have intervened in her son's plight, and I did not. She is right to have called me a coward. I have been running for so long, it never occurred to me that I could have chosen to stand and fight."

Too late. Ridley had realized his error too late.

Gratefully, Peter fell quiet and left Ridley to his own brooding regrets.

The travel back to Devon took much longer than Ridley had imagined. Peter, it seemed, had many friends, and he apparently felt obliged to visit all of them. "To reintroduce you into society," Peter had said.

With every introduction, Peter made it clear that Ridley had his full support and protection. He would not have his brother disparaged. Ridley felt certain that was the purpose of their circuitous and lengthy journey. Peter wanted all of England to know that the Devonshire name was not available for the mockery and censure of others.

On the fifth such stop, and the eighth day since leaving Windsong, they were visiting Peter's old friend Edward Stanley, the

Earl of Derby. Lord Derby's round belly matched his round head, but he also had an easy humor and gossiping tongue that flapped far more than even George's had in the stables.

"You'll never guess who's gone and found himself a ward," Lord Derby said while they walked to his carriage house so he could show off his new barouche.

Peter grinned. "Have you gone soft?"

"You guess me? Oh no! Not I. I barely like my own children. I can't imagine purposely taking on someone else's. No. But the one who has is far less likely a candidate. Lord Grimes. He's apparently found some sort of *charity*." Lord Derby laughed as though he'd made an excellent joke.

"No!" Peter exclaimed. "But what would a man who hates everybody want with a child?"

"He's apparently in some financial trouble. Poor handling of his property mixed with a love of the darker entertainments. His gambling debts stretch from shore to shore, I hear. His ward comes with a rather large financial allowance, enough to keep Lord Grimes from needing to sell off any more of his land."

They entered the carriage house. Ridley could not help but compare it to the one he'd managed at Windsong, immediately noting the inefficiencies and all the places needing improvement and attention, but he kept his mouth closed. Peter would not like it if Ridley began giving advice on how to maintain such a space. He was a gentleman now, not a stable master.

"Poor child," Peter said.

"Indeed."

"How did he manage to gain access to the boy?" Peter asked.

Ridley only half listened as he inspected the carriage house doors. They weren't hung properly, leaving gaps at the bottom and too much overlap at the top.

"I hear he has dealings with a litany of soiled sources. The young baron comes from a place not too far from where Lord Grimes is located. Kendal, I think. Now look at this!" Lord Derby spread his hands wide to the shiny barouche. Lord Derby looked at both Peter and Ridley to admire his new conveyance, but Ridley's blood had turned to ice.

"Young baron from Kendal, you say?" Ridley asked. It had suddenly become too hot to breathe in the carriage house. Ridley wanted to claw his cravat away from his throat.

"Yes. Lord Coventry of Kendal. The boy's father died last year. Sad business, really."

Peter quickly turned to Ridley, watching him carefully.

"If you'll excuse me a moment," Ridley said, even as he turned and left the carriage house. Once outside, he tore off his cravat to ease the pressure around his throat. He sat on a narrow wall separating the main yard from the stable yard, trying to breathe.

Young Edward was in the hands of Lord Grimes. Ridley didn't know much of the man beyond the rumors that he was horrible to his servants and couldn't keep a decent groom in his stables. That Edward should be used in such a manner for his fortune was staggering to consider.

Though Ridley hadn't much cared for the late baron, he had to admit that the man had been careful to hire intelligent stewards to see that his lands were profitable. There was money to be had in the Barony of Kendal. Ridley was certain the late baron never intended for his heir and financial holdings to go to one of the most irresponsible lords in the peerage. He could not conceive of how such a scheme had been planned out, let alone executed to the point where Nora had lost her son to such dark dealings.

Peter exited the carriage house after a few moments and joined Ridley. "I already hear your feet running, brother."

"Running?"

"Back. In your mind, you're already there. In your heart, you never really left. Your feet will follow soon enough."

Ridley eyed his brother. "I am not running anywhere. I shall not return. I was banished." He took a deep breath. "I need a favor, Peter."

"I know."

"We'll need to stop in London."

Peter nodded. "Convenient, since I've already planned on stopping there."

"I'd like to leave now."

Peter rolled his eyes. "I'm sure you would, but Lord Derby has invited us to take a meal with him. I'm famished, and I know from experience that his cook is truly accomplished. We'll eat. Then we will give our apologies and be on our way."

"Thank you."

Peter's expression fell. "I know you don't quite trust me yet. But please know that I am *not* the monster Alexander was and that I do care for you and your well-being. We will help the young baron. If we are unable to return the boy to his mother, I will acquire a writ from the Chancery giving the child to me instead. Then I will bring the baroness to Devon. My Anne will be delighted to have a child in the house. And though I've not had the pleasure of meeting Lady Coventry because you left me in a carriage, I'm sure she and Anne will get along famously."

Ridley blinked back the tears in his eyes. When his mother died, he had not believed he had any chance at a familial relationship with anyone. When Peter had found him at Windsong, he had not believed they could forge a genuine relationship. He only left with Peter because he had no other choice. Now, a new feeling emerged. Peter *was* his brother, in every sense of the word. They were going to be all right.

Peter clapped Ridley on the shoulder. "Let me remind Lord Derby that we are famished. Perhaps that will hurry along his need to salivate over his barouche." Peter disappeared into the carriage house, emerging only moments later with Lord Derby.

The brothers ate as quickly as they could while still being considered polite, and once they were on the road again, Ridley felt glad they had stayed for the meal as it would sustain them through the journey to London. All the better that the food had been everything Peter had promised it would be.

Peter went over details of the people who would be in the best position to petition the Chancery on the young baron's behalf. He also planned on writing his own assessment regarding the matter. "I did visit the lands and the manor. No one need know I only saw what was visible from behind these curtains." Peter swiped at the blue curtains with the top of his walking cane.

"There was nothing to see aside from pain and sorrow."

"Don't worry, Ridlington. Once Lady Coventry has her son in her arms, she will welcome you to her arms as well. She will not be able to stay angry for long."

"I wish you were right. But alas, I do not ask this favor of you so that I might win her back to me. A man cannot always act with the hope of reward. Sometimes he must act because it is the right thing to do."

Peter looked at him doubtfully. "That sounds very noble. But I say the reward does not tarnish the deed."

Ridley let out a small laugh. "I suppose not. But there is no reward to be had here. She is well and truly done with me. Reuniting her with her family is the only way I will be able to proceed with my life knowing she will not be part of it."

"As you say, brother." Peter stretched out his legs and closed his eyes.

Ridley tried to rest, but his back ached, and his muscles had cramped almost as soon as he'd folded himself back into the carriage. Still, he did not regret that they were already on the road. There was much to be done to persuade the Chancery to retract the writ they'd given to the solicitor and Lord Grimes. No doubt Mr. Ashby had been paid a tidy sum to make such an event occur.

When Peter declared that he would put up some of his own coin to emancipate the young baron, Ridley had shown him his own funds that he could donate to the cause. Peter had laughed and told him to stop being vulgar.

Ridley frowned. He really had been away from the lifestyle of his family for a long time. His savings were far from small in his own eyes, but his brother had looked at the few coins as though they belonged jangling in a child's pocket.

Had he ever been so cavalier regarding money? He didn't think so, at least not that he could remember. If he had ever been so careless as a boy, he resolved to never be so careless as a man. He would remember the gnawing vacancy in his belly when he'd been between work opportunities. He would remember the pain in his hands and feet from the cold. He would remember *want* so he might be able to help keep others from its snapping jaws.

Not that he had money of his own aside from that small savings his brother had recently mocked. Not really. He had been a penniless stable hand for far too long. His elevation to stable master was still too recent to have allowed him to acquire savings. How had Nora loved him as such when she would not love him as a titled gentleman?

He imagined no other woman in the country would make such a choice.

Which was why she was the only woman he wanted.

He remembered the little rhyme taught to him in the nursery: *If wishes were horses . . .*

But they weren't. Wishes were wishes. And they seldom came true.

Chapter Twenty-Seven

Nora and Lia had been in London for almost a month with little success. It seemed anyone who had any power to help felt disinclined to be bothered with her affairs. While several women who held sway over their husbands were more than happy to have her to tea, nothing came of those meetings except to foment excess gossip in the *ton*.

Nora's discouragement in the past had always led her to inactivity. Failing to accomplish a task merely increased her insecurities and paralyzed her. But she was not the same woman she had been. Now, each discouragement fueled her to greater action. She would not be bested by these challenges. Her son would not be kept from her. Everything she had learned about Lord Grimes underscored her initial impression that the man had a despicable reputation.

As Nora mentally mapped out her day, Lia joined her for breakfast. Nora set aside her worry to focus on her daughter, who was also dealing with the loss of Edward. Nora asked Lia questions to keep her engaged and gave her full attention to the answers. Serving her daughter in even that small way filled her as well. It forced her to stop sulking and to step outside herself long enough to see the needs of others.

What would I do without Lia to remind me how to be human? Nora wondered to herself.

Lia had gone upstairs when the footman handed Nora the day's mail. She frowned at an envelope written in a hand she did not recognize and cracked open the seal.

She read the letter.

Then read it again.

"It can't be true," Nora said aloud.

She read it a third time, and she jumped to her feet and ran from the room.

"Lia!" she shouted.

Lia's face peered out from the banisters at the top of the stairs. "Yes, Mama?"

"I'm going out. I've no time to waste, but I will hopefully return soon."

"Where are you going?"

"To retrieve your brother."

"Lady Eleanora Coventry, sir," the footman announced from inside the room.

Nora stood outside the chambers of Lord Andrews, one of the Chancery judges. She heard a man's low rumbling voice, and she was then ushered inside.

Lord Andrews stood as soon as she entered. She had to tilt her head back to look the elderly man in the eye. He gave a brief bow, though it caused him to wince and press his hand to his lower back. "Lady Coventry. I'm so pleased you received my letter and were able to come so quickly. Please, do be seated. It is good to meet you as I've heard so much about you."

"You say you have my son?" she asked, unwilling to be sidetracked with banal tea-time conversation. She had fretted for the entire journey and could wait not another moment.

"Yes. Well, not here exactly. He'll be here presently so you may verify his safety for yourself. Of course, he is quite impatient to verify your safety as well. He's been worried for your well-being."

"How did my son come so far south?" Nora asked. She'd spent the carriage ride trying to make sense of the snippets of information the letter contained.

Lord Andrews folded his wrinkled, papery hands in front of him on the desk. "He had apparently traveled here with Lord Grimes, who was here on business. It worked out most fortuitous as it saved my office from traveling so far north to ascertain the situation with Lord Grimes. We'd received your many letters bearing testimony regarding Mr. Ashby's duplicitous behavior toward you and your son. We apologize for any delay—we were having that testimony corroborated by others of the peerage. We are happy to report we have concluded our investigation and found that you were treated most unfairly. Your son is on his way to you now."

"What of Mr. Ashby?" she asked.

"Evidence has come to light that you are not his only victim. As of last night, he was brought to jail and is awaiting trial. Your testimony has been most helpful, Lady Coventry."

She breathed deeply in relief. Mr. Ashby was no longer involved in her affairs. She would be able to manage her own life from that moment on. What was it that had worked such a marvel in her life? Had it been her many letters? This other testimony? "You mentioned someone corroborated my testimony?"

Before Lord Andrews could respond, a knock came at the door. "Enter," Lord Andrews said.

"He's here, sir," the footman said.

"Well, bring him in! We don't skulk around doors like criminals. We enter or we exit."

"Of course, sir." He opened the door wider.

"Edward!" Nora shot out of her seat and rushed to her son, enveloping him in her arms. She had expected him to pull away or insist he did not need her sentimentality, but he returned her embrace wholeheartedly.

"Mama! I am glad to see you. Are you well?"

"Am I well? How can you be worried about me? Are *you* well? How are you here? How was this all managed?"

Edward laughed and finally pulled away. Nora reluctantly released him but did not take her eyes from him. She feared he might disappear again if she looked away.

"It looks like everything is as it should be, then," Lord Andrews said. He'd lumbered to his feet when Nora had stood and was now ambling toward the door. "I regret I cannot enjoy your reunion longer, but today's business is quite full, and as your affairs have been managed, I must untangle the rest." He gestured with his arm as if sweeping them from his office. "I'll have his things sent to your London address. I am glad things have worked well for you all. Lord Coventry. Lady Coventry." He bowed to them both, a soft moan emerging as he pressed his hand to the small of his back again.

Nora took her son's hand and left.

She had expected the entire affair to be far more involved. She had expected to wait for hours. She had expected to have to weep and wail and argue her position. She had not expected to be hurried along and deposited with her son on the front steps with little to no ceremony and no arguing at all.

She laughed and stared down at her boy with wonder.

"Well, then," she said. "For home?"

"Of course. Lia's been far too long without a good tease. I have much to make up for."

Nora laughed again. Where she had felt hollowed out before, she was full to brimming with happiness. Her son was hers again.

As soon as they arrived home, Lia almost knocked Edward over in her rush to hug him. As he had done for Nora, he allowed Lia to hold him for a moment before he gently shoved her away and said, "Enough of that. Get off me already."

She did not take offense, only gazed at him in much the same way Nora still did. They all retired to the drawing room so Edward could share his adventures since they had last seen him a month and half prior. Edward sat in his father's chair as he had done before they'd left London for Windsong—but he didn't fit in it the same way he had before. He filled the chair and—by extension—the room with comfort and confidence. The London home had always seemed cold and unrelenting to her, but now it felt warm and welcoming. She marveled at the change that could come from such a simple act.

"Was Lord Grimes terrible?" Lia asked as she sat upon the sofa across from Edward's chair. "His name sounds terrible."

In another instance, Nora might have gently chastised her daughter for being indelicate, but in this moment, she agreed too much. She sat next to Lia and awaited the answer.

"He was ridiculous, honestly." Edward rolled his eyes. "I've never heard such strange ideas. He was sure his house was haunted by chickens because he said he could hear them clucking at night. And he tried to pay me to poison his neighbor's prize hunting dog so that he wouldn't look bad when they went hunting together. Luckily, he was too preoccupied with drinking and muttering to his paintings to be too much concerned with me."

"What did you do the whole time you were with him?" Lia asked.

"I wandered his house, mostly, which was in terrible repair and wretchedly dirty. And I wandered his grounds, which weren't much better than the house. I consider the whole adventure as a good education on how to be a baron."

"Really? A good education?" Nora eyed her son skeptically.

"Of course. You can learn a lot by a man's bad example. Mr. Ellis taught me that."

Nora scoffed at the idea. "I suppose he *is* the man to teach such things, seeing how he has proven to be such a bad example."

Edward raised his eyebrows at her. "Has he, Mama? In what way?"

Nora floundered for a response. "He lied to me, to us, to everyone, regarding his identity. He put himself forward to be something he was not. And he failed to help us in our moment of need." *In my moment of need,* she thought.

Edward shook his head. "No, that can't be. He's the one who alerted the Chancery to Lord Grimes and Mr. Ashby's plot to steal my money by claiming me as Grimes's ward. Without him and his brother, I would not be here with you."

"Mr. Ellis did that?" The news could not have surprised her more.

"Lord Andrews tells me it is Lord Ridlington now, not Mr. Ellis. That was a surprise, I tell you."

The reminder of his title and position made her clamp her mouth closed with a clack of her teeth. She pretended the news of Ridley being instrumental in returning her son to her did not affect her. She did not let her thoughts wander into the wilds of her imaginations. She instead forced herself to listen as Edward regaled them with stories of Lord Grimes's snuffling and loud snoring every night and of the dreadful food since Grimes could apparently not keep a decent cook employed. He said that Mr. Ashby had told him to mind his tongue and manners and to not be in the way of Lord Grimes.

"I reminded Mr. Ashby that he would be wise to consider that he was addressing a baron when he spoke to me."

"What did he say to that?" Lia asked, her eyes wide at her brother's boldness.

Edward smirked. "He was always quick to apologize and say that it was my very position he was trying to protect. He isn't a very good liar, for anyone could see his intent had nothing to do with protecting me. I had many grievances through the whole of it. But that reminds me!" He stood and hurried from the room.

When he returned, he held the satchel he'd packed at Windsong. He reached inside and carefully extracted Lia's doll. "Thank you for letting me borrow her. You were right. She is a very good listener."

Lia's mouth fell open and her exclamation of delight was joy itself. "She is!" Lia agreed, hugging the doll to her chest.

The day passed beautifully as Nora watched and listened to her children talk and play together.

After she'd seen them both off to bed and had checked on them for the second time to be certain they were both still there, she returned to the drawing room. Mrs. Herold, the housekeeper at their London home, had prepared a tray of tea, cold meats, cheeses, and fruits.

"It is good to see you like this, ma'am," Mrs. Herold said.

"See me like what?" Nora asked.

"Happy."

Nora allowed a small laugh. "You say that as if you've never seen such a thing before."

Mrs. Herold folded a blanket Lia had left on the floor. "I don't think I have ever seen you enjoy this particular sort of happiness. It suits you if I may say so."

When Mrs. Herold had gone, Nora mulled over the comment. She could not deny the truthfulness of her housekeeper's words. She was happy in a way she was sure she'd never been before in London, but she was not as happy as she knew she could be. There had been those few blissful weeks when her children were well and safe and blossoming in Windsong and when she'd also had the assurance of Ridley's love. *That* had been happiness that had suited her.

But Mrs. Herold was right that while Nora had previously been in London, she had not had the smallest idea of what true happiness could be. She had not had the smallest notion of her own strength. She felt gratified to learn of her own capabilities and the depth of her love.

And though she had told Ridley she had no need of him, she wished he could see this version of her. She wished she had not lied to him when she'd said she'd wanted nothing to do with him. Why had she allowed her anguish to speak for her?

Even after all the hateful things she had said to him, Ridley had used his influence to reunite her with her son. How could she ever repay such a gift? How could she express the depths of her gratitude?

She could not go see him. Ridley had to have known she was coming to London but had very likely left for Devon already. Certainly, she would have heard news if the Duke of Devon and his eligible younger brother were still in London. There had been no such gossip, which had to mean he was out of her reach.

She gazed out the window and frowned. "What are you doing at this moment, Ridley?" she murmured. "And what must you think of me?"

The next morning, Lia brought a handful of hollyhocks into the drawing room. Her fingers wove the flowers together into a doll as she inserted a thin stick that Edward had sharpened for her through the whole of it to keep the pieces together. She talked while she worked.

"I've heard that Mr. Ellis is still in town with his brother, the duke. That's strange to say, isn't it? *His brother, the duke.* Though I suppose his name is not really Mr. Ellis. It is Lord Ridlington. That sounds imposing, doesn't it? Do you think he will mind very much if I continue to call him Mr. Ellis? It's shorter and much easier to say."

Nora gaped, feeling her breath catch. Ridley *was* in town. Her heart stammered in her chest at the thought that he was so close.

"Mama?" Lia said.

Edward shrugged. "Don't mind her, Lia. You've given her a surprise, that's all."

"What surprise?" Lia asked.

"She didn't know Lord Ridlington was still here."

Lia groaned. "If you're going to call him Lord Ridlington, then he'll surely expect me to do the same."

"How did you come to hear such news?" Nora asked.

"Rebecca told me while she was removing the papers from my hair." Lia swung her head to make her curls bounce.

Nora brought herself under control. Ridley had to have heard she'd been reunited with Edward and was staying in London for a short while. He knew where she was but had not come to see her. That meant he did not wish to see her.

She didn't blame him. She had been horrible to him when they had parted. She had shouted and accused him most shamefully.

"You should pay him a call, Mama." Edward's voice broke into her thoughts.

"What?"

"Lord Ridlington. You should pay him a call."

Heat flooded her cheeks, and her mind stuttered and stammered that her son should give her such a direction. "Oh, no. I do not believe that would be appropriate."

Edward watched her with his head tilted, as if he could not understand what he saw. "Will you not see him because you love him, and that makes you afraid?"

"Mama loves Mr. Ellis?" Lia asked.

"No!" she insisted. "Why would you say that?"

"I'm not blind. I saw the two of you together."

"How could I love him when he was our stable master?"

"He's the brother of a duke," Edward said. "Besides, he was never just our stable master. He was our friend."

Why was it suddenly so hot in the drawing room? "What would people think of me throwing myself in the path of my previous stable master?"

That was not the reason she would not see him. But it was a good enough reason to tell the children. The truth was that she feared he despised her, and she did not think she could bear to see that feeling reflected in his eyes.

Edward put down the book he'd been reading. "Mama, Mr. Ellis taught me that it is important I respect myself. If I do not respect myself, how will others know how to follow? And if I choose the opinions of society over the company of a good and decent man who makes you happy, that would make me someone I could not respect. So do not turn him away on my account. At the very least, we must thank him for the service he has given us."

Hot tears stung Nora's eyelids. "Why, Edward." She could scarcely see him through the blur. "It would appear you've grown up much more than I had thought over these last months."

"Yes, well. I don't feel very grown-up sometimes," he admitted with a shrug that showed the truth of his words.

"I don't feel very grown-up sometimes either," Nora said. They grinned at each other.

"Mama, I love you, but I might not *like* you very much if you do not go see Lord Ridlington. I like him. I'm certain Lia does too."

Lia, who had become engrossed in building her dolls, looked up at the mention of her name. "Who do I like?"

"Lord Ridlington," Edward answered.

"I don't like Lord Ridlington." Her response surprised them both.

"You don't?" Nora asked.

"I *love* him! He saved Bonnie, and he listens to me when I talk, and he doesn't say I ramble on and on."

"And on and on and on," Edward added.

She narrowed her eyes at him, but he ignored her, turning again to Nora. "What we're saying, Mama, is that we don't know why you're still sitting here with us when you should be going and talking to him."

"I do not know how to begin a conversation with him. The last time we spoke, I shouted and threw him from the house."

"You could start with hello and see how he answers."

"But he won't be home," Lia said.

"Where will he be?" Nora and Edward asked at the same time.

"Rebecca said he and his brother, the duke, would be attending Lord Andrews's ball tonight."

Edward smiled. "Weren't you planning on going to that ball? You really should get dressed, Mama. You don't want to be late." He picked up his book as if that was the end of that.

Nora scowled at her son. She'd accepted the invitation to the ball but had decided that morning that she would have to send apologies because she wasn't quite ready to leave her children for a whole evening.

"Mama. Go," Edward insisted.

Nora stood, her heart both eager and terrified. "He must hate me after how I treated him."

"Only one way to find out," Lia said in a singsong voice.

Edward nodded.

Only one way to find out.

Chapter Twenty-Eight

Ridley rolled his eyes at his brother. "No. For the last time."

"You're right. That is the last no I will hear from you, since I require that you say yes. It will be fun. Besides, I hate going to these things by myself, and Anne is in Devon, so it must be you who accompanies me. Anne says I'm incredibly stupid in social gatherings."

"I'm not in a position to argue with your wife, but I believe she could have just as accurately ended that sentence at *stupid.*" He eyed his brother, who was already dressed for the ball, and thought of all the things he no longer knew how to do in society. Peter had already had him tailored with appropriate clothing for all occasions, but Ridley had no sense of how to feel comfortable in any of it. "I don't even remember the last time I danced."

"So don't dance. I will keep you occupied well enough to prevent you from being forced to the dance floor by some overzealous mama looking to marry off her daughter." Peter glanced in the mirror and readjusted his jacket.

"That's why you want me to go. You're looking to marry me off to an overzealous mama's daughter."

Peter laughed, but Ridley felt certain he'd hit the mark.

"Think of it as you owing me a favor for the favor I have done, and continue to do, for you." Peter turned to his valet. "See that my brother is dressed well enough to catch the eye of every overzealous mama with an eligible daughter."

Ridley would have argued, but Peter had already left the room. He would be attending a ball despite having no desire to do so. He had no desire to do anything at all.

That wasn't entirely true. There were a great many things he wanted to do, but the person he wanted to be laughing, walking, and riding with, the person he wanted to *be* with, would not want his company. He had secretly hoped she would pay him a visit while he was still in London, but she hadn't.

Regardless, he took some happiness in knowing that Nora's family was all together, even if they were all together without him. At least Peter had stopped making jokes about every knock on the door being Ridley's beloved, finally seeing that such teasing was incrementally killing Ridley.

Ridley allowed the valet to dress him. Maybe a dance would do him some good. Maybe getting out of the house and away from his thoughts would push away some of the torment in his own soul.

After having been oiled and combed and dressed and brushed enough to garner his brother's approval, he was stuffed into the carriage and on his way to the ball being held by Lord Andrews.

"Showing up to his party is the least we can do, considering he went to such lengths to liberate the young baron. Though truth be told, I think he enjoyed dressing down Lord Grimes the way he did." Peter grinned.

Ridley did not remember Peter grinning so much when they'd been children. He had remembered a quiet, sober Peter. He knew that hadn't always been the case. Before their mother passed, they had been happy, laughing together often. She calmed Alexander's temper and offered a protection over Peter and Ridley they hadn't realized was there until it was gone.

"I am glad you forced me to come with you," Ridley said.

"Are you?" Peter sounded intrigued. "Why?"

"Because I have just happened upon a memory of us as young boys and you learning to dance. As I recall, you were dreadful. Mama spent a prodigious amount of time coaxing you out of your room and promising that Alexander would not be allowed to laugh at you."

"Ah, Mama." Peter's voice softened. "Her gentle voice often quelled the most wretched storm. I recall those days as well. You were too young to have started lessons, but Mama allowed you to go wherever we were. Your lessons came a few years later."

"Much good they did me since I truly cannot recall a single thing I might have learned. And with dance styles changing so often, what chance do I have of not tripping over every foot in the party?"

The carriage stopped outside Lord Andrews's estate. Ready or not, Ridley was about to be thrust back into society with one great shove instead of with Peter's gentle, individual nudges. His entire reputation would be formed in this one evening. With everything Peter had done for him, Ridley knew he needed to make certain that reputation was one worthy of a duke.

They exited the carriage and were announced as they descended the stairs to the ballroom. Ridley felt as though all eyes were on him, but he reminded himself that all eyes were likely on the Duke of Devon. Who would care whether the duke's brother was at his side?

Music poured from the instruments as a dance kicked up. Laughter floated around him at dizzying speeds. It seemed everyone wanted to speak with Peter, and so the brothers would walk three steps and stop to exchange greetings with one group, walk four steps more and stop to exchange greetings with another group.

With each greeting, Peter pointed to Ridley. "Have you had the pleasure of meeting my brother, Ridlington Devonshire?" If Ridley's reputation had been known already, no one dared mention it with Peter around.

"Do you dance, sir?" an older woman asked, her daughter by her side.

Ridley could not recall her name despite their introduction, but the tune was one Ridley knew and the steps were ones he was sure he could manage.

"I do on occasion. As luck would have it, this is one of those occasions. If you would be so good as to direct me to a partner?"

"My daughter, Miss Oakley, loves to dance." She gave her daughter an encouraging nudge. The girl was pretty but looked barely older than George.

"If you would do me the honor, Miss Oakley?" Ridley asked.

The girl blushed. Peter beamed. The mother all but cackled in delight.

He led Miss Oakley to the dance floor. "I hope you'll forgive me if I stumble. I am a bit out of practice." He wanted to be quick with his apology so the girl would hopefully be quick with her forgiveness.

She asked him several questions about himself, though he kept his answers vague; she did not really want to know what he'd been doing the last thirteen years of his life. He deflected the questions back to her. She said something he was certain he was to take as a joke, so he laughed politely, though he hadn't truly understood what she meant. His laughter cut off when he heard the announcement of the next guest.

Lady Eleanora Coventry, Baroness of Kendal.

Her eyes met his, but her face showed no expression of either pleasure or pain regarding him. Devil take him, could she feel nothing at all for him? She descended the stairs to the ballroom floor. He tracked her every step and longed for the music to come to a halt.

He managed to continue dancing without tripping or falling, but he did not know how much longer he could pretend interest in the girl before him when the woman he desired had disappeared into the crowd.

The music ended, and he was finally able to deliver the young lady back to her mother.

Peter tried to pull him into another conversation, but Ridley whispered in Peter's ear, "She's here."

It was enough. Peter waved Ridley away to find Nora. He headed toward where he had last seen her, his pace just short of a run.

He found her alone on the terrace. He was glad she was in such a secluded place; he wanted to speak to her without interruption. He took a step forward, and when she turned around, their eyes locked.

She didn't look away.

"You're here," he said. He'd been so afraid she would look away and not acknowledge him. Her eyes filled him with a hope he thought had died.

"I am here," she said. "*We're* here. Aren't we?"

He wasn't sure why she phrased it that way. Did she mean that they were together in this moment, or did she mean she hoped to be together at long last and forever?

He hoped for the latter, but in case she meant the former, he spoke first.

"I'm sorry. I'm sorry I didn't tell you the truth regarding my identity." He offered her a bow. "Allow me to introduce myself. I am Lord Ridlington Parker Devonshire, younger brother to the Duke of Devon. I am the next in line to inherit the title and property, though I don't know that such information would actually recommend me to you."

She opened her mouth as if to interject, but he hurried on.

"I ran away from home when I was sixteen. My mother had passed away five years prior, and during those five years, I endured incredible torture at the hands of my eldest brother. When I last saw him, Alexander had been drinking and was complaining that our mother had given me my father's pocket watch. He demanded that it was his. When I refused to give it to him, he threatened my life.

"We struggled, and I hit him hard enough to knock him over. He'd been drinking and was clumsy. He was hurt badly but not badly enough to worry me. But I knew from experience that once he'd sobered up, his anger would become deadly.

"I left my pocket watch with him so he couldn't accuse me of stealing it, took my horse, and ran. Later, when I realized he'd accused me of stealing the horse and trying to take his life, I knew I could never safely return home. So I kept running. And I kept lying. I am only sorry that I lied to you."

She had listened attentively to his tale, her expression filled with both sorrow and pity. "I did not come here to dredge up a painful past for you," she said. "I'm sorry you have endured so much. I wish I had any power to relieve you of the pain that is still evident in your heart." She offered a sympathetic smile. "I came tonight to thank you for all you did for Edward. I am in your debt."

Every word she said sounded like goodbye to him. She came only to say thank you, not because she wanted to be with him.

"You owe me nothing, Lady Coventry. I only did what I ought to have done from the first."

"Your duty does you credit, sir." She lowered her gaze and folded her arms in front of her.

Why did she seem hurt? "Lady Coventry, have I offended you just now?"

"No. Yes. Perhaps."

Though the answer confused him, his happiness depended on clarity. "In what way?"

"You continue to call me Lady Coventry." Her eyes brimmed with tears. "I know I told you to refer to me as such, but had I known how much it would hurt to hear you speak so formally, I would never have allowed such words to leave my mouth. I'm sorry, Ridley. I am so sorry I sent you away."

"Nora, please don't cry."

"I'm not crying." She sniffed.

He would not tease her though, for his own eyes filled with unshed tears. "Nora, do you still love me?"

"Ridley, how could I not?"

Relief flooded him. "I fear I have given you too many reasons, but I am grateful for your answer. I asked because I still love you. And I wondered if perhaps you would do me the honor of allowing me to introduce you to my brother. He will tease us and ask us impertinent questions such as whether we shall marry in the future." He took a deep breath. "And I wondered if you would allow me to answer him that yes, we will marry?"

She glanced into the ballroom where couples danced and musicians played. "Are you serious? Here and now, you're asking me that?"

"I've never been more serious."

"Then you should not delay another moment in introducing me to your brother." A smile blossomed on her face, and he wanted nothing more than to take her in his arms and kiss her and kiss her and kiss her.

He took her hand and led her back into the ballroom. As he searched the crowd for Peter, he caught many curious looks from those who noticed he had a firm hold on Nora's hand. He had no time to worry about what society might think when he had a brother to find and an engagement to declare.

He spotted Peter speaking with a small group. He placed Nora's hand in the crook of his arm and led her through the crowd. They were forced to stop several times so Nora could politely address someone who wanted to talk. They would raise their eyebrows when they noted that Ridley did not leave her side. He offered polite smiles. He was grateful Peter came to them.

After the happy news was shared, Nora thanked Peter for his intervention regarding Edward.

Peter brushed her off. "It was all my brother's doing. He loves you, you know."

Nora smiled at Ridley. "I do know."

Ridley took her hand and pressed his lips to her gloved fingers. "Would you care to dance? I am not a wonderful dancer, but I think I can manage a waltz. I can think of no better way to celebrate our future together than with our first dance."

She allowed him to lead her to the floor where several couples were already moving to the music. "This is not our first dance," she said.

They stepped into position, and he shot her a look of confusion. "I'm sure I would remember if we—".

"I was six years old. We were in Devon, and I was learning to dance. At first, I danced with a boy who called me clumsy and made me cry. I swore to never dance again. But then a different boy, one who loved to ride horses, offered me a piece of pie if I would try again. I would not have remembered except that when I entered the ballroom this evening, you were dancing to that same song we practiced together all those years ago."

He held her close as they moved together across the dance floor. "It would seem we are meant to be."

"It would seem so."

He wondered what the gossip columns would say regarding the duke's wayward younger brother and the widowed baroness. He imagined some of them would be unkind—not that it would matter since Nora and he would never read them—but perhaps one or two of them would get it right as they told a story of love, loyalty, and a match meant to be.

Epilogue

"Mama! Mama! Do hurry! I've waited long enough!" Lia said loudly.

Nora felt certain the child had been heard all the way to Lancaster. She increased her pace because her daughter was accurate. She *had* waited long enough.

Ridley's gaze was on her as she approached, the contented smile never seeming to leave his face. Seeing him waiting for her brought a smile to her own lips.

Edward and Lia and Nora's soon-to-be sister-in-law, Anne, stood near him in the field, all of them clearly impatient to get on with it.

"All right. I'm here. Let us see this spectacular, long-awaited event, shall we?" Nora said.

Lia grinned and allowed Ridley to lift her onto the saddle on Bonnie's back. Bonnie flicked her tail, unconcerned, and when Lia clucked her tongue, the horse began a pleasant, steady walk.

"Do be careful, darling." But even before the words had left Nora's mouth, Lia had eased Bonnie into a canter. Lia was relaxed and steady as she rode Bonnie around the exercise yard. "Are you sure she's safe?" Nora asked Ridley.

"I would never let her on a horse I was not confident she could handle."

He'd said as much at least a dozen times already, but Nora felt certain she would ask a dozen times more.

"Is Uncle Peter really not coming until the day after tomorrow?" Edward asked, already bored of watching his sister ride her horse.

"He said tomorrow in his last letter, but I'm planning on him the day after that because Peter is by far the worst dawdler I've ever met. The last time I traveled with him, it took an entire year to get to London."

Edward laughed at the exaggeration.

Nora loved the sound of her son's laughter. But she scolded both of them for abusing Peter. "He will not be so casual with time when he knows we require his presence at the wedding."

Anne agreed.

"Fine, he will likely arrive tomorrow." Ridley gave Edward a sly grin. "While your mama and I are away on our wedding trip, please take my brother on a tour of your lands and tell him all the ways he could be a more effective duke."

The banns had been read, and the wedding would be in three days. Peter's wife, Anne, had been staying with the family since they'd returned to Windsong. Her presence helped maintain propriety until the wedding took place. Nora, who'd been an only child, was continually delighted by how well she and Anne got on and the way Anne doted on the children. Edward went to walk with his aunt, likely because she told stories about Peter that made Edward laugh.

Nora leaned into Ridley and sighed.

"What is it you're thinking?" Ridley whispered in her ear as they watched Lia.

Nora considered all the unexpected happenings in her life that had allowed her to be surrounded by so much love. "Ridiculous fancy."

"Is that a good thing?" he asked.

"Yes." She stood on tiptoe and kissed him, loving the soft warmth of him. "The education has been a long time coming, but I've learned that ridiculous fancy is perfect."

Acknowledgments

So much love goes to Heidi Gordon and Lisa Mangum. I love how much you both help me grow as a writer. To the entire Shadow Mountain team, I can never be grateful enough. You are all such a huge part of every page. Thank you!

Writing is a solitary business, but writing friends make it less so. I have a huge writing family who encourage me, champion me, and take care of me. You all know who you are. Thank you all for being my friends. It matters. So much.

I am lucky enough to have an incredibly supportive and amazing mom and dad. Let's be real—without them, I wouldn't even be here.

So much gratitude goes to my children—McKenna, Dwight, Merrik, Charisma, Chandler, and Julianna (plus my grandbabies, Theo and Lily)—for putting up with all of my weird. It's not easy.

I can never be grateful enough for my husband, Scott, who always believes in me, always supports me, and always holds my hand through the hard stuff. *Du är min lyckliga någonsin efter. Du är min alltid.* Thanks for always making dinner. I really do hate cooking. I love that you know and accept that about me.

And finally, thanks, Heavenly Father. There was a gorgeous rainstorm today and I just want to say, I love you too.

Discussion Questions

1. Nora struggles with her own sense of identity. She focuses on her titles but ultimately finds her greatest strength is in who she is as a person, not as a title. In what ways do we focus on our titles rather than ourselves as a whole?

2. In Nora's journey to discovering herself, she grapples with the expectations of society and often succumbs to the pressures of her day as she worries about rumors and gossip. Have you ever had an experience where you heard a rumor and allowed it to alter your opinion of someone else?

3. Ridley has run from his past, and he finds it difficult to forgive his brothers. He ultimately chooses forgiveness and healing. Have you had an instance in your life where forgiveness has allowed healing and progression?

4. When Lia's doll is broken, Ridley fixes it and tells her the doll is beautiful with the cracks because it is evidence that the doll had been through something hard and has overcome. What other things exist in the world that could be seen as "cracks" or "flaws" but also as marks of beauty?

5. Ridley tells Edward, "Striking out at anyone who is, by law or means, unable to reciprocate is the basest show of weakness." What are ways we can show strength by protecting others?

6. Edward asks his mother if she will find value in him because he told the truth. She replies that he will find value in himself. In

what ways do our words and integrity matter in how we see ourselves?

7. Ridley tells Edward that it's important to take advice from those who are well-informed. Where do we go to find those with the best information? How can we recognize good information when we see it?

About the Author

JULIE WRIGHT was born in Salt Lake City, Utah. She wrote her first book when she was fifteen after an English teacher told her she would never be a writer. Since then, she's written twenty-six novels and ten novellas. Julie is a two-time winner of the Whitney Award for best romance with her books *Cross My Heart* and *Lies Jane Austen Told Me* and is a Crown Heart recipient. Her book *Death Thieves* was a Whitney finalist. Her books have received several starred reviews and have been listed in the American Library Association's top ten romances of the year.

She's a sucker for almost all things nerdy: Doctor Who, Disneyland, the Marvel Universe, Harry Potter, Lord of the Rings, fairy tales, and Jane Austen. She believes in second chances, getting up and trying again, and in the power of generosity and compassion.

She is surrounded by a loving and supportive family, one dog, and a varying number of houseplants (depending on attrition).

She loves writing, reading, traveling, hiking, snorkeling, playing with her family on the beach, and watching her husband make dinner.

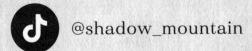
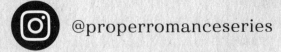
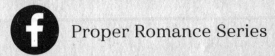